An

EMS

Life

N.L. Seitz

An EMS Life

Copyright © 2016 NL Seitz

Edited By Kassandra Cross

ISBN: 0692694285 (Sawyer-Linwood)

ISBN-13: 978-0692694282

LIBRARY OF CONGRESS: 2016906768

Dedication

To my family who tolerated my many hours at firehouses over the many years, as well as putting up with my hiding away to write, sometimes incoherently at any and all hours of the day and night.

This book is also dedicated to the Cobleskill Volunteer Fire Department along with Paramedics Bill Averill, Andy Cuccinello, and Mike Lent, who taught me the love of volunteering in Fire & EMS, and to my good friend Erik, who always made me laugh. He also showed me the value of hard work and determination over *any* obstacle.

Acknowledgements

I would like to acknowledge all the fire fighters and EMS professionals, both volunteer and municipal, as well as the hospital Emergency Room staff that make our jobs more fun and enjoyable. The relationships between us all only strengthens us, no matter the personal or political riffs between us.

If anyone reading this is interested in joining their local volunteer fire department and/or rescue squad, I can only whole-heartedly encourage you to do so. All you need to do is ask for an application, no matter how gruff the firefighters or EMS personnel seem to be. Once you're in, you are family. You will be surprised what you receive when you put the needs of others first.

Medical Disclaimer

All EMS calls in this book are fictional. The story, all names, characters, and incidents portrayed in this book are fictitious. Any past, present or future resemblance to Fire or EMS personnel or EMS calls or events is strictly coincidental.

This book is a work of fiction and contains general information about Emergency Medical Services (EMS) and certain medical conditions and pre-hospital treatments. The treatments noted in the book are subject to change due to the state EMS protocols and vary by State. The information is not treatment advice and should not be treated as such.

- ONE -

Jake Mitchell was a paramedic for the Montgomery County Fire and Rescue Services. He had been stationed at Engine Company 5 in Kensington, Maryland for the past two years. It was a volunteer owned station, manned by volunteers on nights from 6 p.m. to 6 a.m. and all day on the weekends, and county-manned by day during the week. The volunteers had just purchased a new engine with grant money the previous spring. They had two ambulances, both fitted exactly the same, and swapped out as primary and secondary units as they needed service or for mileage.

Jake had caught a ride with a buddy this morning for his regular 12-hour shift. Though today he was leaving a bit early. The morning routine was pretty standard no matter what station he was at. Inventory the equipment bags and patient compartment, wash the ambulance, check the lights, and then take care of any county required training or paperwork. Sometimes there were patient run sheets that Quality Assurance had caught that he'd have to look over again. Running EMS calls is what broke the monotony of the job. He thought himself lucky to have a semi-regular schedule.

Most days were a mix of simple calls like sprained ankles, kidney stones with the occasional hair-raising trauma call. Jake however was known throughout the county EMS community as a shit-magnet. He still got the stubbed toes, but for some reason, his calls included more obvious traumas. A stubbed toe would turn into a compound fracture with toes pointing straight up, or a simple fall, but with a lacerated temporal artery. These calls however are what kept his focus. He loved every minute of it.

And when he grew tired of the politics and the incompetence of the county management, he found solace in the 10 or 15 minutes of focus, when then world disappeared around him and it was only the problem at hand.

About 15 minutes to 4, Jake was begging not to get a call. His shift ended 2 hours early and today, and the last 30 minutes of every shift are the most nerve racking. Jake wanted to get off the clock on-time, but also knew that a call could come in at any moment. It was a blessing and a curse of Emergency Services, anticipation, reaction and hopefully satisfaction. Erik drove up into one of the visitor spaces in his black Toyota Tacoma. He parked next to a purple PT Cruiser and honked his horn a few times.

Erik Foerter was a flight medic for the Maryland State Police and usually flew on Trooper 6, on the eastern shore, just across the Chesapeake Bay Bridge. The MSP ran all of the emergency medevac choppers in the state of Maryland. He had the day off and had some errands to run in town. At 4 p.m. on the dot Jake verified that a volunteer was there to take over his shift. It was somewhat odd to do this, but they had a cordial relationship with the volunteers, so his captain allowed some things to slide – as long as there was coverage. He let his captain know that he was falling out, signed the log book and ran out of the firehouse. Jake jumped into Erik's truck after moving all the trash and soda bottles and empty cigarette packs behind the seat. The trauma kit Erik kept in the truck almost didn't fit. Erik has been in the process of eating healthier and quitting smoking for the past 3 years to varying success.

"Jesus Christ, Erik," Jake said.

"Hey, don't mess up my trash! That's valuable stuff," Erik shot back.

"I thought you were going to quit smoking," Jake started to complain

"So did I, Boss-man. So did I," Erik replied.

"And eating better?" Jake was tossing the wrappers into the back.

"Man, do you know how much I have invested in this thing?" Erik asked, patting his stomach, trying to stick it out. "Beer and ice cream is expensive these days. I don't want to just up and throw it away."

"Yeah, you're a real fat-ass," Jake said sarcastically.

"Besides," Erik continued, "you, me and Meredith are going be gorging ourselves on roughly 120 million calories tonight. I don't think one trip to Mickey D's or a Virginia Slim is going to make a difference."

Jake snorted. "Wait. Did you just say 'Virginia Slim'? Dude, if you're going to do it, at least be a man about it. Don't puss out on me. That's embarrassing. Do you also jerk off to the Sears catalog?" Jake knew that was a dumb question and got the requisite smart-ass reply.

"Only the Bra section, page 221, *if* the pages aren't stuck together. Leave my cigs alone. It was the cheapest pack they had, and I needed my fix. So taste me, Mofo. Taste Me," Erik said, spreading his legs and pointing to his crotch.

Erik was a bit of an oxymoron, "with emphasis on the latter" Jake would tell people with a joking smile. He was 5 foot 8 inches, weighed about 175 pounds and he had the metabolism of a cheetah. Prior to working in Maryland, he was a Corpsman in the Marines and then an L.A. County Paramedic for a short time. He said he moved back east for family where he worked for Montgomery County Fire and Rescue Services as a Paramedic with Jake before eventually getting the State Police job two years ago. Erik craved junk food, but somehow managed to keep the physique. He still had that "V" shaped cut that the ladies seemed to swoon over, plus the fact that he was a flight medic, one step down from a neurosurgeon to hear him say it. Either way, the man played it up for the ladies, and they more often than not fell for it. He thought he had to impress people, and well, being a flight medic was impressive, at least to Jake.

Jake had always wanted to be a flight-medic, but at 5 foot 11 inches, tipping the scale at 275 pounds, he was hardly fit for much chopper duty. Jake had gotten into EMS as a junior member in his local volunteer fire department while still in high school. He'd worked his way up through the fire department and gotten more experience. They even paid for his EMT and Paramedic training. The job with the county was a municipal job, so was mostly safe. Before this position, he'd thought about flight work on the medical transport side, or working on oil rigs out in the Gulf of Mexico – sweet gigs for a single guy, but then he had met Meredith. That was about a year after he started with the county and all those "single man" jobs went straight out the window.

Erik threw the truck into reverse.

"Ready to pig out there, Boss-man?" Erik was excited.

As soon as they backed out of the parking spot, Jake heard the tones go off in the fire house. The announcement was something about Kaiser Permanente. Jake smiled. Their clinic was just down the street. Kaiser almost forced you to see their doctors before 'allowing' you to go to the hospital. They'd picked up people there in the middle of a stroke. Most times though, it was shucking runny noses or broken bones over to a hospital that had a full medical department. That would've been his call – and all Jake could do was laugh. This was indeed a good day.

They were meeting Jake's wife Meredith at the steakhouse

by their house in Frederick. Erik's family was in extreme southern Maryland. Meredith and Jake effectively took him in like an orphaned puppy (*rogue* puppy was more like it), and Erik adopted them as his surrogate family.

"Man I can't wait to get my fingers on that bustin' onion." Erik was almost drooling.

"Bloomin' Onion," Jake said, "It's called a Bloomin' Onion."

"Yeah, whatever. Just let me at the beautiful, golden goodness."

"Hold up man, do you know what that does to your body?" Jake tried to ask in a condescending tone. They both knew they were going to murder that thing as soon as the waitress placed it in front of them. Like a rib bone in front of starving mutts.

"No way homie, that's your body. You're getting old there, Boss-man. You're going to spend most of the day tomorrow in the can reading the latest treatment protocols or ambulance Safety Regs or worse, the Post."

"Yeah, probably, but it'll be worth it," Jake grinned, and Erik shook his head in agreement. They could almost taste the grease now. Throw in a 20-ounce porterhouse steak, medium rare – if they still let you do that these days – and you've got a heart attack waiting to happen. Good stuff indeed.

Jake sat back in the uncomfortable seat and tried to relax during the hour ride up to Frederick. His back muscles ached. The pain was starting to shoot down his leg again. Jake had blown a disc some time ago while awkwardly lifting a patient over a banister – awkwardly – as if there was any other way to lift a patient over a banister. He had bounced back pretty well, considering he could hardly walk for 3 months and gained 70 pounds. But by then, Meredith and Jake were already married and she had to love him even if his boobs were bigger than hers. He snorted at that thought. Of course, that was before the pregnancy.

They caught some traffic at the truck scales 10 miles out, but it cleared up quickly. They hit more traffic at the Route-70 interchange. Erik took the shoulder and hit the West Patrick Street exit right on time. Coming around the turn, they merged with traffic. Directly in front of them was a familiar looking car but the glare kept either of them from being positive, and it was too high in the air to make any sense. Jake could have sworn it looked like…

The sparks showered and the shattered glass gleamed in the sunlight.

Erik pulled the truck up to the silver car. Jake grabbed the trauma kit from behind his seat and ran to what was left of the driver's door. Erik was on his phone with 911 giving them the pertinent details, heading over to a truck with a crumbled front end. The car had rolled a few times and come to rest on its roof. The driver side door was gone. The 'A' post was holding for now, but the 'B' post had been shattered in the wreck. The driver was a woman of 32, and eight months pregnant. Her body was half in the car, and half on the pavement. She was conscious but not breathing, her eyes wide and terrified. Blood trickled across her nose and down her cheek, following her jaw line into her once sandy blonde hair. *Probably coming from her ear.* Jake thought. Jake was assuming a head injury. She hadn't been wearing a seatbelt, and Jake cursed under his breath, "These pregnant women never fucking listen."

She was trying to scream, but her crushed larynx prevented any sound or air movement. Jake could already see the tracheal deviation pushing her airway to the right. The area of her throat crushed by the steering wheel was starting to fill with blood. The swelling from the impact as well as the structural injury combined to make it look like a sick looking scarf. Jake had to act fast. Erik was yelling across to him the ETAs for both ground and helicopter medical units. According to Erik, the newest and fastest chopper, Maryland Trooper-8 was en route but had an ETA of 13 minutes, having just dropped off a patient in Winchester, Virginia. Trooper-3 was next closest, but was 14 minutes out, coming from a drop at Suburban Hospital.

Jake grabbed a laryngoscope out of the bag. Even with the gag reflex, maybe he could force the airway open? After the second try, he knew it wasn't possible. Jake grabbed an OB kit out of the trauma bag. This is the only piece of equipment Erik carried in the truck that contained a blade, a No. 11 scalpel to be exact. Jake opened an alcohol wipe, and rubbed her neck down with it.

Erik was assessing the driver of the other vehicle. He looked over.

"What the hell are you doing?" he yelled.

The two vehicles were separated by 2 lanes of roadway, and traffic was getting antsy, unsure if it was morally acceptable to pass through a traffic accident this serious, while trying to avoid the debris. As soon as Erik looked up, he knew what Jake was doing if not why. Knowingly going outside of protocols was by law considered to be "practicing medicine without a license". Jake knew he was putting his license on the line for sure, and maybe his freedom into jeopardy, but he wasn't going to sit there and watch 'his' patient suffocate when he was trained to fix this particular problem.

Suddenly her eyes got huge and bulged from their sockets. She lurched forward and passed out. Jake could see that pit in her neck moving, her accessory muscles still straining to help her breathe. He stuffed a rag under her shoulders to lift up her throat and open her airway a little better more as a matter of reflex more than something that would actually help. Jake counted the notches in her neck, checking his landmarks. He made the vertical incision down across her thyroid cartilage and dabbed at it with a 4x4 bandage. It was his first surgical airway on a live patient let alone in the field. He didn't really expect the amount of blood that came out. There was so much blood. He hadn't grabbed any more 4x4's to help soak up the blood. He slid his finger into the hole to find the cricothyroid membrane under the skin and poked through it with the scalpel, turning the blade vertical to keep the hole open.

With the escaping gasses came a spray of blood. Her chest rose instantly with the pressure change of the air being sucked into her lungs, making a sound similar to a low scream. Jake grabbed a number-6 ET tube and slid it in. As soon as the tube was in, Jake popped on the bag valve and pushed a few breaths. Jake had to listen to breath sounds to make sure there were no other blockages and rule out a hemo or pneumothorax. The breath sounds were dull on her left side. He checked the bag for a chest needle, *any* needle. No dice. Not the worst, but not good. It was something he'd have to keep an eye on. Jake secured the tube in her throat with tape and slid a pulse-ox on her finger and set about a trauma exam.

Her legs were pinned up under the dashboard. She was still unconscious, but she was now moving air. Tidal volume was good. The dullness on her left side wasn't getting any worse. Good expirations, even more important. There was no blood pressure cuff in the bag. Jake cursed audibly. Her pupils were sluggish but equal and reactive. The local fire department had shown up and started to secure the vehicle so it wouldn't shift.

They also acted as scene safety officers and someone had brought over a proper trauma bag.

Jake had tunnel vision. A bad thing to have, but he had it just the same. He couldn't say that he'd ever remember having had it before this call or since. The more experienced folks don't get it too much, at least that he'd seen – in any case, he was aware enough to know he had it, but didn't care.

Jake felt strong pulses in both of her arms, the only extremities that he could reach. He felt what he thought was a pulse in her left femoral artery, but he couldn't reach up under the dashboard far enough to be sure – maybe it was wishful thinking. Her pelvis was broken, shattered was more like it. Jake felt and heard the crepitus of the bones rubbing together.

Jake was unaware of the commotion going on around him as the Fire Department and other Emergency Medical Services arrived on scene. Someone handed him an oxygen tube to connect to the bag valve and a cardiac monitor. Jake handed off the bag valve and placed a 12-lead EKG the best he could and started running a tape. He put the blood pressure cuff on her right arm as it was easier to reach. The extent of the dysrhythmia was startling. It was the potassium no doubt. Jake didn't expect it to set in so soon. "She must have a major crush injury," Jake said under his breath. Her pressure was okay. He'd seen worse. But she had a car on top of her, and for now he'd take 'stable' as he could get it.

Jake started two lines all the same, both 16 gauge wide open, dumping fluid into her as fast as he could, saline in one, bi-carb in the other. Checking her lungs again, they were no worse, so he decided to leave that for now. Her O2 saturation was in the upper 80s and holding with the oxygen.

The rescue squad seemed to take forever cutting the car apart from the bottom down. He looked at his watch, and had to wipe the blood off the face to see the time, 1707. Jake marked it on the back of his hand with a sharpie from Erik's bag. It had already been 23 minutes since he and Erik arrived on-scene of the accident.

The chopper had landed and Jake could hear the blades spinning down. He never noticed the downdraft if there was any. The flight medic came over to Jake as Erik had told her who had the priority patient. Erik had relinquished his patient's care over to the County's duty medic that arrived and came over to assist Jake, take over bagging for a bit and do his own assessment of her injuries where he could. A fire fighter was in the partially collapsed car trying to hold c-spine.

The flight medic – like Erik - was technically a Maryland State Police Officer. She started to give Jake a dressing-down over the airway when Erik got between them, trying to calm them both down. He had to show his own badge and gave a quick synopsis of the situation. The flight medic was after all, the one who was going to have to deal with it in the air and explain it to the trauma docs. Erik hadn't met all the new medics that had rotated into the MSP and this was one of them.

Jake was ambivalent. Who cares what that medic thought? His patient had an airway. His patient was breathing. He'd done his job. He saved a life that was gone. He brought it back. Him. Like it was another day at the office.

Erik grabbed Jake's shoulder and pulled him back so more of the firefighters and EMTs could secure the patient and prep her to be moved to the stretcher. That also gave other medics a chance to get in and take over treatment. He handed Jake a towel to dry his face, now smeared and dripping with blood and sweat.

Jake's fears were realized when they were finally able to remove the patient's broken body from the wreckage. With a neck brace on, they slid her straight out onto a long board. Her legs twisted and contorted into shapes not compliant with nature, shapes that would give the most grizzled medic nightmares. They were crushed flat yet at different angles. There was flesh broken here, bone protruding there. And now that she was free of the car that was killing her, while at the same time keeping her alive, her body was filling up with poisons.

There are other worries, like compartment syndrome, but those worries are distant. If all else fails, a worst case scenario could be remedied with a drastic, if somewhat final amputation. No, the big problems were the poisons now coursing through her body. The potassium, and phosphorus, and myoglobin given off by the crushed and now necrotic tissues and bones were attacking her heart and kidneys, trying to ruin her liver. Not to mention that her bladder was ruptured and her intestines no doubt punctured. That's almost instantaneous sepsis.

Jake had no way to know that this would be the last time he'd see her alive. In fact, he rarely ever saw any of his patients again. If he ever did it was because they recognized him, not vice versa. The firefighters and EMTs got Jake's patient loaded into the chopper as the blades were spinning up.

Jake never turned his back as the chopper lifted off, throwing all manner of dirt and debris into the air. He started to crack. His knees buckled, and Erik, standing behind him, caught him as he fell. Others around him noticed, knowing the issue all too well as word had spread as he was working the patient.

"Erik?" Jake said in almost a catatonic state.

"Erik? I need a ride. Can you give me a ride? They took Meredith. They took my wife and I need a ride," Jake's voice was cracking under the stress.

Erik steadied Jake, and then grabbed him by the arm and

led him to a waiting state police cruiser. With a State Trooper driving, they rode together to R. Adams Cowley Medical Center - better known as Baltimore Shock Trauma to make sure that someone was there to meet Jake's wife who would be arriving care of the Maryland State Police Trooper-3 within about 15 minutes. Jake prayed for a strong tail wind. He should have prayed for more.

- TWO -

The chopper landed at Baltimore Shock Trauma in 17 minutes. It took Jake and Erik almost an hour to get there in the cruiser. Even with lights and sirens blaring, rush hour into and through downtown Baltimore sucked as much as any other city. The state trooper was doing Erik a favor, who was in turn doing Jake a favor. Extended family is still family.

Meredith was in surgery for more than five hours before any of the doctors came out to talk to him. He was still wearing the Baltimore Orioles shirt she gave him that morning, now covered in blood. Some of it was his from the glass cuts but mostly hers.

Erik had made himself scarce not knowing what to say, or maybe knowing exactly what to do. He wasn't sure which. Maybe both.

"Mr. Mitchell, I'm Doctor Watts. I'm the orthopedic surgeon called in to consult on your wife's injuries."

Mr. James 'Jason' Watts, M.D., was in his early 50's or so. He was graying at the temples, a tanned man of Hawaiian or some other pacific decent. He walked out still in scrubs, his $1800 Italian leather shoes wrapped in those stupid blue footies. His voice was steady; his demeanor was cool, as if he'd done this too many times. He was a consulting orthopedic surgeon at Shock Trauma. He *had* to be one of the best.

"How is she? Is she out of surgery? Can I see her?" Jake rambled. He needed to see her, touch her. He needed to know everything and he needed it five minutes ago.

"Mr. Mitchell, please sit down. We need to talk about her condition. It's very grave."

Jake sat down on one of the waiting room chairs, the formed vinyl covering ensuring his butt slid into the right place.

"I understand that you're a paramedic, is that correct?" he asked.

"Yes," Jake said. "Why?"

"Good, that means I won't have to dumb this down." Doctor Watts had a way with words in that he didn't mince them. He'd give you the biggest words he could find, medical if at all possible, and then let you choke on them.

"It took about 45 minutes to extricate your wife, is that correct?" he started. Jake knew that wasn't a good place to start.

"Was it that long? I don't know., Jake looked at the back of his left hand. It still had the stick times written in sharpie. He rubbed it with his right as if he could shorten the time, wishing it to be sooner than it was. Erik didn't carry saline or bi-carb in his trauma kit. Jake had to wait until the ambulance showed up. It turns out that it was a fly car that was first on-scene.

To start with a question like that forced him to question everything he did. His mind was racing. *Did he do it right? Was he fast enough? Could he have done more? Of course he could have.*

"Mr. Mitchell? Mr. Mitchell?" Doctor Watts said repeatedly.

"Yeah, Doc," snapping out of his trance of self-doubt. A motion his brain had since raced to continue.

"Mr. Mitchell, the next 24 hours will be the hardest and most telling for us. We still have her in surgery. We could not save her legs. We initially performed a pelvectomy, a disarticulation of her entire right leg, but then the doppler lost the pulse in the left, and we decided to remove the left as well, about 6 inches above the knee. I'm sorry. She will be in surgery and then in recovery for quite some time.

"She did have a slight pneumothorax on the left side, but it was manageable. Also, due to the crush injuries, we operate under the assumption that she has rhabdomyolysis. We're bypassing her kidneys for now with dialysis, trying to clean out some of the potassium and protein, but at this point it may not be enough. We're monitoring uric alkalinity, etcetera, but aside from the obvious trauma to her legs and pelvis, renal failure and damage done to the cardiac muscle are our big concerns.

"What I'm saying to you Mr. Mitchell is that we can bypass her kidneys for a while, but not her liver or her heart – not for very long. At this point, if she goes into one or multiple system failure, I'm afraid there isn't much we can do."

Jake fazed the doctor out again. Her kidneys were there to take a beating and she could live without much kidney function, at least for a while, long enough to get a donor. Weekly dialysis would be a bitch, but she could do it, couldn't she? And she has a strong heart. A *strong* heart. Had to, to put up with him all this time, right? And she was pregnant too, that strengthens the heart, doesn't it? His mind was racing, looking for any ray of hope to cling to. But he wasn't thinking straight. All of his training, all of his skills, and he couldn't put things in order.

"And the head injury? I saw blood coming from her ear," Jake asked tentatively.

"No. No head trauma that we saw. She did have some trauma to her ears, but it might have been from the earrings. Nothing to worry about there., Dr. Watts actually sounded glad to give some good news for a change, no matter how small a pittance it was.

"And my son?" Jake knew the answer to this. He knew it on scene. He didn't know why he asked. She was eight months pregnant with their first child. It was her dream to have a large family. Dr. Watts looked at him, sighed heavily and frowned as if he knew Jake was forcing him to tell him something he already knew.

"Your son died in utero, Mr. Mitchell. It was no longer a viable pregnancy when your wife arrived. To some degree, that takes a load off of your wife, but it also complicates things as her blood gas and chemical levels are in a state of mismatch. We cannot distinguish the injury levels against the pregnancy levels against what should be normal levels, at least not in everything."

He was speaking more softly now. "We also have her on high dose antibiotics to ward off any probable infection which will not help her liver, so it's a balancing act right now."

He hung his head and put his hand on Jake's shoulder. It seemed an uncomfortable action for him. Jake didn't get the feeling that the doctor was used to this, if one ever gets used to telling already distraught family members that their worst fears may very well be realized. The surgeon turned and walked out of the waiting room and left a broken man there to start cleaning up the pieces of what started out to be a damn fine day, now just damned.

Jake prayed. It was the product of growing up a minister's son. He dropped to his knees and begged God to let him change places with his wife and son. The tears echoed in the now empty waiting room. Jake let out a groan that he never thought possible. He'd heard it before in waiting rooms and Emergency Departments that he'd brought patients to. Spouses and loved ones hearing that the bed they'd sleep in that night would be cold forever. The moan of the undead wishing they were. Wolf Blitzer mouthed something on the televisions mounted in the corners. The closed captioning was a second or two behind. Jake heard the pages of old magazines rustling in the breeze. The air conditioning was on.

God gave Jake his answer a few hours later. Meredith's kidneys had shut down completely 2 hours prior. Her liver and spleen were overwhelmed almost instantly. Her heart had also taken a beating from the potassium released into her blood. The massive infection played a big role in that too. In the end, it was her heart that gave out.

It was 2 a.m. on the dot when she went into cardiac arrest, and then starting with her left ventricle, dropping into P.E.A. and then asystole shortly thereafter. Multiple defibrillations and epinephrine injections didn't faze her one bit. There was just too much potassium in her system. The hyperkalemia had done its damage even before the dialysis. Her system just couldn't handle the massive trauma she had endured over the last 10 hours. She'd lost her son, her legs, and now her life. Jake couldn't save any of it.

Meredith was still in the post-op recovery area. Jake wasn't allowed in to see her until she was already gone. Her eyes were still taped shut. The tube he had inserted on-scene was still there, but it was officially stitched in. Her neck and throat were now engulfed by the ugly bruising. They had taken the lines out of her arms, but left the IV catheters in. She lay in the bed, lifeless, legless. There was some swelling in her face, mainly around her left eye.

Jake's knees gave out and he slumped to the floor, holding onto the bed rails of his dead wife. He grabbed her cold hand and he held it to his face, kissed it, trying to recall how her skin smelled. Her hand lied. Both of them did. Neither one showed any signs of the brutality they'd been through. Not so much as a drop of blood. They were young and beautiful and smooth. She had her mother's hands.

My God, how do I tell her mother? He thought. How does he tell her that he could not save her daughter? All of his training, all of his experience, and all of his love could not save his wife or their son.

His mind went over the process of the newly dead. The pressure in the lungs now equal with the current atmosphere and lack of accessory muscles or hypoxic drive. How the cells start to burn sugar instead of oxygen before they die, rigor mortis sets in, and the muscles and tendons tighten up, then relax, only to repeat the cycle. The blood settles to the lowest point in the body in what's called morbid lividity. He'd seen it all before, but never with his own family. He had never even considered it. But now he was seeing it happen right in front of him to the love of his life. It turned his stomach. If he had anything in his stomach other than stale coffee, he'd have lost it. He started dry heaving, wracked with fits of tears. He wanted to scream.

A thought shot into his mind, his wife's eyes just before she passed out. She couldn't scream. Her eyes did that for her as if screaming at him to do something. Jake was lost. Jake's phone started buzzing. He tried to ignore it but they kept calling. Someone in his family had caught wind of the accident – probably from Erik. Jake fished it out of his pocket, and flipped it over to see the caller ID and it read "Mommy". It could have been his mom or dad or maybe even his little sister if she was over there at this hour. Jake held his head against the cool metal of the hospital bed and slept.

Around 4 a.m. they came for his wife and wheeled the bed down the hall to the elevator. They were taking her to the morgue in the basement of the hospital, where it was cool and dry and everything was shiny stainless steel. Jake held her hand as long as he could, only letting go as the elevator doors began to close. His eyes were wet and puffy. The tears left a trail through the dirt and crust of the previous day.

He kept seeing the image of her face covered with the sheet. It was odd seeing that. There was half a human under that sheet. *"Were you still considered a human after death?"*

Jake's mind started racing again. It hadn't really ever stopped; it just took a rest. An inappropriate joke popped into his head. It was a defense mechanism according to the county shrinks. All paramedics had to undergo annual psychological evaluations. Even now, as inappropriate as it was, he knew somewhere in the back of his mind that he was trying to fend off the obvious. If he made light of the subject, if he joked about it, if he could laugh about it, maybe it would go away so he wouldn't have to deal with it. He tried to put the day's events and details in the back of his mind where he put all the other horrors he'd seen and dealt with, or so he thought.

He started walking back towards the waiting room, unsure of what to do next. He was starting his life over and had no idea how to continue let alone what was going on.

"Jake! I've been looking for you," It was Erik. "Your dad and sister are here," He grabbed Jake's elbow and put an arm around his waist to help guide him. Erik knew everything that had happened. He knew half of the people that worked at Shock-Trauma. This was *"his"* hospital, and being a flight medic with the MSP, he knew everyone's secrets and was plugged into all the gossip.

Jake was still in a state of numbed shock. Erik led him to the waiting room where his father, Peter, and sister, Kelly had been waiting. They had come in when Jake was walking his wife's corpse to the elevator. His dad didn't say anything, he just hugged him. Peter was about 5 inches taller than Jake and outweighed him by an easy 50 pounds. Jake all but disappeared in his giant paws and bear hug.

Jake lost it. He balled like a baby. Jake buried his face in his father's chest and screamed. He screamed as loud as he could for as long as his lungs could handle. He sucked in more air and screamed more. His sister Kelly, 4 inches shorter than him, and 120 pounds soaking wet, initially waited to give him a hug until the loudest of his screams abated. She wiggled into their side, their dad lifted his arm to let her in and then hugged both of his children at once.

"We don't know God's plan, son."

Jake's father was a minister. He knew more about the bible than most priests. Jake pushed back, out of his grasp. His sister knew what was coming and curled up into a seat out of their way. Jake's eyes narrowed. At this point his sorrow turned to anger, then mere anger turned into rage.

"Do *not* talk to me about God, dad. Not now, not ever again. I don't give a god damn what you believe! I've seen and experienced too much to believe that any kind of god that you believe in could ever exist, and if he does then he can go to hell!" Jake was just getting warmed up.

"I just watched my wife of 7 years get her legs and pelvis destroyed, dad. I watched as our unborn son was pressed against the steering wheel until he was crushed inside of her! And Meredith wasn't unconscious when all this happened, dad. Oh no! She was awake and aware of it all. She could feel everything. But see dad, she couldn't scream because her throat was crushed. Her eyes told me how much pain she was in. They told me to do something.

"God obviously hadn't done a damn thing. He hasn't been involved up until now, so why bother him at all? Or maybe, he was the one that allowed it all to go down like this. If that's the case, then fuck him."

Instantly Jake recoiled at that one and wondered if he had gone too far in his condemnations. Whether he believed in god or not, the saying goes that 'there are no atheists in a foxhole'. Like most medics, Jake believed there was a God, but not as his father did. Some medics were very religious, some just the opposite, having either experienced more miracles than tragedies or vice versa.

But Jake was in a rage now, and he was taking it out on his dad. He dared to bring faith into this equation and now he was going to pay. Someone had to pay for the things he'd been through. His dad knew what Jake was saying wasn't really his fault. Jake ran his fingers through his hair as if trying to stop the thoughts from coming out but it was too late. "Even now dad, you're not a father. Even now, when I need you most, I need *you*. Not some walking scripture-spouting bible thumper. When you've walked in my shoes, and been through the things I've been through and seen the fucked up things I've seen, then we'll talk about that crap, but not now," Jake was breaking. "Not now! My wife is gone, she's dead!"

His knees collapsed again and Jake crumbled to the floor. He put his hands over his face trying to stop the tears. Kelly ran over hunkered down and threw her arms around him.

His dad started to walk towards him. Kelly put her hand up to stop him.

"No, not right now, dad, please. Give him some space. I'll give you a call when he's calmed down a little more," Erik had been outside the waiting room this whole time, acting as though he was not paying attention or talking to the ladies at the nurse's station. He walked over to Jake's dad and the two of them headed off down the hall towards the cafeteria.

After a few minutes, Kelly and Jake stood up. She wrapped an arm around his and started walking down the hall to no place in particular. They said nothing as they walked. Jake was thinking about everything while trying to think about nothing. And the harder he tried the worse it became until the voices in his head came to a crescendo and then all at once stopped – or they were silenced. Jake stopped crying and dried his eyes. He and his sister walked around silently until they found a break room where Jake picked up a bottle of water.

"And it only cost $2.25. This is a hospital. You'd think water would at least be cheaper if not free," Jake said, Kelly was only listening.

They started walking again, in the vague direction of the cafeteria.

"Where's mom? Did she come too?" Jake asked. Again, knowing the answer. It was her that tried to call him earlier. He might not know the exact excuse, but Jake knew it would be something he considered bullshit.

"She wasn't feeling well at all. As soon as she heard, she instantly felt sick. She started throwing up and everything. She almost fainted."

"Why doesn't that surprise me one bit?" Jake quipped. "It's good to know who not to call when the chips are down." His mother was a woman who was set in her ways, and shied away from any situation where she would have to come to terms with her own mortality.

"That cowardly bitch! She can't stand to see her darling son in this condition. Fuck her." He was still coming down off his rage from earlier.

"What did you expect, Jake?" Kelly squeaked. "You know how she is. She's been like that as long as we've been alive. You can't expect her to change overnight."

"Yeah, well, I didn't expect her to basically ignore the fact that her daughter in-law was crushed to death and that her grandson will be buried next to her." He was starting to feel that anger coming back or maybe it was bitterness creeping in.

Kelly led him to a table just inside the cafeteria. They were out of the line of casual sight, unless you were looking for someone. People walking in passed right on by without giving them a second glance. Of course, that was partly their indifference to them too.

Jake saw their dad and Erik sitting by the windows talking. Their dad was no doubt trying to convert the inconvertible Erik or maybe it was the other way around. Erik was good at making a scene when he didn't fit in and he knew it. He would goose a nun if he didn't think she'd slap him silly, and even then it was still an option. The thought brought a slight smile to Jake.

Peter and Erik spotted the two and began a slow painful waltz over to their table. Jake looked at his father when he got there, stood up and hugged him. Again, Peter wrapped his huge arms around his son and sighed heavily.

"I'm sorry dad, I didn't mean to scream like that, or say some of those things."

"That's okay son, I don't pretend to know what you're going through right now, so I'll cut you some slack. I can't speak for the man upstairs though."

Jake walked away rolling his eyes, feeling the bitterness growing teeth beneath all the other emotions.

Kelly immediately changed the subject. Even Erik was relieved. Apparently he really was getting an earful from the old man. That was too bad.

They all agreed to meet back at Kelly's house later that night, sans Erik, who had a shift to work on the eastern shore. Jake pictured Erik bent over the kitchen sink washing his hair, probably with Dawn or Palmolive. That brought a smirk to his face. He was sure a lot of others would be coming over to Kelly's house. Jake hoped anyway, if not for him, then for Meredith. Kelly managed to call most of them and let them know the bad news, and that no, there was no need to come to the hospital and that they'd be in touch, and if they could pass along the word to anyone we may have missed. Jake hugged his sister and father and thanked them for coming. They parted ways for now and dad and sis walked back towards the parking garage.

- THREE -

Erik, meanwhile had borrowed a car from someone. Apparently most of the people in the Four-State area owed him a favor. He drove them back in the direction of home.

Erik had a folder with some papers for Jake to fill out. Jake started flipping through them when they hit route 70. Insurance, both auto and medical. The state police were reconstructing the accident, as is standard in cases like this. There were some hand scribbled notes from Erik, some part of what the Accident Reconstruction Team had found up until last evening.

The truck that hit Meredith wasn't really a truck per se. It was an old bronco with a 5-inch lift kit on it. The 28-inch mudding tires weren't installed properly and the bearings on the left front wheel hub had frozen up, sending the bronco across the double yellow line and into his wife's Saturn.

They hadn't had her car to the dealership for service due to the fact that Jake believed, as most do, that dealerships ripped you off more on the service than the actual car. They were never told of a 'service advisory' that was out on her model that related to airbag deployment failures.

The driver's side airbag circuit, about the size of a baby's thumb nail had shorted, preventing the airbag from receiving the signal from the front end collision sensor. Not that it would have helped anyway. She wasn't wearing a seatbelt, so the airbag would have shoved her further under the dashboard. Maybe.

The bronco hit her at about 60 miles an hour, even accounting for slowing when the tire froze up, about 7 feet. According to the little black box installed on all GM vehicles, she was going 53 miles per hour. That gives an impact of roughly 113 miles per hour. No brakes. No secondary energy transfers unless you count the passengers. The front end crumple zone took the brunt of the impact, but soon folded under and flipped the car as the 4,380 pound 1983 Ford Bronco with the 5-inch lift kit and 28-inch mud tires plowed into the engine compartment and door frame of his wife's Saturn, glancing off her driver's side door hinges and support beam, causing the Saturn to flip through the air, rolling 3 times and coming to an inverted stop 57 feet away from the initial point of impact.

Jake didn't remember all of that. They were in Erik's pickup truck and just had the odd timing of merging into traffic 2 cars behind Meredith on their way to dinner.

There was some confusion as to whether the Bronco was street legal. Jake guessed it didn't matter, though technically, at this point it was considered a "homicide investigation". The driver of the Bronco, James Callahan, 22, of Manassas, Virginia was transported to Suburban Hospital for treatment and released. They took him there as a technicality. It was the closest Level-1 trauma center, and he had to go to a trauma center due to the mechanism of injury of the woman he had hit. He had a couple of scratches, a broken wrist, and possibly a concussion but was otherwise fine. The police found some empty Corona bottles and some pot residue, but tests were still forthcoming. He passed all sobriety checks at the time.

"Did they say when these needed to be returned by?" Jake asked, holding up the folder.

"Nada, Boss-man," Erik wearing his wrap around Oakley's and backwards hat.

"Where'd you get the wheels?' Jake asked, trying to make conversation, not really wanting anything other than to break the silence that had engulfed the car since they left the city.

"Andy. He's got a ride back."

"The Gooch? When did he start working Shock-Trauma?" again, with the small talk.

"Yeah. He started a few months back. His back is still giving him fits. I worked his old man a couple of years ago when I was a ground-pounder like you. He took 4 shots of epi and some pacing but I got him back, and no deficit, too."

Jake shook his head. Jake didn't know the Gooch's father. Erik had worked on someone in almost every family in the area it seemed.

"Better to be a ground-pounder than a fairy in a unitard," Jake said.

Erik smirked. Things could get back to normal as long as they had someone else's tragedy on our mind.

"Excuse me, 'fairy' is a mighty divisive word, and for your information, it's a flight suit, not a u-ni-tard," Erik shot back, enunciating each syllable.

"Oh and you can do what half a dozen more procedures than me? Push what - another 10 drugs on standing orders? Maybe? All that for keeping your weight under 200 pounds?"

"Not so fast. I get to make arrests and carry *el pistolo* too!" Erik replied cheerfully, pointing his finger and thumb at Jake.

Things got quiet again. A song came on the radio that stuck in Jake's head, "Far From Home" by Five Finger Death Punch. He made mental note to make sure he got that one. The strangest things had started to catch his attention. After that, things stayed quiet until they were about 20 minutes from Jake's house.

"I hate to bring this up, Jake," Erik started. Jake thought he knew where he was going.

"Then don't. Don't do it, Erik. I don't want to hear it. I've had too much shit happen in the last 18 hours. I don't want to hear more procedural bullshit from you. I did what I had to do to keep her alive. She was alive. I gave her a chance!" He was starting to lose it again.

"Well, I was going to ask you to drive me back to my truck. We left it at the scene. One of the officers drove it over to the CVS parking lot across from the hotel. But if you want to talk about protocol breeches today, that's fine too."

"Fuck you, Erik. Not now."

"Promises, promises. Tsk tsk tsk," Erik said. "You know me, Jake. I think you made the right call. It was ballsy. But I can't cover for you. Other people saw you doing it and know I didn't give you the okay. Otherwise, I'd take the heat. There will be a review, and you'll probably get your card pulled. You'll be a desk jockey for who knows how long, that's assuming you pass the psych test to come back."

They were both avoiding saying anything about the situation that had led to this moment. Neither one of them could say anything about what they had just witnessed.

Jake had done a surgical airway on his wife while in the field. It's something that is outside of his scope of practice, let alone standing protocols. He was schooled and trained on how to do it. It was on the National Registry Exam, and by state licensing requirements, he's required to understand and have the ability to perform the procedure. But he isn't *allowed* to do it. It isn't in Maryland State ALS protocols – or protocols for any state that he was aware of. At least not for the ground pounders – paramedics that ride in the ambulances. Flight medics like Erik can perform the procedure, but not the 'common' paramedic. Jake was too tired to fight. Erik sensed it too because he shut up.

This wasn't the time or the place. Jake would get his soon

enough and Erik had to be there for support. He closed his eyes and took some deep breaths and dozed off. About half an hour later they dropped off Andy's car at the Comfort Inn and got into Erik's truck. The remains of the trauma bag, bloody gloves, wrappers, and other trash crammed into it, was sitting on the passenger seat. Jake zipped it up and threw it in the truck bed.

Jake didn't realize his mistake of going home until it was too late. As Erik pulled into the driveway, the house loomed over them. The morning sun behind it now, casting the front in shadow. Jake was scared to death to go in. It was the last place he wanted to be. It was empty and hollow. He knew it was empty. It would always be empty now.

His legs felt like stones grinding on the steps up to the front door. He tried to put on a brave face. He knew he looked like hell. Felt like it and smelled like it too. The blood still on his shirt had dried to the point that it was making the shirt curl up at the bottom. The plasma cells contracting, drawing the cotton fibers closer together. Jake managed to find his keys. Erik had held them for him this whole time.

"Do you want me to go in with you, Boss-man?" Erik asked.

"No, thanks. I'm good. I'll be fine," Jake lied, Erik knew it, but allowed him to do what he felt he needed to do.

Jake couldn't imagine what Erik thought as he watched him walk up the last step. Jake popped the key into the door knob and turned the lock, then the knob. There was a click as the lock opened and the latch retreated into the door. It seemed incredibly loud in the foyer. The door squeaked open letting the mourning shadow pour in.

Jake stepped inside and closed the door behind him. He leaned up against it and heard Erik drive off. The room darkened and the silence enveloped him. Jake couldn't stand it. His mind had kicked into high gear again. A thousand different thoughts at once. Some made sense; some he didn't want to think about, others still were just smart-ass and inappropriate even by his own standards.

He needed some sleep. But he wasn't about to head upstairs. Not yet. Not without some chemical assistance from his friends Tylenol and Codeine. He found the bottle in the kitchen above the fridge that was covered in pictures of him and Meredith. He couldn't help but look at every one. Jake was numb now, cried out and hopeless. Jake was done.

His stomach churned and he knew he was going to puke, but he still hadn't eaten anything aside from day old coffee. Jake started dry heaving over the kitchen sink. He dropped the folder that Erik had handed him on the counter and grabbed the Dewar's and the Jameson from the cupboard. Jake wondered what a shot of Irish whiskey and 12-year old scotch tasted like. He tossed 4 pills in his mouth and washed it down with 2 double shots of the cocktail. It tasted as he thought it would, just like ass. Twice. The Dewar's burned going down, but then the Jameson warmed his stomach. Hopefully, the alcohol and the drugs would hit his system faster on an empty stomach.

Jake started up the stairs and grabbed Meredith's jacket that was hanging on the end of the banister and dropped it into the hamper at the top of the stairs. Old habits die hard, especially when you don't really know they're gone. Jake stopped at the hall bathroom to use the bathroom and addressed himself in the mirror. Yup, he looked like hell. He staggered back to the master bedroom and collapsed on the bed and felt a tear run down his nose as he realized he could still smell Meredith on the sheets, her skin, her perfume, her shampoo, everything. He remembered crying and then sleep stole him from the stress of the day.

He woke up what he thought was about an hour later to the sound of the telephone. The room was dark; the whole house was dark. And quiet. Why was Jake surrounded by so much silence now? So much darkness? The phone, it was his sister, Kelly.

"Jake, thank god! Are you okay? Where are you?" Jake smirked, those were some stupid questions.

"Hey Kelly, yeah, I'm alive. I'm at home, where you called me, remember? I'm not the only on who's been drinking, ha!"

"Yeah yeah, its 5 p.m. are you on your way over? It's a 90-minute drive with no traffic" The concern in her voice glowed through the phone.

"I don't think I'm in much shape to drive right now. I'm not going anywhere today, Ha!" Jake started laughing. "Oh yeah, I'm plastered. No work for me tomorrow. Woo Hoo!"

"Okay, well, it's too late for mom and dad to come over, but I can still come if you need some company."

"Nope. No company needed right now, thanks for playing." He was slurring his words. "hmmm" he could almost see Kelly's furrowed brow.

"Okay, but we'll all be over first thing tomorrow, dad and me. Mom is coming too" Jake could hear Kelly rummaging in her purse, probably for her chapstick. Kelly and her damn chapstick. "Dad has been calling your in-laws for you."

That was nice of him actually. He got along better with them than Jake did, mostly anyway. But then, he didn't preach to them for whatever reason.

Jake hung up the phone and laid his face back on the bed,

only to be reminded why he was drinking himself to sleep. The mix of Secret and Pantene and Meredith's skin swirled around him. The smell was strongest on her pillow. Jake hugged it tightly and inhaled deeply. In the back of his mind he was worried that he'd ruin the smell on the pillow with his own. But right now, this was as close to Meredith that he would ever be again, and he cherished it, a grown man caressing and crying into a pillow.

Jake woke the next morning with a pounding in his head. And it was loud. It took him a moment to orientate himself and realize that the pounding wasn't in his head, not all of it anyway. His brother in-law, Randy was down stairs with Jane, his mother in-law. Apparently the door bell was either broken or wasn't loud enough to wake him, so Randy resorted to pounding on the door, ensuring the neighbors 3 blocks away would be aware of his presence.

Randy was the consummate redneck. 6 foot 2 inches, and most of his shirts were plaid flannel. He was the hunter-fisher type, very manly as the stereotypical definition goes. A good guy deep down, but you *really* had to dig. Jake found him to be kind of superficial and judgmental on the surface. He meant well, he just went about it in a different way. The wrong way for most people.

Jane, his mother-in-law, stood behind him. She was one of the sweetest most naïve women Jake had ever met. He didn't mean that in a bad way, she was just oblivious to most of the goings-on around her, which these days was a blessing.

Kelly, Peter and Jake's mother, Anna pulled up as Jake answered the door. To his surprise, it was just the 5 of them. Meredith had a pretty large family. She was the youngest of 4, but had 17 nieces and nephews, so for only her oldest brother and mother to stop by it was a small coup in his favor.

His sister, mother, father, Jane and even Randy had to hug him as they entered the living room. It was then that he realized that Jake hadn't changed clothes. He still had on the bloody Orioles shirt and jeans from the previous day.

2 days ago? Had it been 2 days already? A day and a half, technically, Jake thought.

Randy stood staring at him, at the shirt, at his sister's blood. He knew at least to some degree what had happened to his sister, thankfully not the details. The tears were welling in his eyes, and Jake hugged him. Randy turned to his own mother and continued with the tears. Jane started crying and then all of them were at it. Jake turned and went upstairs, hoping that this time he really was cried out.

"I'll be back down in a few. You all know where everything is." he needed to get out of these clothes. He remembered he'd left the scotch and whiskey out on the counter.

To hell with 'em Jake thought. *If anyone needed to get drunk, if anyone deserved it, it was me.*

Then he wondered if there'd be any left when he got back down stairs.

Showered with a change of clothes, Jake felt somewhat better. He used Meredith's shampoo. It actually helped him feel like she was still close by. Downstairs, Kelly was showing them all what she had done in the past 24 hours regarding the funeral. Jake hadn't even begun to think about that. He still didn't want to think about that. Kelly had some of it planned out thankfully. The phone rang. It was Erik.

"Hey hommie, how's it hangin?"

"I'd be lying if I said I was sober," Jake said still somewhat sleepy.

"Drunk again? Lucky bastard. Hey, I just got off the phone with Cap'n Jostler down in Rockville. She's putting you on leave for at least the next week. And she wants you to see the doc before reporting. No questions. Got it?"

"Orders is orders, right?"

"Oh, and Boss-man, keep shakin' that bush, man. Keep shakin' that bush."

"I'm shakin' the bush boss, I'm shakin' the bush." The thought of Paul Newman tying a string to the bush made him want to do something like that now, make a quiet getaway. Jake didn't want to be here, anywhere but here that was for sure. Having to face his mother in-law feeling like he'd let her down, let her daughter die, and her grandson. They all knew it was an accident. They all knew it wasn't his fault. All of them knew it except Jake.

Back down stairs, his family stirred and cried and stared at the pictures and memories that He and Meredith had created over the past 10 years. Jake loped down the stairs and went over to the counter where Jake had left the folder that Erik had given him. Jake didn't want anyone to see what was in it. Not that the medical forms of the dead are a big deal, but her death certificate was in there are well. Heart failure secondary to crush injury was the official cause of death. There were also notes from the reconstruction team. The accident laid out in dry mathematical form.

He threw the folder on top of the refrigerator as nonchalantly as he could. Kelly came over and gave him a hug. From that point on, it was all Meredith. That's all they talked about, what she may have wanted, and things of that nature. She didn't like talking about death. She said it was depressing.

No shit! Jake thought. But now it was something Jake had

to do and there was no reference from her. Jake left a lot of the information and decisions to her Mother and Brother. They decided that there would be two caskets, one for Meredith and one for his son, Jonathon Luke. A name Meredith and Jake had tentatively agreed on. Kelly and Jane took it from there. Everything from getting the bodies released, to the viewing. It was all very depressing indeed. Kelly went upstairs and picked out a few dresses for the funeral and burial. Jake went to the kitchen and started drinking. Randy followed. Jake's mom and dad just sat there, trying to make heads or tails of the situation. They were there for moral support he thought, but didn't do or say much. Misery loves company.

Jake gave Randy a glass and threw in two shots of Whiskey and two of the Dewar's. Randy looked at him strange, one eyebrow up. His bushy mustache tilted with his mouth, trying to figure out what Jake was trying to do to him.

"It's my own concoction, though it may already have some fancy name in Boston's. Personally, I call it 'double-shot-of-ass'."

That elicited a smile from Randy.

"Works for me," He said as he threw his glass back and chugged it. He came back coughing and hacking. Jake had to laugh.

"A double shot of--Yeah, that about sums it up. Why in the world would you drink that on purpose?" He coughed some more.

"Well, I've only had it once, you're number two." It does the job it's supposed to when you need it to. Just sit down a while, give it time."

Jake thought it was strange that Randy came over to share a drink, but considering the circumstances, he was guessing 'strange' would be the new norm for the foreseeable future.

- FOUR -

The next four days were a soul numbing experience. Jake tried to stay somewhat buzzed while still being able to focus and function on details for Meredith's funeral. It wasn't working out very well as he wasn't much of a drinking man before this mess started. Kelly and Jane had taken care of most of the technicalities with the funeral home. There was no will, but Jake wasn't going to argue with anyone. He had a precious few items that had belonged to Meredith that he had squirreled away. The rest was open to anyone who wanted something to remember her by.

The engagement ring – so small that Jake was embarrassed to give it to her - one of Meredith's most prized possessions, was something she would be buried with. A necklace that her sister had given to her on their wedding day. Her nails painted a soft earth-tone brown with a shiny sparkle on each index finger. And then there was his son, Jonathon Luke.

Fuck the details for an adult. How the hell does anyone do that for a kid, let alone a baby who died on his birthday? He was 5 pounds, 12 ounces. He was to be buried with a small teddy bear and an ambulance Matchbox car.

It was the small details Jake couldn't handle. He wasn't even sure if he'd go to the funeral at all. He didn't want to remember her that way – he wanted his memories of her to stay fresh and alive. Though he knew the memory of her eyes while she was in the car would haunt him.

Kelly and Erik worked to give all of their friends the schedule and time table for the viewing and the funeral. Jake made sure he was completely sauced for both. Erik, always the experienced one with these issues allowed Jake to drink right up to the closest possible time, then he'd thrown Jake into the shower and force him to brush his teeth just before the viewing and funeral. This way, people would see the bleary eyes of a man in mourning, and not the bleary eyes of a drunk – even though they were essentially the same - without the annoying smell of alcohol and unwashed funk.

It was a beautiful day that belied its purpose. After the funeral, pretty much the most depressing parts of the whole ordeal were completed, everyone went back to Jake's house where the standard thing was to bring food. Kelly had set up a lot of food on her own. A few people brought wine, a few beer, and a few came to mooch the wine and the beer.

In the end, it had been decided to cremate Meredith and Jonathon together. It was done more out of budgetary concerns than out of anything else. The costs of the funerals and plots were too much for Jake to handle even with the offers to chip in. Now the only odd question was who 'gets' to keep the ashes and where. Jake always found that odd when he'd go to people's homes for EMS calls and he see an urn. Now it was his burden. Their urn was an ivory colored porcelain, rimed with gold. It had blue flowers and some doves in flight in the distance. Certainly not something Jake would have picked out in terms of decoration, but it fit Meredith's personality.

Jake had gone all week without talking to anyone from the station. His ambulance chief and the county medical director both came to the funeral as well as a few others that he worked with normally. Captain Jostler was there too as was his union rep. There was even a police officer there that he had worked a few months back.

He knew he'd have to call in at some point, probably when his vacation ran out. He didn't really care about any of that at this point. He was only 45 minutes into some nightmare of sobriety and didn't really care about work at this point. Or life, for that matter. Work could wait. Of course, what Jake didn't know was that Erik was giving Jake's supervisors the information they needed.

When the last of the visitors left, the last of the family was still milling around, cleaning up the paper plates and plastic cups. Erik had retrieved a large canvas bag from his truck and hauled it downstairs. No one really wanted to leave, knowing that once they did, the finality of it all would hit. Jake among them knew this the most. He was just waiting for the last door to close. He wanted the silence, but he feared it at the same time.

Unbeknownst to Jake, Erik and Kelly had hatched a plan – more so Erik, but he kept Kelly in the loop. Erik was in the process of moving in for the time being. He needed to be out on the eastern shore a few days a week for his shifts, but would otherwise be free to look in on Jake and his "recovery". Jake seemed to perk up at learning Erik was moving in. The two were like brothers, and though Erik didn't exactly ask, he didn't exactly need to.

Jane was the last to leave. It seemed that the finality was hard on her as well. She kissed her fingers and touched the urn, gave Jake a hug and the two sobbed for a bit. Randy was out in the car waiting to take his mother home, clearly unnerved by all the emotion and unable to deal with it publically. Jake broke the embrace and kissed Jane on the forehead. They said their good-byes and he closed the door as Jane stepped into the waiting car. As they drove off, Jake wondered if he'd ever see her again. Or anyone from Meredith's side of the family for that matter.

There were still a few things to clean up, and the stillness in the house was hard to take. Erik was downstairs unpacking, just trying to stay out of the way – as he had grown accustomed to of late. After a bit, he came upstairs and sat down at the kitchen table. Jake opened the fridge and grabbed a couple of beers, handing one to Erik.

"Man, if this isn't a fucked up day," Jake said, summing it up the best way he could.

"Yeah, so now what? What's the plan? *Is* there a plan?"

"I don't have a clue. I haven't talked to anyone back at the station – aside from today at the funeral, so I don't know if I have a job, I don't know what the hell is going on, or what."

"Ah, well, this came for you in the mail. It's from State EMS."

State EMS – also known as MIEMSS, or Maryland Institute for Emergency Medical Services Systems. A fancy name for people who need to justify their jobs. Kind of the way a judge or minister wants to be referred to as 'right honorable'. In any case, it was the state agency for regulating Emergency Medical Services within the state of Maryland and if you wanted to get anything done, you had to go through them.

"Hmph. I'm guessing this should be interesting," Jake murmured.

"Well, have a looksee and let me know. I'm going downstairs to go grab a shower. Try not to flush the toilet, would you?"

"Yeah, no problem," Jake replied, turning the music up on his phone. He'd downloaded that song he'd heard the day after the accident. He had it on repeat. "Far From Home". It just seemed to speak to him. He slid his finger under the corner flap of the envelope, ripping it open across the top. Opening the letter, a single page, folded into three sections, Jake read it while walking around the kitchen.

"Dear Mr. Mitchell... Yadda yadda yadda," Jake was half reading half skimming aloud.

"'On the afternoon of June 6th... MVA... Blah blah blah... 'surgical airway'. Ah. Here we go."

Jake took in a deep breath, walked over to the sink and turned on the cold water to fill a glass of ice to dilute the booze of the day.

Jake continued skimming, reading aloud, "'Your license to practice in the capacity of a paramedic within emergency services in the state of Maryland is hereby suspended until further notice... hearing before the review board... plead your case... you may bring your own counsel if you so choose... in case there were extenuating circumstances...'.

"Extenuating circumstances? Circumstances like you assholes require us to be trained a specific way then you fuck us when we use the training that you require us to have." Jake was talking out loud, telling no one in particular.

He was pacing the floor and wondered into the bathroom to straighten up and replace the hand towels. He cleaned up a bit, and tossed a tissue into the toilet, which he then flushed. *Goddamn was he domesticated,* he thought.

In the back of his mind, Jake wondered if any of those jack-holes at the agency level had any recent and relevant pre-hospital or field experience. Considering most had "MD" after their names, he guessed not. EMS was the dirty step-child of the medical world.

He looked over the letter again for a specific date for a

review board hearing. There was none, only an inference that a second letter would be forthcoming. In either case, he'd have to send this up the chain from his county supervisors to see what – if anything - could be done.

There was some yelling and cursing that came from downstairs and it broke his concentration. His thought pattern was still tied to the letter, but the yelling became more distinct and focused. Focused on him. Then he understood. Erik had still been in the shower. Even though it was completely innocent, Jake had managed to suck up all the cold water in the house – subconsciously, that may be a different story. He looked over at the kitchen sink and the faucet was still running. A smirk hit Jake square in the mouth, and with it the faintest glimmer of hope that he might – everything might, just turn out to be okay.

The next morning, the phone rang about 9:30. Captain Madelyn "Maddie" Jostler of Montgomery County Fire and Rescue Services had called to check on Jake. She was a 51-year-old mother of 1200 county Fire and EMS personnel. Maddie had been in the fire service for almost 30 years. Most of that was fire side, but she had done enough time in EMS to know she wasn't cut out for it. Maddie was also the classic "shit-magnet", so it didn't take long for her to come across something that convinced her to stay on the engine. She was careful to give her boys space, but didn't stop taking care of them from the fringes. After a while, Maddie was the one that everyone looked to for comfort or solace or just a shoulder to cry on. She was 'one of the guys' that people could talk to and she would understand or at least not judge them. Maddie had known, and had been through a lot of what her boys – and more and more over the past few years, her girls - had been through.

Jake was planning on heading down to Rockville to start

the process of figuring out where exactly he stood with his job and paramedic license. He just didn't know how to start the process of starting the process. They made an appointment for the next week. There was no point in talking to someone the day after the spouse's funeral.

Maddie met him at the county office building, which was the same building that held the medical team and a few other administrative offices for emergency services. It was directly across from the county courthouse, and sandwiched in between the two was a movie theater and a burrito stand. Presumably in case the county workers got bored; the matinees wouldn't dig too deep into county coffers.

"It's good seeing you Jake. You're looking better than the last time I saw you," Maddie stated, referring to the funeral. "Oh look, and you're sober too! You can't get Jameson past this nose. Even if you try to cover it with Irish Spring."

"Heh, yeah. I guess it's been a while since I've seen daylight. Erik has been keeping me somewhat vertical though," Jake replied.

"How's that rat bastard doing anyway? *Some* of us still miss him," Maddie asked.

"He's doing okay. He's pulling a 48 across the bay. The State P.D. keeps him pretty busy, aside from keeping all of his certs current. Pennsylvania updated their protocols, so he's got to take another course to keep his license with Pennsylvania." As well as the rest of the states he may touch, Jake didn't say aloud.

"Okay, let's see what we've got here. Do you have your paperwork from MIEMSS?" she asked, pronouncing it "mems". "We've got all your other paperwork. It looks like your PALS is coming up for renewal."

Jake huffed when she mentioned PALS, the Pediatric Advanced Life Support class. It was too personal. He might have been a father by now.

"What's the point if they've yanked my credentials? They aren't exactly known for being lenient on medics. God forbid we do something we're fucking trained to do."

He was starting to preach to the choir. Maddie had her own issues with MIEMSS, and in her eyes, they never sided with the medics.

"The point is that it shows them that you're still dedicated. Yes, they can be assholes. In fact, that's all we ever hear about them – but in their defense, most of the time they're dealing with medics who've broken an actual criminal law like stealing drugs, or selling medical supplies out of the back of the rig, or worse. What you did was heroic and if anything shows that paramedics should be trusted with *more* responsibilities."

"Yeah, well my understanding is that they're looking to charge me with practicing medicine without a license. Imagine that. Those peckerwood's feeling encroached upon by a medic. Cowards."

Jake didn't truly hate the agency; he'd never had a run in with them until now. He understood that everyone had protocols to follow. Fire, EMS, the police. Everyone. He just wished they weren't so gung-ho about taking his livelihood away from him. It's like someone was getting off on it. All because he tried to save a life – albeit his own wife's. It just didn't seem right.

Maddie went through all of his paperwork to make sure it was in order. Aside from the Pediatric Advanced Life Support, or PALS certification, they found the blood borne pathogens annual renewal had expired in the three weeks that Jake had been out.

His HazMat Operations refresher was due soon too. Thankfully those two could be done online. The PALS cert would need to be a couple of days' worth of class to get back. The thought didn't sit well with him.

"Okay. Can I still take the classes through the county? I guess that's the big question here. Am I still a county employee?"

"Yes, technically you're on paid administrative leave. Then you can use your vacation, but that won't last too much longer. At the very least we can put you on desk duty, so you will still have some paychecks coming in. I've already talked to someone over at HR and they have a direct line to the union folks. It might take a few weeks, but there are already a few positions being advertised, so we may be able to slide you into one of those."

It's a known fact that county, state and federal governments exist most only to grow and serve themselves, but unions aren't much better. One of the few good things to come of his forced union membership in the IAFF, the International Association of Fire Fighters was that they managed to keep their people employed while investigations are ongoing – that whole 'due process' thing. In Jake's case, which had been receiving somewhat more public attention due to the personal nature, the county wasn't about to make a fuss.

***

As Jake's license to practice had been pulled by the state pending the outcome of the investigation, the county gave him a desk job doing quality assurance on the ambulance run sheets. He had to make sure the guys he ran with from the varying firehouses were filling out the reports properly and crossing all the T's and dotting all the I's. It sucked, getting to read all the calls that he couldn't be on. True to form, most of the calls were running old people to and from the retirement homes or assisted living or half-way houses. A lot of falls and stubbed toes. One call came in for 'dehydration', but upon deeper inspection, the call came in from a new dispatcher and the patient had explosive diarrhea. Jake made of copy of that run sheet, taking care to black out names and addresses and dates. That was one for the cubical wall. He would have puked for sure if that were his call.

A month in and the monotony was starting to get to him. While he craved the solitude and the routine, not being able to do what he considered his 'calling' was eating at him. At times, living with Erik only made it worse. He and Erik would stay up swapping stories or helping one another with certification requirements or what Erik called 'that fancy book learnin'. He also spent time trying to forget the accident, while at the same time talking to Meredith. Every day he'd go home and expect to see her in some form or fashion, maybe even just a sign of her presence. But each time, there was nothing but disappointment.

- FIVE -

"Ambulance 4, Ambulance 4-1, Wagon 4, Rescue 4, Engine 2. Respond Route 340 Northbound, just prior to Marlowe Road. Motor Vehicle Accident, car versus tractor trailer, possible DOA, 1239."

Jake found himself in the driver's seat of an ambulance at his old volunteer fire departments in West Virginia, with Erik next to him.

Erik grabbed the mic. "Ambulance 4 responding. 340 and Marlowe.

"Ambulance 4-1, Rescue 4, County. Same traffic." One of the other crews added.

"Copy that. Ambulance 4, Ambulance 4-1 and Rescue 4 all responding, 1242"

Jake was already out of the parking lot by the time the rescue engine fired up their lights. It was a quarter to one in the morning and who knows what they'd find. They were already talking about a possible DOA, which meant that whatever it is, it must be pretty bad.

"County, Ambulance 4, go ahead with supplemental," Erik said.

"All units, you're responding to an MVA, at 340 North and Marlowe Road. Car versus tractor trailer. PD on-scene reporting at least one obvious DOA. Unknown if there are others at this time."

"Copy that. Can we get a bird on stand-by?"

"PHI is spinning up now," The county dispatch replied.

"Copy that. Thanks."

As they pulled on scene, Engine-2 had already set up a perimeter and blocked the right lane. They were beginning to direct traffic, and some of their firefighters who were also EMTs were assessing a man standing outside of the flatbed tractor trailer. Pulling up to the site, they could tell it wasn't going to be an easy call. They saw an old yellow Buick crumpled mostly under the back of the flatbed. Mostly.

The truck driver had stopped on the shoulder near the intersection to get some coffee and use the restroom at the nearby gas station. He didn't want to pull all the way into the station because that would have been hell getting out with the full load, six tons of 2" stainless steel pipes. The driver said he'd left his hazards on.

The passenger side of the car had hit the left side of the flatbed like one of those off-center crash tests. At the speed the car was going, it was sheered in half, from the engine compartment to the trunk, leaving the passenger side of the car crumpled into the tires and pipes, while the driver's side of the car slid down the side of the pipes. From the look of it, sliding the driver down the side of the truck as well. The side of the truck and pipes were smeared with all manner of blood, gore and brain matter, as the driver of the car was ground down to a nub.

Jake found a finger with a wedding ring on, shoved under one of the nylon straps holding the pipes down. The car was old enough that there were no airbags, and the driver wasn't wearing a seatbelt. Not that it would have helped in this case. He was definitely DOA, or 'dead on arrival'. He didn't smell any alcohol, but what was left of him was still wedged between his seat and the pipes.

The ambulance crews had nothing to do, no people to help or save. In obvious cases like this, the police can pronounce death with a call to the Medical Examiner, so they all went back in service, letting the helicopter crew know their services were not needed. The truck driver wasn't there when it happened so there wasn't a need to get a medical release form from him, though he had his hands full with the police officers.

Soon, the engines left and Jake found himself alone. The darkness was broken only by the headlights and LEDs of his ambulance. Even Erik had seemingly abandoned him. It was just Jake, the ambulance and the lights fending off the darkness. The headlights shining on the back of the truck and the passenger half of the car shoved against it. About the time he noticed he was alone is when he saw it. There was blood on the back of the truck. He hadn't noticed it before. He wondered if anyone else had before they left.

As he walked closer to get a better look, the angle he took towards the pipes showed more and more blood, dripping from the pipes. Then he realized there was someone in the other half of the car. Jake hurried over to the car to see that there was half of a body slumped in the seat. The upper half had been crushed by the impact, the unforgiving seat shoving the upper body, head and shoulders into the 2" diameter stainless steel pipes.

In what seemed a natural move, Jake pulled the car away from the truck to reveal even more gore than the driver. The lungs and skull clearly visible in as many pieces that he could count, all covered with hair, blood and brain matter. The legs had been shattered as they were forced through the floor boards. Jake was used to scenes like this and mostly immune, or so he thought.

He called out to the police officers who were at the front of the truck, but no one answered. He stuck his head around the corner, but he didn't see anything. And he didn't hear anything either. He turned back around, looking at the pipes and froze. Setting before him, in the end of the pipes were two eyes, staring at him, wide and terrified. The wind kicked up, sending a shriek through the pipes. He felt the warmth of urine running down his legs as the wind slowed and the sound in the pipes changed from a scream to a low howl and then into the moan of the dead.

The eyes that were stuck in the pipes followed him as he walked to the other side of the truck, his shadow from the headlights and flickering lights walking along the back of the truck didn't show his how much his legs were shaking. The wind gusted, forcing the sound of the ghost rattle through the pipes to reverberate in Jake's head. His mind was spinning. The sound of the wind sounded exactly like the last breath Meredith took as he opened her throat, the blood spraying and the sound of air being sucked in involuntarily, and of course the eyes, staring at him, accusing him, and never blinking.

***

Jake woke in a sweaty circle on the sheets. The oscillating fan in the bedroom circulating the air the only sound other than his gasping for breath. It was just another nightmare. He didn't sleep well any more. Every time he closed his eyes he saw more and more of the faces of the people that he couldn't help. And the eyes. He always saw a pair of eyes. What rest he did get was either from the Ambien the doctor prescribed him, or from the Bourbon. He preferred Maker's Mark, but this week his usual liquor store was still waiting on a shipment, so he went with a new brand, unfortunately.

Jake was afraid to tell the county shrink. He was required, as part of his continued employment to see the county shrink at least once a week. If they found out about his inability to sleep to the point that it was, then there would be no chance at getting his card back.

He knew it was at least a touch of PTSD. That was all the rage now. It seemed *everyone* had PTSD. It was one thing for a soldier to have it, having been shot at in a war, sheep in a field of wolves, unable to go on the hunt, waiting to be shot at before being allowed to shoot back. But people today claimed PTSD because daddy didn't buy them a pony or mommy didn't hug them enough or they didn't get the promised 'participation medal'.

No. Jake may be undiagnosed, but he wasn't going to waste more county resources on it than need be. For the time being, Ambien and booze was going to have to do. He'd figure out how to deal with it in the long term. He hadn't had to deal with the 'Ambien Walrus' yet. Hell, he'd heard Erik screaming in basement before, nightmares of his own. Maybe that was why he liked to cut loose all the time. Erik had been a medic in the Marines and had been deployed to the overseas shit storm in the Middle East. Jake had never asked about it and Erik never brought it up. At the very least he knew Erik was dealing with some heavy stuff.

But damn it if Erik wasn't always 'on point', Jake could learn to be too. He'd suffer through the bad dreams and shitty booze if it meant he could help people in the end and continue to live his dream of being a paramedic. It really was a calling for him.

Jake had gotten his date to plead his case in front of the MIEMSS board, but it was a few weeks away. Every time he went over the paperwork for the case, the accident, the run sheets, the formality of it all just brought Meredith's death back to him – or more so his inability to save her. He could only manage 15 minute blocks before needing to take a break. Erik had asked around for a good personal injury lawyer. Mr. Llewellyn Masters, esquire. Basically, the one all the cops hated because he could find cracks in almost any legal paperwork. If it wasn't written down, then it didn't happen. If it didn't happen, then his client was not guilty and/or needed to be compensated for it.

He wasn't cheap, but considering the nature of the client, and the reason for the hearing and of course the little bit of publicity, he gave Jake a break and knocked 30% off the bill. *What a guy,* Jake always thought, sarcastically. The union couldn't help much beyond helping keep 'a' job for the time being as it was medical protocols at issue, and he wasn't on-duty at the time. They did tell him that they would write what letters of support they could and that included 'friend of the court' briefs if the need arose in any kind of civil court action.

In any case, the hearing was still what seemed forever away. Two more weeks of the same cookie cutter cube farm life that Jake hated. He just wanted it over with. One way or the other so he could get on with some semblance of his life. He still had the sleepless nights to deal with. Hopefully once this meeting is done and over with, the nightmares would subside.

Jake passed the time by signing up for and renewing his PALS certification. He was allowed to do this during his work day to accommodate work schedules for county employees. For the time being, he was still treated like any other medic for the county. It was brief – just a 2-day class, but it made him feel at home again for the first time in a while. He soaked it all in. The smell of the classroom, the comradery, the fact that he knew half of the class and they could all insult each other with the gusto of lifelong friends while still engaging in teamwork and group learning. The fact that he was going over advanced life support skill for pediatrics didn't bother him in the slightest – This was somewhat odd, considering his previous aversion to the class. He was afraid he wouldn't be able to take the class. He'd always been lucky with kids. A few busted noses, a few seizures, but nothing on the scale of horrific injuries that he'd heard of and the aftermath that he'd helped other medics get through.

The instructor was a younger woman in her mid to late 20s named Brandy. Her last name he didn't catch, but she had a pleasant voice and a soft teaching style. There were no greenhorns in this particular class, so it went a little smoother and a little faster.

The toughest part of the class for Jake was the Broselow Bag. It was all based on the length or height of the child. There were weight variations as well but overall it was a clumsy guessing game at best. The problem was that there were no better options. He'd used the bag system just once in his 15 years in EMS, though he knew medics that swore by them. Erik loved it. Jake thought it was more because he could ask the medics and EMTs out in the field about them and they'd just stare at him with a quizzical look as if he'd just asked what color a 3 headed Orangutan was. Jake had hoped they would phase it out along with MAST pants, but it was not to be. And the MAST pants were just brought back in a different form on a different protocol anyway.

The two-day course was a breath of fresh air. The exam was a breeze, though he only scored an 88. Erik would bust his chops on that one, which is why Jake would tell Erik that he got a 92. Passing is passing. The joke is "What do they call the guy that graduates last in his class at medical school? Doctor." So he skipped out with his passing grade, and got home just before the rush hour traffic got bad on north-bound 270.

When Jake got back to the house, Erik was still sleeping. He had just finished his shift and was taking a well-deserved nap. The door closing behind Jake is what woke Erik up. He stumbled up the stairs, wearing only his boxers and socks.

"Hey Boss-man. What's up?" Rubbing his eyes, not used to the bright afternoon light.

"Nada mi amigo. You?" Jake replied.

"Same shit, different day. How'd class go? I take it you passed?" Erik asked.

"Yeah. Did okay. A 92. Not bad for a rusty old man."

"A 92 huh?" Erik said with a crossed smile. He knew Jake was looking for a break. Erik wasn't about to give him one. At least not now. "That's not what I heard. A 92? Really? Are you sure you want to go with that?"

"That's what the paper said, and that's what I'm sticking to, officer."

"Okay, well, I'll let you talk that over with Ms. Samuels."

"Ms. Who? Samuels?"

"Yeah, you know Ms. Samuels, 26, short, blonde hair, blue eyes, bubble butt, first name is Brandy."

"God dammit – is there is chick out there you *haven't* dated? And how is it that you're still on good terms with most if not *all* of them?"

"Trade secret my friend, trade secret. Actually, you'd be surprised how far treating a woman like gold will get you. A few flowers every now and then, out of the blue. Things like that make them melt."

"You're a slut and Cops are assholes."

"Don't hate." Erik walked over to the laundry room and

grabbed some clothes. "It's my job to keep an eye on you."

"Hmmm. So what's the plan for tonight? Our usual Ozzie and Harriet night at home?" Jake asked.

"Nah man. I need to get trashed," Erik said, putting his boots on. "The sooner the better. It was a rough shift." Erik grabbed his Jacket.

"Aw. Big bad twooper had a bad day in the office? Come tell me all about it," Jake stated in his most condescending parental voice he could muster without laughing, throwing his arm around Erik as they walked out the front door. Jake always seemed to be the designated driver when out with Erik.

***

They headed out Route 85 to a local pool hall called 'Champions'. It was a local bar, but it had that 'chain' feel to it. It was big enough to have live music, restaurant seating and a dozen or so pool tables. The bar was a big enough draw in and of itself. Jake and Erik were probably considered part of the 'regular crowd' more so than they would have liked.

Erik was always the life of the party when he had a few in him. It helped that people wanted to hear gory stories. They always wanted to hear, just not experience what the two of them had to deal with on a semi regular if not regular basis. Jake would always snap back with something along the lines of "It was all cleaned up by the time you got there." Or "I don't think I've ever seen a flight crew go around looking for a limb." But still there were the stories Erik had. The hard tubes, the thoracotomies, and Jake's personal favorite, the escharotomy – having to cut through the dead skin of burn victims so they can breathe. People tend to turn away when you're describing skin sloughing off while they're eating barbeque – but again, that was all in the purview of the flight medic. Jake wasn't allowed to do most of the things Erik would talk about.

For the most part, Jake let Erik have the spotlight in the "world's grossest call" contest. When Erik told the story, he really got into it. He would mention breaking a tooth while trying to get the laryngoscope into the back of the mouth of a fat man who has vomited his dinner and then aspirated it. He'd act out the motion of straddling a patient and trying to direct imaginary EMTs to suction or some such thing. Sometimes he'd use one of the ladies nearby as a prop if she were game. Sometimes it worked. Sometimes he'd get the guys who had to one-up him or folks who saw something "way cooler." Though they rarely had to actually work the patient. Every now and then Erik would come up with a new call that he hadn't told Jake about. Not always gory, but usually very dark and macabre.

This evening's story was entertaining, though no less gory.

"Okay, so this was a few weeks ago, back on the 4th of July. Out on the eastern shore. It had been a quiet day, and that was probably part of the problem. About 9 p.m., we get this call from a squad out in Preston. It seems while everyone was saving their seats to watch the fireworks, it cut out the people that came later from getting a decent spot. So, one guy got the bright idea to get a cherry picker and hauled it out to a field to watch the fireworks. The problem being that it was getting dark and the guy wasn't overly familiar with the field.

"He fired it up. Thankfully it was just him. His buddies were still getting there and getting the beer out of the trucks. Anyway, he jumps in and starts raising it up. He didn't see the power lines above him. He had parked the cherry picker directly below some powerlines. He was holding on to one of the rails and saw the powerlines at the last second. His friends said that he grabbed the powerline as a reflex, just before it would've hit him.

"The electricity shot through him and into the cherry picker, blowing out the hydraulics on the way to the ground. Then the cherry picker came crashing down. So at this point, he had a few things wrong with him. The shock and the 25-foot fall. Anyway, the electrical current traveled through his arms, down his torso and out of his left leg, into the cherry picker.

He had fourth degree burns on 3 of the four limbs, meaning that all the tissue was burned off the bones. His right hand was burned off, some of the bones included. What was left of the radius and ulna were burned, gray and jagged. It was fucked up, man. His left foot basically exploded. He lost that one just below the knee. His right one might be saved, but that's up to the docs. He lost at least one eye. Maybe they can save the other, but I doubt it. The one eye was effectively cooked. I can't imagine what that will do to the other. Let's see" Erik said, looking up, trying to remember all the details of the call. "He broke some ribs in the fall, and punctured a lung and lacerated his spleen. He also had some internal burns, but we'll let the folks at the burn center deal with that."

"Jesus Christ!" someone gasped. "How do you even begin to help someone like that?"

One of the guys in the group that had surround them was taking the story in and trying to make sense of what he considered to be horror.

Erik chuckled. The beers were setting in.

"Well, first it wasn't very bloody at all. Most everything was cauterized. It was what we call a 'distracting' injury. Once you realize that, it's pretty basic. You've got to take care of your ABCs. Your airway, breathing and circulation. He was unconscious, so we didn't need to worry about pain meds at the moment. The local squad did a decent job securing him and getting him stabilized. They intubated him, and popped his lung and got him out to a safe spot for us to fly him out. When we landed, they were still looking for what was left of his foot and the fingers that were blown off."

"Popped his lung?" someone asked, unsure of the euphemism. Erik looked at Jake and rolled his eyes.

"Yeah, popped his lung. He had a collapsed lung. The fix is to allow the trapped air to escape so it doesn't crush the heart and prevent it from pumping. There are a couple of ways to do this, but the fastest and most effective way is by using a 14-gauge needle at top of the lung," Erik said, holding his pinky up as if to say it was the size of the needle. "Maybe a 16, depending."

Jake raised an eyebrow as if to say it didn't matter much.

"So, now this guy who was in such a hurry to see fireworks has changed his personal life in ways he'd never thought of. It wasn't anyone's fault but his own. He was too hasty and didn't check his surroundings. Assuming he makes any kind of recovery, his life is going to be drastically different."

"Wow." One of the guys listening in said.

"So what did *you* do?" He asked.

Jake tried his best to stifle his laugh down to a chuckle, but he couldn't hide his smirk. It was the innocent equivalent of "so what?"

While Erik had taken great strides to make this particular episode of 'adult story fun time' as detailed and grotesque as possible for the small crowd that had gathered around to hear it, he didn't realize that he wasn't framing the tale so he was the 'white knight' of the story. *Erik was slipping. It was probably the beers*, Jake thought.

"What do you mean 'What did I do?'" Jake asked incredulously. "I flew his ass out of there and got him to Bayview for treatment."

"No, what I meant was, he was unconscious, so he didn't need pain meds. The county medics tubed him, so he had an airway. I mean, what did you do for him, outside of getting him to a hospital?"

This guy was determined to dig himself into a hole with Erik, Jake thought. He had been drinking as well, no doubt.

"We stabilized him, threw the 12-lead EKG on him and made sure he survived. We pumped him full of warmed saline. We kept the burn center apprised of the ongoing changes in his physiology in real time to make sure the right people were there when we arrived to give him definitive care. Other than keeping him alive and stable I guess we didn't do much of anything," Erik said sarcastically, while glaring at the guy.

"Do you know why the saline has to be warm? Because you're a Jackass," Erik said, trying to end the conversation.

After a couple more hours it was time to head home. Jake was getting tired; the sodas were getting flat. Erik was coming down off his buzz, almost to a point of sobriety. Almost.

"Come on Erik. It's getting to be that time. We have to get going."

"Alright. Let me pay my tab and we can bounce up out of this mofo'!" Erik's voice getting louder with each syllable.

The bill came, was paid and the two 'brothers' fell out of the place. Erik all but singing, belting out the theme to "The Jefferson's" in an off key manner reserved only for the semi-sober or borderline drunk. *Strange, but not all that out of place for Erik,* Jake thought, amusing as it was. They hopped into Erik's truck, Jake making sure he had the keys.

The ride home was uneventful though Jake sensed something was on Erik's mind as Erik had gone quiet.

"Hey Erik, how're you sleeping these days?" Jake asked, hoping Erik hadn't gotten too sober. Prodding a bit too see if his symptoms matched Jake's.

"I sleep fine and dandy, Boss-man," Erik slurred his S's. "No problems here."

He decided he'd let it go until Erik approached him about it. If it came to that. Erik was almost too good at masking his emotions. Jake was just the opposite and wore his emotions on his sleeve. It was a good night they both agreed, something they both hoped would become more plentiful.

***

To Jake, the few weeks between the class and the hearing passed like molasses. It was torturous watching the clock day-in and day-out. Reading run reports that only pointed out to him what he wasn't doing. Telling him what he would have done on this call or that. How he would have done things differently or not. He even learned a thing or two. Though mostly just new abbreviations for drugs or diagnosis from patient transfers.

The MIEMSS office was on West Pratt street, a block over from Shock-Trauma, 2 blocks from Camden Yards where He and Meredith would go to watch Orioles games. It brought back some memories that he had to suppress. Though, he wasn't sure he'd be able to in the hearing.

Jake's lawyer, Llewellyn Masters, showed up on time, and had a stack of folders and papers. Most had absolutely nothing to do with the current case before him. Jake was resigned to resign. He had all but given up.

"Hey Jake." Llewellyn shook his hand. "I haven't had much experience with this type of thing, but I'll try to keep your commenting to a minimum. You may need to answer some basics, 'Yes'. 'No'. That type of thing. I've got a stack here that *should* keep your license."

The cases he held in his hands were all current or former paramedics from the state of Maryland, with one case being from North Carolina. It just so happens that one of the members of Jake's current review board was at one time a member of the North Carolina Office of EMS. It looked as if Llewellyn had actually done his homework after all.

30 minutes later, with only sparse questions for and replies from a teary-eyed Jake, Llewellyn had quite easily shown the review board the error of their ways. Playing to several of the members' previous opinions usually published elsewhere outside of the bureaucracy that was MIEMSS, as well as the very nature of helping one's spouse, being akin to helping a child. No one sitting in the room would sit idly by and watch as a child died choking on something when any one of them could 'fix' the situation. Llewellyn also kindly pointed out that Jake – and all paramedics – had to recertify every 3 years, whereas the doctors on the board only needed to keep up with their CMEs, or Continuing Medical Education credits, something the medics also needed to do.

The point being that Jake was the only one in the room who had any recent training – allowed by protocols or not – on how to complete a surgical cricothyrotomy in the field. The doctor previously from North Carolina was actually in favor of allowing paramedics, at least some ground-based paramedics do surgical airways in the field. The case Llewellyn had brought was a case in which the doctor had praised a young paramedic who had a 30-minute wait for a flight medic. His patient was a 17-year-old male who had crushed his own throat trying a new trick using a couple of skateboards. Rare instances indeed, but no more rare than some other procedures that paramedics can do on standing orders, without having to contact MedCom – or medical command.

However, the issue remained that Jake had indeed broken protocol and gone outside the boundaries of his license. So while the review board understood why he did so, they still had to do something to discourage others from doing the same. The board had effectively decided his fate before the hearing. Jake would keep his license to be a paramedic, however his license would be suspended for 6 months to include time served. His job would still be waiting for him when he got back, but he had to survive for the next 3 months.

There were mortgage payments, car payments, and of course he was upside down on both. The economy sucked too, so getting a quick buyer for the house or blue-book on the car would be difficult. Maybe he could teach. That wouldn't be up to MIEMSS. That would be up to the county, and he already had an inside track with Maddie. He'd have to hit her up for something to bridge the gap. All in all, he was feeling pretty good all things considered. He had an out.

Maddie was expecting his call. She had eyes everywhere. One reason 'her boys' were so protective of her.

"Jake! Congratulations! I heard you got a longer vacation."

"Yeah, I guess." Jake didn't ask how she knew. She just did. "Do you happen to have anything open for the next few months?"

"We do, we do!" She was excited for him. He could start to put everything behind him, sort of. "You still have the choice to keep doing the QA on the run sheets, though we'd have to drop your pay since you're not an 'oh-fficial' paramedic at this point."

"No. that would be a worst case scenario for me, I think. It's driving me nuts. Is there anything else?"

"I figured you'd say that. Let's see. We've got an instructor position coming up, but that's not for another month – mainly Advanced Trauma Life Support. Same pay though, no 'medic' license needed. Of course there are other classes you'd have to teach, but ATLS is the biggie. We'll have to check your test scores to see if you qualified for the instructor's class. It's more about how to teach than the actual material, since you've already taken and passed that one."

"Yeah, let's do that one. Can you let me know on that?"

"Absolutely, Hon. Other than that, how're you doing?"

"Well, I'm still sober. Mostly."

"Good, we'll get you taken care of. Don't you worry. I'll give you a call when I verify that everything is a go."

A voicemail from Maddie later that afternoon confirmed that he could slide into the instructor position after he took the ATLS instructor class. She would assign the training center as his new 'duty station' and he would be responsible for getting the class taken care of. The time and place of his choosing, and of course at his expense.

"Hey you fat bastard!" Erik exclaimed walking through the door. Jake was lying on the couch watching TV.

"I see you're not drinking, so that means good news, right?" Erik asked.

Jake, replied while rolling off the couch, "My license is suspended for another 3 months, so 6 months total. But after that I get to go back to work, a letter in my file. I talked to Maddie and they've got an instructor position open, but I've got to take the ATLS Instructor course somewhere."

"Somewhere, huh?" Erik asked.

"Yeah, ATLS is private national certification so the class is the same everywhere. It's not state spec...." Jake tailed off, all of a sudden wondering why he had to explain this to Erik.

"Look, Boss-man. I've been wanting to talk to you about something." Jake felt the air get tense. Erik had a serious look on his face, something he'd rarely seen.

"What is it?" Jake replied.

"It's nothing, really. It's just that I think you need a change of scenery. You need to get out of this place." Erik was pointing around him, referencing the house and everything in it, including the memories.

"You're wallowing here, wasting away. You don't eat, you don't get out unless I drag you. You don't even fit your clothes anymore."

Jake accepted that he was a shadow of his former self. How does a shadow eat, sleep and live? He'd lost his best friend, his partner. He'd lost the meaning of life. To this day he hadn't been in Jonathon's room. It was exactly the way it was the day of the accident. The fire engine curtains – they couldn't find ones with ambulances on them, Jake cried 'Discrimination!" at the time they bought them - the crib in the corner sat waiting for a baby to fill it, now gathering dust. He could hear the mobile clink and clang together like a wind chime when the air conditioning was on. He had given up in his own mind with nothing left to fight or live for. That his clothes were big on him never really registered until now.

"And what would you suggest? I can't deny that I need an

actual vacation, but I can't afford Hawaii, or my dream trip to Wyoming or Alaska."

"How about California?" Erik was serious.

"California? What's out there? In California, that mad crush of people? Seriously?"

"Yeah. I've got some contacts out in L.A. that can get you into the right classes, hook you up with the right people. Your sister has that timeshare. I figure you could use that for a place. All you'd really have to pay for is food and a ride. I can help you with the airfare."

"No, man. You've already helped me enough, moving in and all. You don't need to spend any more money on me."

"Okay. I offered." Erik smirked walking away quickly. "You've got the time. If you waste it here, I'll kick your ass, and then leave what's left for Maddie to bury." He yelled up the stairs as he retreated to the basement.

Jake mulled it over. The house was a sanctuary for him, but he also knew it to be taking a toll on him. He didn't know how to move on without letting go of Meredith. He was afraid of losing her again. He needed an anchor.

"Are you coming with me? I have the place; you have the connections," Jake yelled downstairs.

It surprised Erik. Hopefully this would be Jake's push out of the nest he needed to find his wings again.

Erik stepped back over to the landing, looking up the stairs at Jake.

"I hadn't really thought about it. If I can do it, then I'll probably be working everyone's shift until kingdom come. Let me make some calls." Erik really was going to be working holiday shifts for everyone.

"Okay. I'll check on plane tickets; you call your people out west."

And just that fast, it was a done deal. In a week, they'd be in sunny Los Angeles, California.

The night before the trip, Jake woke up again in a pool of sweat, another nightmare, another person he couldn't save. This time, the eyes were watching him from over his shoulder. The howling wind ringing in his ears, unable to get away from the sense of the eyes, staring at him, pleading with him to do what the both knew he couldn't, only reminding him of his failure. He could only hope the nightmares would subside after a vacation. They were set to leave out of Baltimore early the next morning.

- SIX -

Arriving at L.A.X. was pretty easy. They'd gotten a direct flight from BWI airport on Saturday morning, arriving just before 1 p.m. local time. The airport was busy but not packed. Erik picked up the luggage while Jake went to the rental car desk. A few minutes later, they headed out to meet the shuttle to the rental lot.

Getting off the bus, the two walked down along the numbered parking spaces. Jake stopped short and Erik almost ran into him.

"Hey Boss-man, what's the deal? Did you forget something?" Erik asked, picking up the sunglasses that he'd dropped trying to avoid the collision.

Jake just stood in front of parking spot 86 and sighed heavily. He started fidgeting with the two keys that the rental agent had given him, tied together with some kind of cable so they wouldn't get separated.

Erik looked at him, and then the car with confusion on his face. The realization struck and Erik saw red.

"Dude, I should kick your ass back to the east coast. What the hell were you thinking? Not only will we not get any respect, we'll be lucky not to get laughed at," Erik fumed.

Jake had gotten the cheapest car that wasn't a hybrid. That got them a light maroon Toyota Corolla. It was the base L model with a 4-cylinder engine, automatic transmission, manual windows and an odd smell. There was a rainbow air freshener hanging from the rearview mirror.

"Could you have gotten a more pussified car? I didn't even know they made an 'L' model," Erik asked, snatching the air freshener off the mirror.

"Hey, the next car up was an extra $40 bucks a day, and it was a pink smart car, so shut up and get in."

The car started with no problems and the GPS that was suction cupped to the dash turned on automatically.

"Kelly gave me the directions to the Marriott she has her timeshare through. It's over off Olympic Boulevard," Jake said, handing the address to Erik to enter in to the GPS.

Before he finished, Erik told Jake, "The fastest way is going to be the 105 to the 110."

"Hmph," Jake grumbled, looking at the GPS after Erik had put in the address. Erik was right. He was always right, the fucker. "Yeah. But let's get something to eat. I haven't had anything since that overpriced burrito back in Baltimore. Even the flight snacks sucked," Jake was getting grumpy.

"Okay, take the Exposition Boulevard exit off the 110 and hang a left. That will put us in the area of the USC campus and the law school. Hopefully, that will give us something to look at, enjoy the scenery if you will," Erik stated.

Erik was testing the waters. He and Jake never talked about Meredith or the accident. They never talked about how Jake felt, if he was thinking about ever moving on. Erik didn't know how much time to give the guy. He hadn't even so much as looked at another woman even in the carnal-lustful way that all guys looked at women with at some point. Erik didn't understand it. How do you get over something like that? Jake and Meredith had been married 7 years, together for 10. It had only been 3 months since the accident. But to Erik, it had *already* been three months.

"Hmmm. USC in September. I can go for some decent scenery right about now," Jake replied.

Jake had been dealing with his own feelings. He still felt connected to Meredith, but still had the same wants and desires as every other man. Single or otherwise. It caused Jake a lot of confusion internally, feeling he had betrayed Meredith if he looked too long, or allowed himself to feel – anything, really. *The healing process takes time, and each person is different. It's only been 3 months.* The little voice in his head kept telling him.

"Where is there a place to eat around there?" Jake asked, passing the DMV, still trying to get on Exposition Avenue, still technically on South Hope Street.

Passing the ubiquitous Starbucks, and all the lightly colored brick buildings, the street somehow was magically renamed West Exposition, and they were where they were supposed to be, according to Erik. Now, to find a place to eat.

There was a glint of light in front of them, and then they saw a car roll up on the left side jersey wall and roll over, almost in slow motion. And then there was a wall of red brake lights. The cars slamming on their brakes forcing their rear ends up as their front brakes grabbed and forced their front ends down. Jake was sure they were going to eat the back end of the pickup truck that was in front of them. Lucky for them, the Corolla was a lot lighter and able to stop sooner. The wreck was four cars in front of them.

Erik was amped up, grabbing his cell phone.

Jake, meanwhile, was fighting back memories of the last car accident he was at. This time, before him was an overturned silver Mercedes instead of a Saturn. It didn't look like much of an issue, though for a car to be overturned, there was enough energy transferred to be of concern. There was a woman in the car screaming. The box truck that sideswiped it was stopped on the side of the road just ahead of them. The driver was out and walking back towards them.

The side windows were either shattered out or already rolled down. There wasn't as much glass as he'd expected. There were fluids from the car leaking, mostly antifreeze. The woman inside was moving around alright, and screaming loud enough to know that she was moving air. She was just so frazzled about being upside down that she couldn't think straight, possibly a panic attack in the process. Erik was sarcastically irritated.

"Dammit, Jake I am *not* on the clock. Three thousand miles away and you're *still* a god damn shit-magnet," Erik said with that smirk on his face that showed off his dimples. Walking over to the overturned car rather nonchalantly, Erik was fishing for his phone to call 911.

Jake got down on his knees and peered into the car. The woman was still screaming her head off. He had to calm her down enough to get an idea if she was hurt. She was in full blown panic, screaming about how someone needed to get her out and how she was going to die and yadda yadda yadda. Jake had heard it all before. The hard part was getting their attention and then getting them to shut up long enough to let him help.

"Hey. Hey! Hey Lady! We're EMS. We need you to calm down a bit. We're here to help. What's your name?" Jake tried.

"Screw you! I can't breathe! I can't... My hands are tingling! I can't breathe, I... I... I feel like I'm going to die!" the woman screamed, sounding out of breath. "Get me out of here!"

"Should we just wait until she passes out? They're much easier to deal with after they've passed out," Erik asked.

Jake shook his head in agreement, almost as if he was considering it.

"Lady, I'm here to help you but you have to listen to me. I can't help you if you don't listen to me. Are you hurt anywhere? Are you bleeding?" Jake asked. He wasn't about to crawl in there with this 'Tasmanian Devil' thrashing around inside.

Erik had walked up next to him talking to the 911 operators.

"Yes, ma'am. There are two out of state Paramedics on-scene… Maryland… Yes, we've started assessing. There is so far a single patient, so far I think she's okay, we'll let you know of anything serious…. Yes, I'll stay on the line," Erik said to the operator, conveniently forgetting to mention that technically, Jake was no longer a paramedic or that he was a Maryland State Trooper, neither of which really mattered as both were outside of their jurisdiction.

The woman in the car must have heard part of the conversation because she almost stopped screaming. Almost.

"Paramedics? You're paramedics?" she half asked, half yelled at Jake, who rolled his eyes and gritted his teeth in frustration.

"Yes. It's a long story. Are you hurt anywhere? Can you move your hands and feet?" Jake asked.

"Uh, yeah. My hands are tingling though." she said, still hanging upside down by her seatbelt. She was fighting back the panic.

"Well, at least you were wearing your seatbelt," Jake said with a sarcastic tone. "My name is Jake, my partner here, who has the finest calves that you can see at the moment is Erik. We flew 3,000 miles just to help you out of this mess. What's your name?"

"Heh. Well, I appreciate that. But technically, you haven't done anything yet," she replied with noticeably more calm and the same sarcastic wit that Jake had taken with her.

"I'm Terra." she added, her voice still holding a tremble.

"Nice to meet you, Terra," Jake said.

Fit and trim, Terra was a leggy brunette, with very wavy

hair. He couldn't tell how long it was since she was hanging upside-down. She answered all the questions Jake asked, could move everything and was insistent that she get out of that car, afraid it was going to explode, something that Jake laughed at. She was well enough to extricate herself, but just needed a calm voice to tell her how, which Jake did.

"Thank you so much," Terra said.

She was climbing out through the driver's side window, slowly letting her weight shift on her knees, crawling around the small slivers of glass. Still a hint of panic shivered in her voice. Terra was a bit more shook up than she was letting on.

"So what happened?" Jake asked.

"That truck swerved to miss something in the road and side wiped me. After that, I don't remember much," Terra replied, clinging to Jake as she stood up.

Erik was still on the phone with the 911 operator, trying to get some idea of where they were. There were no street numbers on the buildings, but there were a lot of students starting to gather and gawk. There was some sort of subway system or light-rail to the left of the road. The dispatcher seemed to know about where they were and had dispatched an ambulance and an engine crew along with a police officer. At some point, all you need is a traffic jam to follow and you'll get to the scene.

The officer was just pulling up as she was getting out of the car. The driver of the box truck had brought over a moving blanket to put around her, and then went to talk to the officer. Neither Jake nor Terra really understood why the blanket was offered as it was a balmy 84° out. They just assumed that he was a bit shaken as well.

"Okay Miss Terra, I've got to ask you some questions," Jake said.

"Okay. Shoot," Terra perked up, thankful to concentrate on something.

"Do you have any medical issues we need to know about?"

"No. I've been to rehab for alcohol, but I've been sober now three years. No other medical issues."

"Good, good. So now we know you're a menace to sobriety," Jake retorted with some dry humor. "When was the last time you had something to eat?"

"I had a latte and some stale popcorn for breakfast. I was on my way to lunch with friends."

He noticed people taking photos with their phones. He hated people like that. Too damn high and mighty to get their hands dirty, but stoop low enough to take pictures of someone else's problems.

"Okay. Let's have a look at those pretty eyes," Jake blurted.

He couldn't catch himself in time. He was used to working on attractive patients, but was also used to focusing on his professionalism. Usually, even the most attractive patients were at their worst by the time they needed EMS.

Terra smiled though. She was used to being hit on – as she took it to be. Terra stood a little taller and a little straighter and tried to look directly into Jake's eyes. He noticed, but he was back in 'Medic-mode' after his slight loss of focus. Not having a pen light, he covered both of her eyes with his hand and then uncovered one, noting the pupil dilation. Then he repeated the same on the other eye. Terra seemed a bit let down by this. It was so clinical and impersonal.

Jake noted both pupils were equal and reactive.

"Now, is there any chance you could be pregnant?" Jake

asked, again highly aware of his earlier slight.

"Meow, honey. Sadly, no. Absolutely no chance of that for some time," Terra answered, showing some sass.

Jake laughed out loud at that one. "I'll just mark that as a 'no'."

Terra huddled against Jake, leaning in, almost asking for him to put his arm around her. Jake noticed but backed up a bit, but still catching a whiff of her perfume.

The ambulance showed up with the engine right behind it, both driving on the wrong side of the road in order to reach the accident scene.

"Nice to know some things don't change," Erik mused, referring to the fact that the ambulance always beat the engine to the scene. Jake got a chuckle out of that too.

"Yeah, I bet that looks *real* shiny during parades, though," Jake said, talking about the fire engine. While the 'Fire' side and 'EMS' side worked hand in hand, they always had a bit of a competition going on between them.

The ambulance pulled up next to them and a paramedic jumped out of the passenger seat, after putting the radio mic back on the console. They weren't in any hurry. There was no need to be.

Jake gave the patient information he had to the medic that came up to him.

"These guys are going to take good care of you. They'll probably ask you the same questions I did and a few more. But let them take you to the hospital to get checked out," Jake stated to Terra.

"No. I'm fine. I don't need to go to the hospital. I need to figure out how to fix my car and get to lunch," Terra replied.

"Terra, dear, do you remember flipping your car?" Jake

asked in his most authoritative tone.

"Hmm. No, not really." Her expression changed instantly.

"Is that bad?" She feigned.

Jake guffawed, "Yeah, I'd say that's a bad thing, not remembering flipping your car."

The L.A. County medic stood there, a gob smacked look on his face. Jake just chalked it up to the situation or something had he had to deal with earlier. It *was* a nice car after all, looked to be a six-figure car, probably totaled the thing, having just rolled it, even if it *was* a 'gentle' roll. The medic guided her to the stretcher where she sat down. They strapped her in sitting up, and started rolling her towards the ambulance.

Jake and Erik started walking back to their car. Erik, again with his trademark smirk. "You know who that is, right?"

"Know who who is? I don't get it."

"Wait, wait! Wait!" Terra cried out. "Jake! Please! Come with me to the hospital. Please."

Jake started walking back toward the stretcher.

"What? Why? These guys are good. They'll take care of you, right. Mr...?" Jake said, looking over at the county paramedic.

"Jackson," The medic replied.

"Right. Paramedic Jackson here will take care of you. You'll be fine."

"Please. I haven't been in a hospital since my rehab days. Please," she begged.

Jake relented. "Okay. Okay. Let me let Erik know. Is it okay for me to ride in the back, Mr. Jackson?"

"Usually not, but I won't tell if you don't. Just make sure to stay on the bench, and out of the way."

"No problem."

A slight breach of protocol, but not unheard of to let non-patients in the box. Jake was walking back to Erik. It seemed nothing would wipe that smirk off of Erik's face.

"Hey homie, she's really freaked out. She asked me to go to the hospital with her," Jake told Erik.

"Ha! Yeah, I bet. No problem. I'll follow the rig to the hospital and pick you up there."

"Hey. Who is she? You asked me if I knew who she was. I have no idea."

"Nothing Boss-man. I'll tell you later. Go save a life."

The last line was as sarcastic as Erik could be, equating saving a life to holding the patient's hand was polar opposites to say the least.

"Still," Jake said pointing at people, most with their phones up, taking pictures. "Fucking vultures taking pictures. It's not even that bad of an accident. These people must be sheltered."

Erik laughed at the irony, both for the reason why they were taking pictures, and the fact that Jake had no idea who his patient really was – and he had just complained about people being sheltered.

They had just slid the stretcher into the ambulance when Jake stepped up on the folding bumper and into the back of the ambulance. Terra's face relaxed noticeably. Her breathing slowed. Even Paramedic Jackson noticed.

Sitting on the stretcher, Terra thought to herself that Jake did have a confident presence. Maybe not a commanding presence, but definitely a confident one. He obviously knew what he was doing. She couldn't explain it, maybe it was just the nerves after an accident. She felt safe around him, that nothing would happen to her with him around. Security was it? Whatever it was, she hadn't felt it in a long time.

On the way to the hospital, they exchanged pleasantries. She had a thousand questions about what paramedics do, and what her paramedic, Mr. Jackson as they'd come to call him, was doing, and so on. Mr. Jackson picked up the mic and called into the hospital, giving basic patient information: female driver, restrained in a roll-over MVA, self-extricated, and GCS of 15, vital signs within normal limits, with an ETA of 3 to 5 minutes, which is what Jake was wanting to know. This was his first time on a call, in the pre-hospital environment since *the accident*.

Terra looked confused.

"15. Is that good?" she asked about the GCS number.

"Well, even dead people get a 3," Jake started, "but 15 is the highest you can go. So yes, it's good."

Jake looked over at the paperwork. He hadn't paid much attention, but it listed her last name as "D." Just "D." That's odd, he thought, but just assumed it was shorthand for the medic to remember. As the ambulance backed in to the ambulance bay, Terra asked the same question everyone wants to know, even other medics.

Just as the ambulance was backing into the hospital bay, Terra asked "So, Jake. What was your worst call ever?"

Even Paramedic Jackson looked up for this answer.

"Oh wow. Being all open about things now are we? That's getting a little too personal." Jake said, allowing him to avoid the question.

The decision was made that she could walk out of the ambulance on her own, without being brought in on a stretcher. She insisted. Jake didn't think much about it as patients sometimes prefer to walk than ride. Jake got out, and he helped Terra step down, holding her hand for stability, with Mr. Jackson following on his own. The three of them walked through the ambulance bay doors of the California Hospital Medical Center's Emergency Department. Jake looked around and saw Erik pull up in a spot on South Hope Street, adjacent to the ambulance bays.

He held up a finger as if to say, "Wait a minute", and Erik shook his head in acknowledgement, popped a Virginia Slim out of his pocket and puffed away. He knew it might be a while. Erik noticed a hotdog truck when he pulled up. It wasn't the best thing, but it was something. He'd pick one up for Jake, too.

Back in the ER, after a quick once-over by the attending physician, the charge nurse there said that Terra was basically just 'walking wounded' and would be discharged as soon as possible. There was no trauma, and no signs of a concussion. Terra was making some phone calls and telling people that she was okay, and where she was at and what had happened. Every time Jake tried to leave, she'd put the phone down and grab his hand.

"No, no, no. Please stay!" Terra pleaded. This last time she took the hint that he wanted to leave. "Please stay, at least until Angela get here. She's my assistant."

"Your assistant?" Jake asked, a quizzical look on his face

"Yeah. My assistant, why?" she shot back, almost on the offensive

"Nothing. I guess I really don't know who you are. Erik said something but didn't finish."

"Wow. You really don't know who I am, do you?" Terra replied in half shock, half amazement. "Oh now I really *do* like you. I wasn't sure if you were just playing it cool or if this is how you treat all of your patients."

"Well, yeah. I guess." Jake wasn't sure which of those two he agreed to, or what the situation with her was.

"Okay. Have you seen the movie *Moonlight Storm*?" she asked.

"*Moonlight Storm*? Sounds familiar, but nothing obvious comes to mind."

"It 'sounds familiar'?" Terra said, putting up air-quotes.

"A $700 million movie, and it only 'sounds familiar'?" she asked, astonished to hear someone who hadn't known of her latest blockbuster. "It was the largest 4th of July Opening in history. It just premiered in China last month."

"Oh. So you're *that* Terra Dee?" Jake replied in a notably sarcastic tone.

Jake was enraged at what he considered her arrogance, and the presumption that people have nothing better to do than fawn over a movie star.

"Well, I'm sorry Ms. Dee. I've had a lot of issues to deal with over the past few months," Jake said as he turned to leave the room, his anger starting to show. "You'll have to excuse me. I have to go. You're in good hands here. You take care."

And with that he was gone.

Terra was left there in the emergency room alone. It was the first time she felt alone in a long time. She hated it. Terra let her guard down for an instant because of a connection she thought she'd made, but now, that connection, and her security blanket was gone. She didn't understand why. Terra wasn't alone for long before her assistant, Angela walked in with her purse, a change of clothes, and a sycophantic attitude. Usually, Terra loved it. Now, however it seemed as hollow to her as it did to most people.

Jake stormed out of the Emergency room doors, using the ambulance bays for an exit to the street. He found Erik leaning against their car waiting for him.

"How'd it go, Boss-man?" Erik asked.

As Jake approached, Erik's smile faded and he questioned, "Uh oh. What happened?"

"Nothing. Let's just get the fuck out of here. I need something to eat and I need to get the fuck out of here," Jake said, so enraged that he was on the verge of tears. His emotions had been so messed up the past few months.

"Okay, okay, Boss-man. We're gone. We're gone. Let's head back to the hotel and get settled in, cool?"

Erik was going to let Jake settle down before pressing him for more. He was dying to know what the story was with the famous Terra Dee. He even forgot about the two wadded-up hotdog wrappers in the back seat.

Erik turned the car on and headed out. He knew the way, mostly. They were only about 15 minutes from their hotel, and no more highway to drive if they didn't want to. They worked their way back over to South Grand and took a left on Olympic Boulevard. The buildings were a lot taller than Jake had expected, who was looking up with his mouth open, obviously a tourist.

Erik stayed in the left lane, instinctively finding that the even-numbered addresses were on the left side of the road. He noticed the Residence Inn on the right. Erik saw the building numbers in front of the hedge row of the shiny building and turned in. Then it hit him that this wasn't a regular old Marriott or the Residence Inn. The sign said it was the 'JW Marriott', but upon further inspection, this was *also* the LA Ritz Carlton, and here they were driving up in a car that might have been worth $15,000 if it was brand new. It looked to Erik that this car was a good investment after all – only now he was wishing there was more rust. He liked making a scene. Pulling up next to a blue shuttle bus and a $150,000 Bentley, Erik was falling in love already. There was a lot of potential here to make people uncomfortable. There was an Aston Martin that was pulling out. Both Erik and Jake got out of the car, and a valet driver was waiting for them with a smile.

- SEVEN -

Good Afternoon, Sir. Welcome to the Ritz Carlton," the valet said with what seemed to Erik as a genuine smile.

Erik handed the keys to the valet, who then handed him a plastic tag that matched where ever they were going to park the car. Another valet moved their bags to the curbs where they were promptly picked up by another employee who was just as gracious and happy as the first.

"Hey, fellas! How are we doing today? Welcome to the LA Ritz! My name is Jake, but people here call me T.J. If you need anything at all, call down here and ask for me. I'm the man around here that can get you anything you need. Alright fellas?"

T.J. was a tall black man with an infectious smile. He was dressed very sharply, even for a Ritz employee, and very welcoming.

"Hey Jake!" Erik said with and enthusiastic handshake.

"My name is Erik, and this is my buddy, Jake."

"My name is Erik, this is my brother Jake, and this is my other brother Jake," Erik said in homage to Bob Newhart.

T.J.'s face lit up at the reference, as did Jake's. T.J. shook their hands. He liked them instantly, or at least the façade of what was there.

"You guys in town for work or play?" T.J. asked.

"Mostly work, but if we happen to have a little fun, we won't tell anyone if you won't," Erik replied.

"Uh huh, I see," T.J. nodded with a knowing smile. "Well, how long are you in town for?"

"Well, technically I think 2 weeks, but I'll only be here half that. I'm going to try and convince Jake here to stick around and decompress. He's had a rough time of late," Erik replied, a little more open than Jake would have preferred.

"Erik! Come on man. Knock it off," Jake said, still irritated from the hospital.

"No, no. That's cool," T.J. interjected. "I don't want to press. But like I said, if either of you cats need anything, you let me know. I can hook you up. And if I can't, then I know someone who can."

T.J. put the bags down away from the check-in desk and held his hand out to Jake, who promptly shook it. Erik, a little more in tune with protocol slid a $20 bill to T.J., and shook his hand again.

"Like I said, he needs to decompress a bit," Erik said with a smirk.

"Understood. No problems, and thank you," T.J. replied taking the tip, and walked off.

His booming voice and positive attitude preceded him as he walked back out the front door, the sun glinting off the top of his shoes. Erik and Jake both took an instant liking to the man.

Jake was the one that had to check in. Kelly had booked them an executive suite with a separate bedroom that Jake took and although they could have requested a second bed, Erik just slept on the couch. There were two bathrooms, but only one had a shower so as long as they could both go to the bathroom without having to wait on the other, Erik was happy. Jake just wanted to relax some.

Aside from the size, the room could have been any other room in the Marriott family. The couch was comfortable enough, but the fabric was still stiff an unused. The furniture was made from real wood though, not the Ikea, flat-pack fiber-board stuff that's in most hotel rooms.

As soon as they hit the room, Erik grabbed the room service menu and ordered a couple of $15 hamburgers, $5 fries and $5 bottles of water. The one meal, with tip was over $60 dollars. Erik just signed the form to charge everything to the room when the meal got there. Neither of them had the immediate scratch to pay cash, and neither wanted to deal with it.

Jake was still running the time with Terra over and over in his head. The car accident, the ambulance ride, the time in the emergency room. Had he over reacted? Was he too touchy? Was she *trying* to be arrogant? To show that she thought she was somehow *better* than regular people? He didn't know. The fact that he couldn't stop thinking about her eyes, the way she stood up and looked straight at him on-scene. He was just looking *at* her eyes. She was looking *into* his. He couldn't get her out of his head and that worried him. He figured he'd never see her again anyway. His brush with a famous person.

Thinking of Terra only led to him thinking of Meredith. He had to figure out how to accept that Meredith was gone. Was it something you just did? Was the guilt just a cut, over and over again causing a scar or a callus? He didn't know. He was already numb.

Jake and Erik ate their lunch with little said between them. They were both beat, Jake more so. Jake finished his burger, left some cold fries on his plate, and then headed back to the bedroom. He closed the curtains on the windows, which had a view of a highway, turned off the lights, and crashed on the bed, fully clothed.

Erik finished about as much as Jake, and was tired, but didn't want to sleep. At first, he turned the TV on. The news was coming on, with a TMZ commercial ahead of it. If there weren't hot women and big explosions, he wasn't interested so he turned it off and headed downstairs to see what there was to do. He had arranged to meet up with some of his friends the next day, and the class was scheduled for Monday through Wednesday, which was time that he wouldn't have to babysit Jake for the day.

Erik hopped on an elevator down to the lobby. He grabbed his cigarettes out of his pocket as he was walking out the main entrance. T.J. looked over at him and they exchanged nods. Erik walked over to the corner of the building, following the sun. It was almost 5 p.m. and he wanted to soak up the rays while he had the chance. Erik lit a cigarette, took a long drag and let it out slowly. This was his 3rd cigarette today. He was slipping back into old habits. Erik had decided to hit the hotel gym when he got back upstairs. As he turned, T.J. had walked up behind him.

"Hey Boss-man, what's up?" Erik asked.

"Not much, man. Just came over to see if you needed anything, and maybe bum a smoke," T.J. answered.

"No problem, boss," Erik said as he took out his pack and shook one up.

T.J. grabbed it and then noticed the cigarette was thinner. Then he looked at the pack.

"Virginia Slims?"

"I know, I know. They were cheap when I started smoking again, now I'm hooked," Erik responded, defending himself.

"Hey a free cigarette is a free cigarette. I'll make sure I return a Camel or a Marlboro to you."

T.J. had his own lighter and started puffing away on the thin smoke.

"So what are you two in town for, if I may ask? That fine set of wheels you rolled up in tells me you're not used to these fat cats," T.J. said, pointing to the cars with his thumb.

"No. No indeed. Neither one of us is money. We're both

paramedics from back east. Maryland. Just outside of DC."

Erik usually doesn't tell people that he's also a police officer, mostly because he knows that people will trust a paramedic before they trust a cop.

"Okay. I've got some family back east. Mostly the Philly area, but I'm pretty familiar with Baltimore. I grew up watching the Phillies and Orioles. DC is right down the road."

Erik nodded his head. "I dragged my buddy out here for a change of scenery. He lost his wife a few months ago and he needed to get out of the house. We're going to be headed over to the EMS offices for some training during the week. I'm hoping a change will do him some good."

"Right, right. I got you," T.J. said, nodding his head. "Well, like I said, if you need anything, I'm the man. I'll let the desk know to call me if you need something off the record. Just tell them to call me and I'll hit you back."

"Thanks," Erik replied, handing T.J. another cigarette for the road.

"Be careful with that. You smoke two of those and you're hooked," Erik warned.

"Ha! That'll be the day, Virginia Slims. But thanks."

T.J. rolled his eyes and tucked the cigarette behind his ear as he walked away.

Erik stubbed out the last of his cancer stick and put it in the ashtray that was at the end of the driveway. He walked to the elevator and poked the "11" button with his knuckle. Erik needed to change before heading up to the gym on the 26th floor. That should be a cool sight, to hit the treadmill with a view 300 feet off the ground.

Later in the gym, Erik's lungs rebelled against him. Those cigarettes were costing him big time. He couldn't break a 10-minute mile. Who can't run a 10-minute mile? He'd been doing it since the 8th grade. Erik was sweating more than he should have, which only went to remind him he wasn't eating right. Smoking and eating crap wasn't going to help him stay in the air. He wasn't ready to drive a cruiser, busting speeders and meth heads. Erik would have to double up on his efforts.

After the workout, Erik headed back down to the room. Walking in and taking a seat on the couch, he heard Jake stirring. It was about 90 minutes all in all. Erik sat down at the kitchen nook and looked at one of the hotel brochures, waiting for Jake to come out. The shower was in *his* bathroom. There was some coughing and hacking, and some spitting and then the toilet flushed before Jake came out to the living room and plopped down on the couch, still half asleep. The room was darkening with the sun behind some of the buildings now.

The view from the room was overlooking LA Live, the Regal Cinema, and the Harbor Freeway beyond that. Not much a view that he could see. Jake was supposed to call Kelly and his folks when he got to LA and he completely spaced out on them and forgot. The afternoon's excitement had been a distraction. He searched for his phone and realized it was dead. He found the charger in his luggage and plugged it in. Jake found the remote and turned the TV on, hoping for some news.

While Jake was looking for the remote, Erik had stolen into the master bathroom for a shower. Almost 6:30 p.m. and the local news was just about over. At least on Fox. A commercial for TMZ came on and what Jake saw froze him solid. Jake was looking at himself. On TMZ. The car accident scene, him standing next to her. It was all still photos, most likely from the smart phones people were holding, but it was him. It was her. It was apparently national news. He turned the volume up, but the commercial was over.

He did see it, right? That just happened, right? Erik was in the shower. Jake's head spun.

"What the fuck!" he exclaimed more as a statement than a question. "What the fuck was that? Aw Christ, now I've gotten into some shit I don't want. God dammit!"

Just then his phone started chirping up a storm. The battery had powered up enough to start and the texts and voicemails were coming fast and furious. There were dozens of them. He had also forgotten about the 3-hour time difference between the coasts. That meant that everyone back home had already seen this stuff. Some of the texts were asking where he was. Impatient little bastards, but he was sure he knew what most were about. He was going through the texts and was about to get to the voicemails when Erik came out of the shower wrapped in a towel. Jake turned and looked at him, and Erik saw him as white as a sheet.

"Hey Boss-man. What's the issue?"

Jake picked a particular text message from Kelly that had a picture embedded in it and turned it around to show Erik. It showed a picture of a TV screen from *Entertainment Tonight* showing him almost huddled with Terra next to her overturned car with Erik in the background.

"Of all the moments we stood next to each other, they chose *that* one?" Jake was not taking this well. "Are they *trying* to make it look like something is happening between us? And where the hell is *your* phone?"

Erik's trademark smirk reappeared with those dimples, mostly in relief that nothing was really wrong, but partially because he was in the shot as well. And damn, the camera really did add 25 pounds.

"Oh, *my* phone is over there. I took it with me to the gym to listen to music. Apparently AT&T sucks across the whole country, not just Maryland. I haven't had signal since we got to the hotel. I have to go to the 26th floor, lean over the railing while wiggling my ears to get a measly 2 bars worth of signal. I'm not that worried about it. Who wants to talk to me anyway? I'm certainly not as famous as you are now, Boss-man," Erik said, getting excited for Jake, even if Jake couldn't be excited for himself.

"What the fuck am I going to do, man? Everyone back home has already seen everything. It seems most of those assholes filming the wreck were fucking paparazzi. God dammit!"

"Dude. Calm down. What's the big deal anyway? I mean, what's the worst they could say? That a friendly driver helped out Terra Dee after an accident? Come on. It can't be that bad – and if it is, what's the big deal. People will think you're laying it to one of the hottest movie stars out there."

They didn't have long to find out. Jake didn't bother with the rest of his voice mails. He sent Kelly a text message telling her that they were at the hotel and that was it. *Entertainment Tonight* came on at 7:30 p.m. They just had to find the CBS station among the maze of hotel channels. There was never a good TV Guide around when you need one. It seemed like forever to find the right channel, but when they did, Erik was ecstatic, Jake, horrified.

"...shining armor. Miss Dee was treated and released, and seen leaving only with her assistant. There was no other sighting of the *hunky* paramedic." There was a short piece of video showing Jake holding Terra's hand as they came out of the ambulance. "…more Hollywood news, when we come back."

"The 'hunky paramedic' was sitting in the car waiting for you," Erik snorted.

"Yeah, and as I recall you downed a couple of hotdogs in the process," Jake reminded him.

"Well, technically, I got one for you, too. You know, it's the thought that counts, Boss-man," Erik replied.

The time waiting and the commercials ate into Jake's brain. He needed to know what was being said. When the show came back on, they had moved on to something with Billy Bob Thornton and then some kid musician. Neither of which Jake cared about. They had completely missed whatever was being said about him and Terra. He wasn't sure if he wanted to know what they were saying about him, or what they were saying about her. Erik rummaged through his suitcase and found some fresh clothes to throw on.

The nap had managed to quiet the voices in Jake's head. His conscious was having a war with itself. After the nap, he hadn't thought of her, until he saw the television. Now, though, he couldn't stop. Her eyes, her hair. The whiff of her perfume that he took. That must've been the moment the bastards took that picture. He cursed himself.

"Come on Boss-man. There's a movie theatre across the street. This place is surrounded by sports bars. I'm in love already. *Goddamn* I miss this place. We can do something around the block, or maybe something over at the Staples Center. Let's just get out of here," Erik interrupted Jake's thoughts.

Erik was right. Jake put his shoes back on, freshened up a little bit and the two went out to see what could be done within walking distance. Jake welcomed the distraction. They both decided to leave their phones in the hotel room.

They got back to the hotel a little before midnight. They were both tuckered, and looking forward the week that lie ahead. Jake was hoping to be fully engulfed in head trauma and eviscerations and learning how to train other medics. He and Erik were meeting some of his friends over near the EMS building. Jake just wanted to get back into something he could focus on. He didn't bother turning his phone on again. He called down to the concierge and asked for an 8 a.m. wake up call. Jake didn't have the time or patience to play with the hotel's damned clock radio. Falling asleep was easy for him. Erik stayed up a little longer to see if he could catch himself in any more photos with Jake and Terra.

The next morning arrived without any issues, and even better, no nightmares, no night sweats. A sunny Sunday morning. The guys got up around 7 and were already dressed by the time the wake-up call came in. Apparently they were still on east-coast time.

"What time are we meeting your friends?" Jake asked, scouring the room service menu for breakfast options.

"10 o'clock down near the EMS building. There's an IHOP kind of down that way. They're pretty common, so there's no looking for Pedro's Taco Shack or Sammy's Subs. It will also give us a chance to scout around and get a feel for the area," Erik replied.

Jake knew when Erik said 'us', he really meant 'him'.

"Sunday morning at an IHOP. Should be interesting. Have you ever *seen* an IHOP on a Sunday morning?" Jake chuckled.

Thankfully, Erik knew the area to some degree as the area had changed a little in the years Erik was away, though Jake didn't know how long it had been, exactly. They retrieved their car from the valet at the Ritz, Erik smiling the entire time. Jake got in on the passenger side and Erik drove. They took the I-5 down to the Lakewood Boulevard exit and took a left. A couple of blocks and they took a right onto Telegraph Road.

"The EMS building is off Telegraph and Pioneer," Erik repeated, mostly to himself. Only then did Jake realize that Erik didn't need the GPS.

A few miles and a lot of lights later, they came to the EMS building. Driving down Telegraph, Erik made the right turn into the driveway just past the intersection. A few cars littered the parking lot. The EMS building had the fancy dark reflective glass covering the entire exterior of the building. There was some sort of odd fountain in the front.

Jake made note of it all and tried to figure out the best ingress and egress points. He had only heard traffic in the area was horrible. He hadn't really had a clue what it was really like to experience it. He'd heard stories of people living 25 miles from their office only to take 90 minutes to drive the distance, and doing it each way, every day.

- EIGHT -

After the small tour was over, Erik turned left back out on to Telegraph and headed down to the next major intersection and a couple of minutes later they were at a packed IHOP, tucked behind a Jack-In-The-Box. Jake saw a couple of ambulances parked out back. Erik checked his phone and sent a text to someone telling them that they were there. The two got out of the car, only Jake took the time to lock his door. Erik debated on leaving the keys in the ignition. A moment later, a head poked out of the front door of the IHOP and looked in their direction.

"Erik, baby! how's it hangin' my man?" the owner of said head exclaimed.

Darrius Patterson was essentially the black version of Erik. From the get-go, Jake knew exactly how the two got along so well. A big smile, short and stocky – he had that gym-cut figure, again like Erik. Darrius was dressed in the standard EMS uniform. Blue cargo pants, black steel-toed boots and a black golf shirt embroidered with the county EMS logo, his radio resting at his hip, with the strap slung over the opposite shoulder.

"Darrius Patterson! You sexy bitch! I'm doing good brother-man. It's good seeing you again. How's the fam?" Erik lit up at seeing his old friend. The two exchange a strong heart felt hug as if they really were long lost brothers.

"Good, man. Doing real good. Sally's inside. She's just getting back on duty. She wrecked her back carrying some fat ass out of a house fire a few weeks ago, but the doc cleared her last Friday, so she's back on shift this morning. Who's the white-bread you got with you? He looks familiar," Darrius said with a sly smile, having already seen and heard about the previous day's adventure.

"Darrius, my brother from another mother, let me introduce you to my other brother."

"Your *what*?" Darrius replied in fake shock, and a mock gesture of putting his hand to his chin as if studying the man.

"Yeah, well, he's the one that's been taking care of me back east. Jake Mitchell. He's good people. Jake, this is Darrius. The whitest black man this side of Bel Air."

And with that, Darrius broke out into the dance universally known as 'The Carlton'. And he was good at it, too.

"Darrius and I were in the service together," Erik explained.

Darrius shook his head in the positive and added, "Well, if you're *his* brother that makes you *my* brother. Come on in and meet the rest of the finest L.A. county rejects."

Darrius threw his arm around Jake's shoulders and escorted him through the IHOP doors that Erik had already opened for them. For the most part, the conversation centered on Erik and his latest exploits and antics. Some were the juicy EMS stories that Jake had heard before and some were of the pre-Maryland variety. He was apparently as much a womanizer around L.A. as he was back home.

Jake met Darrius, and his driver today was Sally. He was letting her take it easy today due to her back injury. There was Rocco and Sal – names heard more often back east, though 'Rocco' was short for Ricardo, and Sal was short for his last name, Salvatore. Jake was having a good time, listening to stories of the past and telling a few of his own, learning more about Erik than he ever thought possible.

"What's this I hear about you being on television, Jake?" Darrius asked.

Jake started to get flustered. He'd managed to not think about it all morning. Now this.

Just then, the radios chirped, and the tones blared. Jake sighed and said a small prayer of thanks.

"Medic 20, Engine 20, Charlie response for abdominal pain to the eleven-thousand block of Sproul Street."

Sally and Darrius grabbed their things and started heading out the door. Darrius keyed his mic and answered, "Medic twenty-one, headed to the bus. We'll be en route momentarily."

Thankfully the waitress had thought ahead – apparently this had happened a few times before. She let them know how much the check was and would hold it until they got back.

"No," Erik said. "I've got theirs. *This* time."

Erik and Darrius exchanged nods before they took off and were out of sight.

"Alright guys, I think it's time to break up this miniature United Nations," Sal announced. "Chief wants us back at the house in time to clean up and take inventory."

"How many times a day do you take inventory out here?" Jake asked. They only did it once at the beginning of their shift.

"We've got a new chief. Former military schmuck. Likes to say jump, just so us SOBs have to jump. Fool thinks he's *still* in the military."

"Ah. Got it. Carry on," Jake said in what he thought was military manner.

"Anyway we can get the legendary Erik "Moneybags" Foerter to pay for our food this fine morning?" Sal asked, looking in Erik's direction.

"Sorry guys. I don't want to support illegal immigrants who take jobs from citizens," Erik said, egging them on. It worked. They took the bait.

"Then take your honkey ass back to Europe! And give this here IHOP back to us Mayans," Rocco intervened.

"Then the Native Americans would have no place to build a casino, Holmes," Erik said in his best parody of a Hispanic accent.

"You're so wrong Erik. Get the fuck out of here, and take white-bread here with you," Sal laughed with Erik.

Jake was suddenly intricately aware of exactly how many Latinos there were in this particular IHOP. The guys at the table all stoop up and Jake shook hands. Erik stuck his hand out to Rocco. Rocco's hand engulfed Erik's as they shook. The obligatory shoulder bumps were exchanged. The fist and shoulder bumps were also exchanged between Erik and Sal.

"Be safe out there guys. I'll be around this week. Let me know what you want to do. I can probably swing by the station too. Bring a pizza by, maybe meet this bad-ass Chief you got over there," said Erik.

Rocco and Sal paid for their meals and headed out in front of Jake and Erik. Erik paid their bill and Darrius' and they walked out. Apparently, the fire station was only a block or two away because they heard the sirens loud and clear, heading away from them though. Erik was glad to leave last so he wouldn't have to explain their car to anyone.

Jake had never seen so many taco or Mexican themed joints in his life. At least back in Maryland there was a little more variety. Indian, Afghani, and of course the somewhat spurious, but no less tasty Peruvian Chicken joints that only accepted cash. That was when you knew it was good food, cash only.

This was Jake's first time to L.A. – really in L.A. – outside the glitz and magazine cover scenes and it looked a lot like Florida. It seemed that every road ran through an industrial park and everything was in long strings of single floor buildings, like strip malls. There were 'Professional' buildings, and a couple of the newer two-story buildings that had businesses in them, selling cell phones or carpet, and a tax preparer, well, a *lot* of those. A lot of signs in Spanish. Everything was tucked away inside these "Corporate Centers". He had no idea how anything was ever found around here.

"What's the plan now?" Jake asked.

"I have no idea, Boss-man. How about we just drive around and see what we can see? Things have changed a lot since my last blow through."

Erik liked not having a schedule, whereas Jake felt better off tied to one. Less time to think about things.

"Come on little brother. Live a little!" Erik yelled as he revved the car engine and all four cylinders screamed in defiance.

"Careful there. The hamster under the hood of this thing is on its last legs. I'll roll down the windows on my side, you roll them down over there," cautioned Jake.

It was a strange undertaking to roll down windows manually anymore.

They drove around the city and saw some of the icons. Jake was amazed at how much traffic there was on a Sunday. They drove down to Long Beach and walked around for a bit with Erik leading the way. With more sightseeing to do, they drove down the Pacific Coast Highway. Jake always thought the highway was supposed be surrounded by cliffs and grandiose views of the Pacific Ocean and coves. Not so much down in L.A.

They pulled off at Seal Beach and walked the pier. Erik was quiet, more reminiscent and seemed introspective. Jake wanted to ask more questions, but it just didn't seem right. It seemed they were both uncomfortable there. Jake because of Erik, and Erik for his own personal reasons. About 3:30 in the afternoon they headed back to the car.

"One place I *have* to show you. It's the one and only reason I come back to the left coast. Well. Aside from those assholes you met this morning. If I could open a shop back home, *this* would be the place," Erik said.

"Any other clue?" asked Jake.

"Nope. Other than to make sure you have an empty stomach."

Erik unlocked the door through the open window. Jake saw that this time that Erik *had* left the keys in the ignition.

Erik took an exit off the Pacific Coast Highway and headed north to Anaheim. The highways around here were starting to leave Jake dizzy. He just let Erik drive and watched the scenery. Every now and then he'd think of Terra and he'd have to force the thoughts from his head. After about 30 minutes – a New York second by L.A. standards – they arrived in front of a sandwich shop called "Tummy Stuffer".

"Now look Boss-man, go easy. It will be a mind blowing experience going inside that place. So slow down, act like you've been there before," said Erik, again talking more to himself than to Jake.

"Ah. Tummy Stuffer's. Well, you have been talking about this place for some time. It's only right that I find out what the hell you've been talking about all these years."

"Hey! Show some respect, man. It's 'Tummy Stuffer'. No 'S'," Erik corrected as he opened the door.

Jake walked in and didn't see anything out of the ordinary. It was a sub shop. He liked Italian subs, so he ordered a number 45 to go. He grabbed some chips and a bottle of water. The total came to $9.77, considerably less than the Ritz. They put the sandwich in a bag with the chips. Erik however was all but drooling when he reached the counter. He ordered some odd-ball sandwich and grabbed a water.

"No room for chips man. That was a waste of money," he said, pointing to Jake's chips.

Ten minutes later, both were stuffed to the gills. Jake wasn't able to finish his sandwich and never opened his chips. He certainly did not expect some mythical culinary experience, but Erik was right. This would definitely be a go-to spot for food in the future. He could honestly say that was the best Italian he'd ever had. Erik finished his, and looked to be in afterglow.

"Hey Boss-man. Just think, that was only one sandwich. There are another hundred-plus that you haven't tried yet. Good times!" he said, pulling out a cigarette. Jake still chuckled at the fact that he smoked Virginia Slims.

"Absolutely. It's the bread that makes it. That place makes a fat man proud to be fat. You were right about that place; I'll give you that. How are you doing on quitting smoking?"

"Better I think. This is my first one today. Yesterday was bad. I had three."

"Yeah, but yesterday was travelling and the car wreck and hospital thing."

Dammit! Jake cursed himself. This was Erik's way of getting him to open up.

"So yeah, about that. What's the story?"

"What's the story? You were there! You *saw* the story, or lack of one. Look. I know you want me to come out of my shell. I know I've been losing weight and I'm an emotional wreck. But I am not ready for any kind of relationship with anyone let alone a busty starlet with an ego problem."

Erik had an inquisitive look on his face, ruining his post-

Tummy Stuffer glow.

"Who said anything about a relationship with her? And you brought her chest up, saying she was 'busty'. Holy shit, dude. You need to slow down. No one is pushing you to do anything you don't want to do. It's just that we miss the 'old' Jake. We all want him back."

But Erik wasn't going to let Jake get away, now that he'd opened up the door.

"But," Erik started, dragging out the word, "Since you're obviously thinking about it a lot more than I am, let's explore..."

"No, Erik. No. God dammit I hate when you try to psychoanalyze me."

"What? I just want to know what's going on up there." Erik was pointing at Jake's head.

"Do you realize that we're supposed to be the other's best friend, and yet we haven't once talked about what happened to Meredith? How do you know that I don't need someone to talk to? I lost *two* friends that day."

That caught Jake off guard. He didn't know what to say.

"This is where you want to have this conversation? In the parking lot of 'Tummy Stuffer'? I'm going to need a few drinks in me to go over this."

Jake was caving. He knew he needed to talk to someone. Hell, that's all EMS ever did when a bad call came in. The county would call what amounted to a therapy session called Critical Incident Stress Debriefings if there was a bad incident either with kids, or with people close to the fire and EMS community, or maybe a mass casualty incident also known as an MCI. They helped some, certainly better than nothing. Jake realized just then that neither of them had really had one for Meredith's wreck. He never thought about Erik losing *two* people. And now he felt like a shitty friend.

"No. This place is my Nirvana," Erik said, relishing the Tummy Stuffer. "I don't want to fuck up my Qi with this bit of history. Let's get back to the hotel. There are more than enough bars around there within walking distance that we can find a corner in and drink ourselves stupid, even on a Sunday night."

"Okay, class starts at Oh-Eight-Hundred. If I walk into class tomorrow morning hung over, I'm blaming you."

"Don't sweat it, man. I've got you covered. Have you checked the back seat since this morning?"

Jake looked in the back seat and there lay two bags of saline, two IV kits and a couple of starter kits.

"All we need are some B12 shots and we are hangover free my friend!" Erik said.

Jake started smiling again. Someone, exactly who only Erik knew, had dropped off a couple of bags of saline into the back seat. Jake could only assume it was one of the guys at the IHOP. It was a standard paramedic recipe for avoiding hangovers.

It took them an hour to drive the 30 miles back to the hotel on the I-5. An accident near East Washington Boulevard had traffic backed up for miles. By the time they got back, it was well after 5 p.m. and they headed into the L.A. Market, a bar inside the hotel for their first round.

They settled into a semi-circle booth away from the main restaurant and bar area, each taking an end seat. Erik ordered a top-shelf whiskey straight-up, and Jake ordered a whiskey sour with Maker's Mark, doubles for both. Erik laughed at Jake every time he ordered it.

"We're in L.A. and *still* it's like I'm drinking with Grandpa," Erik said.

They ordered some appetizers to soak up the vast amount of alcohol they intended on drinking. After a few sips, Erik broke the ice as only he could – very direct. No sugar coating.

"So talk to me Boss-man. What's on your mind? Are you thinking about Terra?"

"Jesus, Erik. Give me some time to drink, man. No. I..." Jake stuttered, "I don't know what to think. I don't know what to feel. I have this, I don't know, a hole, I guess in my gut. A piece of my soul is missing and I don't know what to do to fix it."

Jake took a long drink from his tumbler. He wasn't giving any time for the ice to melt.

"For the last eight years, I've talked to Meredith every day. Even for the past 3 months. She was my best friend."

Erik feigned mock surprise and insult that *he* wasn't Jake's best friend. He was also trying to keep this as light as possible. It was his natural reaction to turn horror into humor. Jake understood. It was an EMS thing.

"Yeah, sorry there, big guy. She had better looking tits than you," Jake joked back.

"Yeah, but only after she got pregnant," Erik shot back.

Jake signaled their server for another round.

"I don't know. For 10 years of my life, she was my best friend," Jake started over. "I told her everything. Even things she probably didn't want to hear."

"Wait. You didn't tell her about the New Year's party, did you?" Erik asked.

"Relax. That will remain in the clouds with the 'Lore of Erik'. I may have to tell Darrius though."

"Sheeeeee-it. Who do you think taught me some of that stuff?" Erik laughed off the threat.

A former squad-mate, Darrius would just as soon give his

life for Erik, and vice versa. And of course, neither would let the other forget about it – even from beyond the grave.

"Well, now I am positive. You two really were separated at birth," said Jake.

They were getting off topic. Maybe it was because of the drinks, or maybe it was because neither of them were ready for this discussion.

"Yes. So back to the accident," Erik said, getting back on point.

"I did everything I could on that wreck," Jake started back. "I did everything I could, and it wasn't enough. The look in her eyes, man. They haunt me. Her eyes are in every one of my nightmares, *screaming* for me to do something."

Jake dared not speak of the howls and screams that accompanied the eyes. Even through the dim lighting and twinkling reflections, Erik could see the tears welling up in Jake's eyes.

It was Erik's turn to take a hard drink. Another signal to the server for another round.

"I know. I know you did. Hell if the accident happened in the emergency room at Shock Trauma, they wouldn't have been able to save her. *She* knows you did. She knows you loved her. You're all she talked about, at least to me. She put me in charge of making sure you were safe. 'Bring him back safe,' she'd say, all the damn time. And I loved her for that. I loved the two of you. You gave me hope."

Erik's own tears were welling. He wasn't much of one for the emotional stuff. He always seemed able to lock things away. "Compartmentalization" they called it, usually not a good thing as far as phycologists were concerned, but critical for folks to be able to function within EMS. Jake knew some things got to him, but gave him his space. Now the compartment in Erik's mind with all the emotions and all the fucked up experiences was full up and it had to go somewhere.

"Aw hell, you're the one I learned that it was okay to give your woman flowers for no reason. I mean, who the hell does *that*, man? No reason? I'd never seen that before. And it's so simple. You two were always so happy. You all were my hope that people could make it. You were..." Erik paused, "You *are* my responsibility, to make sure you're safe. I let you both down. And I don't know how to make it right Jake. I'm sorry."

The sentence faded from Erik's lips and with that, a tear tricked down Erik's face. It was the most emotion Jake had ever seen with Erik. After three torturous months, Erik finally let it out, and Jake followed with sobs of his own.

The booze was being refreshed pretty regular now. The appetizers arrived, but neither of them touched anything. They were ordered more out of habit than hunger.

"Those were the last words she said to me. 'Bring him back safe, Erik.' I can't get that out of my head. She's gone and you're not the same Jake and I can't put anything back the way it was. I couldn't keep you safe, and I couldn't do the *one* thing she asked of me."

That set off another tear from Erik. The server came by and asked if they needed anything else. She was surprised to see two grown men so solemn, their faces still wet from the tears.

"No, thanks. Just another round please. We're celebrating life, tonight," Jake replied, managing not slur his words.

Up until tonight, Jake hadn't been sober for more than a few days at a time.

"Okay, well, you're on your sixth round of doubles. I can't serve you if you're too drunk to function," the server said as she looked a bit concerned, apparently having never seen people drink their feelings to death.

"Too drunk to function?" Jake asked.

After the not so small task of finding it, Jake held up his room key, showing her the Ritz logo on the back of the card.

"It's okay hon, we're not going anywhere tonight. Thanks for the concern. Please proceed with the drinks," Jake said, while receiving a glare from Erik, who got up to use the restroom. More drinks were ready when he returned.

After they'd gotten most of the tears out of the way, the conversation turned to more mundane things. They were both happy to talk about anything else. Too much emotion for one night. They talked about everything, like the upcoming class and a few more details about Darrius. But Erik's original question was eating at Jake. Jumping around looking for an acceptable answer. Last call came at 9 p.m.; the bar was closing at 10 p.m. since it was Sunday in a hotel bar. And about this time, Jake was drunk enough to come to a conclusion.

"Erik. Do you remem. Do you memember?"

Jake's face wasn't working right. Erik started giggling.

"No. No. No. I'm serious. This is serious," Jake managed to compose himself a little. "Do you remember the first question you asked me tonight?"

"Are you kidding me? I don't remember unzipping my fly when I went to the bathroom."

"Heh. Serves you right. Go with me here. You asked me if I was thinking about Terra. Well. The answer is 'yes'. But, Terra isn't just Terra."

"Well then who is she, Boss-man? If Terra isn't Terra? You tend to get all metaphysical when you're drunk, and *you* my friend are drunk," Erik said, slapping Jake on the shoulder.

"No. What I mean is that it's what she represents. You see with Meredith; she was more than my best friend. I told her everything. I still do, most every night. Everything except for what happened with Terra yesterday. I don't know if I'll ever see Terra again, chances are probably not. But what happens if or when I'm attracted to someone else. How do I deal with that? Talking to Meredith, telling her everything. If the time comes, how do I tell her when it's time to move on?"

"Oh shit!" Erik exclaimed, almost falling off the bench. He corrected himself and sat upright.

"Look Broham," Erik started, holding his drink and pointing at Jake with the same hand. "first off, *you* don't tell *her* anything except that you love her and you miss her and you want her back. The issue you're going to have is when *she* tells *you* when it's time to move on, and she will. At some point, she will. Look at it this way, did she love you?"

"Yes."

"Are you sure she loved you?"

"Very."

"So then wouldn't be logical that she'd want you to be happy?"

"Yeah, but that's not what I'm worried about," Jake said, starting to sober up if only slightly.

"Look, Boss-man. You're thinking too far ahead of yourself. Are you ready for another relationship now? No, you're not. You already said that. So stop worrying about it. You will know when you know. Until then, don't beat yourself up because you like to look at some T and A once in a while. Meredith would understand."

And that was it, in essence, for Jake. He still loved Meredith, but still had the desires of every red blooded, heterosexual man and he didn't know how to mingle the two. He wasn't ready to let go of Meredith yet.

"Yeah. I just hope it's that easy, man."

"You and me both, brother. Hey, let's get the hell out of here. I'm not entirely sure I was in the men's room the last time."

"What?"

"Well, either they took all the urinals out of the men's room, or I took a leak in the lady's room. Either way, all the feet pointing in the other direction," Erik said with his smirk and dimples.

"Check, Please!" Jake needed to not be there anymore.

The bright lights of the lobby were in stark contrast to the dimly lit bar. Both Erik and Jake squinted coming out while trying to maintain their balance. Erik sauntered over to the front desk and asked for a 5 a.m. as well as a 6 a.m. wakeup call then walked outside. Jake waited in one of the stiff lobby chairs, figuring Erik went for a smoke.

A few minutes later, Erik came back in with the saline bags and IV kits wrapped in a shirt. A truly discerning security guard may have taken it to be a drug kit in some way, but nothing he had was illegal, and either security wasn't discerning, or they were used to their posh guests' bad habits.

"We get up at 5, pop these in and then sleep until 6. Pop a few Tylenol for the inflammation and we're right as rain," Erik stated.

Erik seemed to have had more than a little practice at this. Jake was looking forward to the bed and dreaming of Meredith. He'd managed not to puke all night and at this point thought he was past the point of concern. He felt better about the answer he gave Erik. He was pretty sure he'd never see Terra again, and he was fine with that. He could now focus on trauma done to the human body in all various situations.

The next morning, Jake realized how wrong he was. By the time they woke up, the paparazzi had not only tracked down where they were staying, but had already effectively done background checks on the two. From voice analysis of the 911 call that Erik made, to calling up MIEMSS to inquire about their past performance. A suspended paramedic gave them the blood in the water they needed. Until that is they found out why. And that's when things *really* got interesting. A paramedic, suspended from his job for trying to save the life of his true love and child.

For the paparazzi, it didn't get much better. This guy, for all intents and purposes was the real deal. He was the gentleman, the healer, the man who could stay cool in the face of certain defeat, and more times than not snatch people from the grip of death itself, if only temporarily. The gossip rags were abuzz with the story. They more they read into it, the more glorified it became. Of course, MIEMSS couldn't release any details of the disciplinary hearing, but the hard facts of the police report and ensuing investigation were there for the world to see.

He was their new "golden boy". And Terra being the darling of Hollywood for the moment, it was a match made in heaven for them. The stories flew fast and furious, each magazine trying to one-up the other with how they met, what they did, and how long they'd been doing it. All that, and it was only 7 a.m.

"God dammit! Why can't people just leave me the fuck alone?" Jake fumed, pulling the IV out of his arm, hitting the power button on the remote, and throwing the remote into the cushions on the couch.

"Come on, Jake! It's your 15 minutes of fame. Relax and try to enjoy it," Erik said as he came out of his bathroom, ready to go.

"Yeah, well, they're digging into areas that I don't want dug into," Jake noted, primarily talking about Meredith. "I swear if anyone asks me a damn thing I'm going to rip them a new one."

"Relax, Boss-man. I don't think anyone in the class will notice or care about this. Besides, it's L.A., who really looks at this garbage? People have more important things to do. We have to get going if you're going get there by 8 o'clock."

In the lobby, they passed T.J. coming in to start his shift.

"Gentlemen, there has been quite the buzz surrounding you two around here with all the reporters and photographers. I've managed to hold the jackals off, but eventually you're going to have to deal with them. Don't be surprised if you see some cats out in the bushes snapping photos of you," warned T.J.

This freaked Jake out even more.

"Thanks, T.J.," Erik said, sliding him another $20-dollar bill. "We'd appreciate it if you could keep running interference for us, at least until we can figure out how to handle this."

Erik noticed that the man was dressed as well as could be, not in his Ritz uniform yet, just coming in to work. T.J. walked with them outside.

"Not a problem, fellas. I like messing with these guys, but I have to tell you, they pay a hell of a lot more than $20 dollars. If not me, then one of the other guys out here. I can only do it for so long," T.J. was telling them in a matter-of-fact voice.

"Sorry, T.J. We don't have the coin for much more of this. Do what you can for us please?" Jake said with a hint of desperation in his voice.

"I'm on your team, guys. You don't have to worry about the sharks getting any chum from me. I'll see what I can do with the other guys," T.J. assured them.

"By the way T.J., do you always dress this well on the way into work?" Erik asked.

"No, man. This is how I always dress. It's called style. Something you D.C. boys don't know anything about," T.J. ribbed, showing his huge smile.

Erik rolled his eyes, and Jake just accepted that yet again, someone told him he lacked style. The valet pulled their corolla around to the front of the driveway and any argument over style went out of the manually operated window.

The drive over was peaceful. Nothing on the radio but traffic reports and pop music. If Jake thought traffic was bad on a Sunday, he was in for a treat on Monday. The EMS training building was about 15 miles away. Maybe on a bad day in Maryland it would take 30 to 45 minutes. On a good day in L.A. it was going to be at least 45 minutes.

Jake slid into a seat just as roll was being called. The class had about 10 people in it; all were locals, except for Jake. There was the obligatory scan-tron sheet to fill out with the number 2 pencils. Some introductions were made. Jake only gave his first name, and that he lived outside of Washington, D.C., hoping that would be enough to throw anyone off. He was getting paranoid. The rest of the introductions were made, and that took up half of the first day.

The rest of the day, they re-hashed the material that they had already studied with the initial class. Jake enjoyed most of it, until they started getting into the 'communications' part. What the best way to relay information to other paramedics was as well as a few clinical differences on how some things are perceived by nurses and other medical professionals who would also be taking the course. The instructor teaching the class acknowledged it was a bit slow, and promised it would pick up over the next 2 days. At the very least, there were some curriculum changes that they needed to go over, and if there was anything the students themselves wanted to go over in depth, they could do that.

The day actually left Jake a bit deflated. He much preferred talking and learning about the actual medical procedures and protocols over the 'train the trainer' and 'how to communicate' type of stuff. Procedures and protocols gave him something to focus on. He could forget what was happening in the rest of the world and focus on the situation at hand. One person – or multiple people – needed his help at a given moment and that's what mattered.

Class got out a little early and Jake checked his phone. He'd had a few text messages with Erik, but nothing much. There was strange one that asked how he was doing, but the area code was from Wisconsin. He had to look it up. Somewhere near Milwaukee. He didn't know anyone from Wisconsin, so he just ignored it. Jake was only a few minutes out of class when another message from the same Wisconsin number popped up.

"Are you out of class yet?"

Well, only a few people knew his number and knew he was in a class, so he figured he'd bite. Maybe someone he knew got a new number?

"Just got out. Who is this?" Erik texted back.

There was no immediate reply back, but by then Erik was pulling up and Jake let it go.

"How was class Boss-man?" Erik asked, seeming to be

unusually happy.

"It was a class man. Not as much meat as I was hoping, but we'll see. Only two more days of this mess, right? And we leave when? Saturday?"

"Well, I leave Saturday. I'm still trying to get you to stick around. I'll have T.J. sit on your ass if I have to."

"You don't have enough $20 dollar bills," Jake sniped back with a smile.

- NINE -

Erik pulled back out into traffic. It was early, just after 4 p.m. but traffic still sucked. They decided to grab some dinner before tackling the highway back to the hotel. Maybe they'd try the neighborhood roads and avoid the gridlock. They picked a non-descript hole-in-the-wall that served what it called 'Delicious, Authentic Mexican Cuisine', and as they only accepted cash, Jake had no doubt that it would be both 'Authentic' as well as 'Delicious'. He was *finally* starting to loosen up, again. Stuffed on chips and salsa and enchiladas and burritos, the two finally meandered back to the hotel. They made it back about 6 p.m. or so and the sun was just starting its decent below the horizon, another hour or so of full sun light. As they pulled into the driveway, they noticed the normal number of high-end cars, though there was a silver Mercedes that caught Jake's eye. He nudged Erik and pointed.

"Look familiar?"

"Yeah. But the one you're thinking of was totaled. That's funny though. Same model and everything." Erik knew why that particular car was there, at this particular moment. He even helped set it up.

Just as they were walking in, T.J. was walking out to meet them, again dressed in what Erik would have called his 'Sunday Best', although different from the set of clothes he had on that morning, before his shift.

"Do you carry a wardrobe with you everywhere you go or something?" Erik was perplexed. "I like your style and would like to subscribe to your newsletter," Erik said in the most 'nerdy' voice he could muster.

T.J. smiled. "Sorry, you just wish you could pull this off like I can. Besides, you never know who's going to show up."

Erik nodded, and T.J. slipped Erik his room key back to him. Luckily Jake was oblivious, and didn't see the exchange. T.J. reached inside his jacket pocket and pulled out a cigarette. Though Erik, didn't see the brand, it looked thinner than most. A smirk crossed his face and he made a mental note to verify his suspicions.

Jake and Erik walked through the lobby, and while he didn't say anything, Jake did notice that some of the people behind the hotel counters were looking at him. He hoped his paranoia wasn't getting the better of him. The elevator got up to the 11th floor, and Erik popped in his room key. Jake walked in behind him. He wasn't in the room but a step or two when he noticed a different smell in the air. It was familiar. He even lifted his nose up to get a better smell, but as he did, he saw her.

Terra was sitting on the couch, watching the two walk in. Erik made himself scarce yet again, and left the two alone, without leaving the two alone, and headed to the bedroom. He wanted this to run its course, but he wasn't foolish enough to assume that Jake wouldn't need him if things went south.

"Hi Jake!" Terra said standing up. "I've been trying to find you two since you left the E.R."

Jake, just then realizing this had been an ambush,

"Hey Terra. You're feeling better it seems."

Instantly uncomfortable with the situation. He had run a similar scenario in his mind a hundred times if he had ever seen her again, how he would act, what he would say. But now he was dumb. His on-scene acumen had failed him. He walked over and sat in the chair across from the couch.

Terra started first. "Look, I'm sorry we got off on the wrong foot on Saturday. It's just that I don't get to meet too many honestly real people anymore."

She sat back down, and laid her purse on the table in front of the couch. She had left her shoes by the door.

"It seems that everyone around here is always working an angle, is always trying to get me to do something or say something for them. Everyone wants a piece. To endorse this product or write something for that blog or podcast. It's just... I don't know..."

"That's fine. I understand, kind of. I don't know the specific details, but I know enough to understand. Anonymity has its rewards."

Jake was still trying to get his mind straight.

"It's funny. I..." Jake paused, "I've run a scenario like this over and over in my head a hundred times and I have no idea what to say to you at this point."

Jake was a little brutal with the honesty sometimes. Terra smirked.

"Well, look. I'm guessing what the papers have said is true about you and the last few months." Erik had filled her in on some of the more exact details, but she wasn't going to throw him under the bus. "I was initially looking to maybe buy you dinner as a 'Thank You'. I'll understand if you decline, but the offer stands."

"Are you hitting on him?!" Erik yelled from Jake's bedroom, obviously eavesdropping on the conversation.

"Maybe!" Terra yelled back, smiling. "Are you jealous yet!?"

"Have at it, sister. His back is *way* too hairy for my taste." Erik's voice almost cracking at that insult, trying not to laugh. "And I prefer at least a C-cup."

"Keep eating like that and you'll be a C-cup in no time," Jake yelled back at Erik, everyone trying not to laugh at this point.

"So? What do you say? Can I take you to dinner to say 'Thank You'?" Terra repeated the offer.

"Sure. As long as it's a regular place. Nothing more expensive than a regular low-key steakhouse or something. A meat and potatoes kind of place."

"Steakhouse it is. The closest one that I like if just off Olympic here – only about 10 miles, but it will give us time to talk. I'll call ahead to get private seating."

Jake pursed his lips. *She can't even go to a goddamned steakhouse with getting uppity*, he thought to himself. *This is starting off lovely. I should have demanded the Outback.* And then the memory struck him like a bat to the gut. They were meeting Meredith at the Outback the day of the accident. *Fuck! And now you're going to dinner with her?* he screamed in his head. Just then Erik opened the door, breaking his train of thought.

"Okay. Do you want to go now or...?" Terra asked leading for an affirmative.

"Yeah, just give me a few to change clothes, lay down some plastic and throttle Erik."

"No problem. I'll go get the car and meet you out front," Terra said without missing a beat.

"Be careful. We've been told the 'pap' are out there staking the place out" Jake warned.

"No problem. I've met your friend T.J. and he's got that taken care of." She looked over at Erik. "Talk about a man with some *style!*"

"What? Why do you have to look at me when you say that? I've got *style!* Oh, I've *got* style!" Erik protested loudly.

Terra was laughing "Okay guys. Jake, I'll see you

downstairs?" As Jake nodded and turned to head to the back of the room, Terra mouthed a 'Thank You' to Erik, and he nodded back, adding a 'hang loose' sign with his thumb and pinky.

Jake didn't know how to feel. He desperately wanted a shower, but didn't think he had time. He wanted to be mad at Erik but really wasn't. He did avoid eye contact with him on the way out. Erik smiled because he saw the smirk on Jake's face.

Jake made it down to the lobby and was walking through the vestibule when he saw someone holding a phone up. He didn't think the person was a 'pap', but rather just taking a selfie, but it still put his senses on alert. He didn't like his life being published at the whim and viewpoints of others. Terra was waiting in the car for him. It was still pretty nice outside where he would have usually rolled the windows down. The windows were tinted extremely dark. As he started to put the window down, Terra stopped him.

"Nope. Not here. Too many people. We don't want to give the bastards any more material to print."

"Or any reason to print it," Jake replied, still on edge about going on what amounted to a date with someone other than Meredith.

As Terra pulled out of the hotel driveway, Jake was still a little shy.

"So," Terra began, trying to jumpstart a conversation, "Jake, Erik told me that this is your first time in L.A.? How are you liking it so far?"

Jake chuckled, "I didn't think anything could be as bad as D.C. traffic. Wow, does your traffic suck out here. At least back home we can stagger our drive times or drive on off-hours. Out here, it doesn't seem like there are any off-hours. There are just way too many people out here."

Terra smiled. It was pretty much a given that traffic was the biggest complaint.

"Yeah, well that's what happens when you've got the best weather in the country. Everyone wants to be here," Terra tried to keep up the conversation.

"Eh," Jake winced, looking out his window.

"I'm not too fond of any place where the ground moves on its own. It just isn't natural," Jake joked.

It took Terra a moment to get it.

"Yeah, well we haven't had a nasty one in quite a while. They build to some pretty strict codes out here."

"May be overdue," Jake stated as a fact more than anything.

Terra just raised her eyebrows in agreement.

"Erik also said that you were in an EMS class today? How did you get into being a paramedic?" Terra asked, trying to draw him out of his shell.

"Now if *that* isn't the million-dollar question. Ah, well, yeah, I was in a trauma class today. It's mostly a 'train-the-trainer' type of class. As for how I got into EMS, let's see…"

Jake sat back in the car seat, and straightened up his back.

"When I was 17, I was a senior in high school. Me and a buddy of mine joined a local volunteer fire department. We couldn't do much at first, but eventually after rolling enough hose, and maintaining the equipment on the engines, we got enough training and experience that we could do things. From then on, it was a no-brainer for me."

"And you didn't get paid for any of this?" Terra asked in disbelief. She was somewhat interested, but also trying to keep him talking.

Jake laughed, "No. That's what 'volunteer' means. Most of the country is serviced by volunteer fire departments. It's just that no one really stops and asks themselves who they are. They just pick up the phone and expect someone to be there. Well, that 'someone' has to be someone."

"Do you still volunteer?" Terra said, smiling, still trying to get her head around doing something that dangerous and that extreme for free.

"Eh. Not so much anymore. I'm on the roll call at a station out in West Virginia, but time and politics take their toll. I wrecked my back, and I had some professional issues with the way things were managed in that county. They treated the volunteers like shit. One thing led to another, and I guess you could just say 'Life Happened'."

It was the best excuse he could come up with at the moment.

"Yeah, I can see that you're not exactly the most politically correct type of guy," Terra said, referring to the way he left her in the emergency room.

Jake grimaced at the reference and gave an uncomfortable, nervous chuckle.

"Sorry about that. I've been a bit on edge for a while. That's why Erik brought me out here. He thinks the change of scenery will do me some good."

"Well, has it so far?" Terra asked

Jake looked at her with a smirk, "No complaints so far."

Dammit man! Straighten up! Jake's internal filter faltered.

Terra smiled at what she assumed to be a compliment. She didn't really know what to expect from him. She was bored with the people around her, who knew everything there was to know about her and it seemed the more people she met, the more people knew everything about her. Terra spent most of her time trying to be what everyone else wanted her to be like. Jake however was a clean slate and knew virtually nothing about her, and here she was unable to really talk to a normal person about normal things. In her closed off world, there was no one to share anything with. She had a precious few friends, mostly back home. Terra didn't trust easily, yet Jake somehow broke through those doubts and fears. She felt the same kind of connection now as she did in the ambulance and in the emergency room. Terra was just afraid that it was wishful thinking.

"So, what's it like, being a paramedic? It seems exciting," Terra said.

Jake smiled and replied, "Yeah. Sometimes, and sometimes it's a shit-show."

Terra laughed at the comparison.

"What's it like?" he repeated the question, looking up through the sunroof, looking for the words. "What's it like? Sometimes, it's like you've got the world in your pocket and you can't do anything wrong. Sometimes, no matter what you do, it doesn't work. Erik once told me that war was basically 'hours of boredom, seconds of terror'. And that's the best summation of EMS I've ever heard, only mostly without all the shooting and things blowing up."

"So what's the difference between what you do and volunteers?" Terra asked, passing San Vicente boulevard.

"Aside from the paycheck? Nothing," he replied. "The politics are different, mainly because vollies can walk away almost any time they want, whereas the paycheck tends to be a bit of a leash for us county folks. If we don't like something, we pretty much just have to suck it up and deal with it."

"Walk away?" Terra asked.

"Yeah. Vollies can walk away whenever they want, either before or after any call. If they're frustrated, or tired or sick, or what have you. Now some departments have shift requirements, and they may need to finish their shift, but at the end of the day, they are free to come and go as they choose. It's a great gig."

"So how do you *keep* the volunteers?"

"Most of us love what we do, in spite of the bullshit politics and 'old boy's club' a lot of departments have in management."

"'Old boys club', huh? Sounds like there's one of those no matter what business you're in," Terra lamented.

Their timing was perfect and they were able to pull straight into a parking spot almost in front of the steakhouse. Jake was a bit surprised, as all the Ruth's Chris Steakhouses he'd ever seen had been fairly impressive restaurants. This one could have passed for a mom & pop shop like he'd wanted in the first place. Terra fished around in her purse to find change for the parking meter.

The maître d' came out to meet them and held the door.

"Ms. Dee, how wonderful to meet you. How are you this evening?" he gushed.

Obviously used to it, Terra played it off like a pro.

"I'm fine thank you. Is our table ready?" Not mixing words, and not paying much attention.

"Yes, Ma'am. Right this way, please."

The maître d' had a waiter following them, and the menus were already in place as was a pitcher of water.

"Your waiter tonight will be Antonio. If you need anything he will be more than happy to serve you," the maître d' said.

He patted Antonio on the shoulder and was off. Antonio

asked if they wanted drinks. At first, Jake was going to order his normal, then remembered that Terra was still in recovery. Both went with water. They made polite chit chat until the waiter returned and Terra ordered the lobster, Jake the filet. The sides were table portioned, so Terra ordered the baked potato for Jake's sake; after all, he wanted steak and potatoes.

"Just so you know, this is going to *suck* in the gym for the next few days." Terra tried the guilt card. Jake wasn't having it.

"Oh live a little. Do you have another movie to go to tomorrow?" Jake asked, not quite getting the lingo right.

Terra chuckled but wanted to change the subject. She was taking a small break from the studio marketing requirements and didn't want to talk about "the business".

"So what's the worst call you've been on, what moves you to keep getting back on the ambulance?" Terra asked, getting a little more articulate in her questions.

This was a pretty common question; Jake had all but memorized the answer, and usually a one-line response shuts people up since they don't want to know the details underneath. It was a practiced response, almost automatic.

"The worst call? You sure you want to know?" he asked.

"Yeah. What was your worst call?"

"Define 'worst'," Jake said.

Terra gave him a strange look in reply.

"Well, you asked me what my worst call was. Most people mean 'What was the goriest call', but my *worst* call – the call that keeps me getting back on the ambulance – was a car wreck with a little three-year-old girl asking her daddy to wake up."

Jake took a drink of water to let that statement hang in the air, to see if it would sink in a bit with Terra.

"That is the worst call I've been on," Jake said, putting his glass down. *That will stop* that *line of questioning,* Jake thought, as it usually did. No one wants to hear the stuff they go through as paramedics, especially over dinner. Terra, however, was a bit more jaded, wanted to know more.

"So, what? Did he have a heart attack or something?" Terra started to dig.

"No. Not that I know of. Do you really want to know this stuff?" Jake questioned, a little uncomfortable and surprised that she wanted more details.

"Yes, I really do," Terra replied, picking up her glass of water and taking a sip.

Jake took a deep breath. The call was never far from his memory anyway.

"So, like I said, when I was 17, and at my first fire department. One night, maybe 8:30 or so, it was dark outside, and had just finished raining, we get this call, an MVA and I finally got to ride on the engine. I wouldn't be allowed to do anything on my own, but I get to ride and that's a start. It was a move up from washing trucks, rolling hose and carrying ladders. So, we pull up on-scene. The ambulance pulls up in front of the wreck, we drive past it and stop to block the back and protect the guys on scene. The last thing we need is some dumbass to come barreling through the area and hitting the cars again when we've got people in there in precarious positions.

"So, anyway, as we pull up along the car, overall, it doesn't look too bad. Certainly survivable. There was a hole in the windshield, covered in blood, some hair too. It wasn't too big, maybe the size of a softball, pushed out a bit so you can tell someone hit it from the inside. We pull up a little further as the cops are moving debris and directing traffic.

"The driver's door is open. The guy is either out cold or dead; I couldn't tell, but he's leaned back in the driver's seat and he had a bloody face. I didn't see too many details. But there was a little girl there, maybe two or three years old, tiny little thing, biggest brown eyes you've ever seen, sitting on his lap crying, and begging her daddy to wake up. She was scared, crying and pushing on his chest, saying, 'Daddy, wake up! Wake up daddy!' and he wasn't responding to anything, just his head shaking back and forth from her pushing on his chest."

Terra gasped, put her hands to her mouth, and whispered, "Oh, my God."

"Now, imagine all the colored lights, the white strobes, the red flares, the sounds – people running, and shouting, and the sirens the horns, and this little girl is sitting there, basically all alone. She doesn't know what happened, she's scared out of her mind, and her daddy – the one constant in her world up until that point – the very instant when she needed him the most - won't 'wake up'. The tears, the fear in her cries were – are *still* - palpable. Between sobs, she was looking around for... I don't know, answers I guess, help maybe, certainly someone to help her, help her daddy. To this day, I can still see her eyes, wide and full of fear."

And that's when Jake's memories crossed from one wreck to the next, now it was her eyes, Meredith's eyes, screaming at him to help, and his voice tailed off. His glance shifted and Terra could tell something had changed. She wasn't sure if it had to do with the little girl or not. Erik had told her some of the details of the wreck, but she was sure there was details left out, and even things that Erik didn't know. Jake was telling the story of the little girl with such enthusiasm. She didn't think the pause had to do with her. It had to be Meredith. And she wanted to stay away from *that* subject. She wanted to hear the story of the little girl, though. Jake said it was what kept him on the ambulance all this time.

"Was she okay? The little girl, what happened to her?" Terra asked, her eyes starting to water.

Jake's were too as this was one of his personal horror stories. It was always in the back of his mind, number two on his "most horrific" list, only just recently knocked off the top.

"Huh? Oh. I don't know," Jake said, snapping back to real time. "She was apparently in a car seat in the back of the car. We saw that too, but somehow she either wiggled out of it or someone unhooked her from it. Hell, for all I know she was thrown from the damn thing. But either way she was sitting on his lap when we got there. The cops had been on scene a few minutes before us, but they said they didn't get her out of the car seat, so that remained a mystery, at least to me. Maybe the medic figured it out. In any case, I made sure I didn't go near that car – I think I went to start throwing kitty litter on the fluids or something with the other car. No one was hurt in that one. I didn't want anything to do with that call. That little girl scared the shit out of me, still does."

Jake showed her his arm, where she could see the goose-bumps had already come up.

"Just the thought of her, the memory of her crying gets me every time, and it's been – what? Over 15 years?"

"So what happened to them? Do you know?"

"Nope. Like I said, I didn't want anything to do with that call – that little girl, any of it. And remember, I was 17 at the time. I was still learning that people don't die like they do in the movies, nice and clean like."

"What do you mean?" Terra asked, admittedly having never seen someone actually die.

"Well, in Hollywood, by in large when someone gets shot, they roll over and die or they're dead before they hit the ground. In real life, people die gasping, grunting or begging and crying. They're afraid. Death is visceral, and *dammit* their eyes don't stay closed when they *are* dead! But at 17, I was pretty sheltered – if someone can consider a 17-year-old who had never seen someone die 'sheltered'. It took a while, but passing that car at that particular moment messed me up pretty good."

"What do you mean?"

"Well, after that call I stuck around the firehouse more, I went on more fire calls instead, like dumpster fires or car fires, things like that," Jake said. "But I could never get that scene out of my head. I kept going back to it. That little girl alone, crying, the tears in her eyes, the fear. That's what it was. Her fear is what got me. I couldn't handle her being in that much fear. It struck me to the core of who I was – even at 17.

"So, after thinking about it for a few weeks, I went to the fire chief and told him I wanted to ride the bus – the ambulance. One the many terms of endearment we have for them. Anyway, the chief and I had a discussion about the 'why's' and so forth, and from that point on, I was determined to help kids, and people in general not be so scared when something happens. Fear and panic are what get people killed.

"Kids are great patients – the conscious ones, anyway. The unconscious ones freak me the hell out. There are really only two rules when treating kids. One: always tell them the truth. If something is going to hurt, tell them. If I need blood, I tell them that the needle will hurt. You'd be surprised at the reactions I get, just because I told them the truth. I lot of them suck it up and take it like champs. If you lie to a kid who is scared, you've lost their trust and its *hell* getting it back."

"And the second rule?" Terra was getting in to it too. Jake's enthusiasm was contagious.

"Two is 'Stay calm'. Kids look to adults when they don't know what's going on. So if they see mom or dad or the other adults are scared shitless, they're going to freak out too. So no matter what, we as EMS providers need to stay calm – if only for the sake of the kid – and it usually helps the parents too. Now, inside we might be freaking the fuck out, but as long as that stays on the inside, we're good."

"So you have to be a decent actor," she said, trying to relate.

"Yeah, I guess you could call it that. If you need something to compare it to. I'd say that would be a fair comparison. The only difference is that every call takes its toll. I don't know if your roles do that to you."

There was a knock on the wall next to them. Jake had never seen that before. It was the waiter.

"Your steak, Sir," the waiter said as he entered the cubby and placed the sizzling platter in front of Jake. He reached back and grabbed the potato and Terra's lobster and placed it in front of her.

"I'll check back in a bit to make sure everything is to your liking."

Then he backed out of the cubby. The towel on his arm never shifted. Terra smiled and thanked him. Both of their plates looked and smelled incredible.

"Absolutely they do," Terra said, getting back to the subject at hand.

"Maybe not to the same extent for most of us, but some

actors have serious problems once they get into a role," Terra protested.

"Well," Jake said drawing the word out and squinting his eyes. "Yeah, I guess if you look at it just right. I'll tell you what. The next time you need help, I'll call an actor. 'I'm not a doctor, but I play one on T.V.' kind of thing."

Jake was trying to be lighthearted about it, but as he watched Terra's demeanor change, he knew he'd crossed a line. Terra huffed a bit at that. She took her skills and her job very seriously. To her, acting was no less difficult than doing what *he* did. Jake noticed the temperament.

"I'll tell you what. Let me talk to a friend of a friend and see if we can't get you a ride-along in an ambulance. You may have to get some initial training, CPR, blood borne pathogens, things like that, but let me check on the ride-along thing. We'll see if you've got the chops for EMS."

"Fair enough. When do we start?"

Terra was getting defiant. Jake chuckled. But he was intrigued. He hadn't expected a Hollywood starlet to be so adventurous when there was no money on the line. He had certain expectation set up in his head about people "in" Hollywood.

"Whoa there, Honey, slow down. If you want to get some of the stuff done behind the scenes, I can get you some online training to do, and we can find a CPR class around here I'm sure. Though I have to warn you, they may not allow ride-alongs on their ambulances. Some places have insurance issues with them, so they don't allow them."

It struck Jake just then that he called her "Honey". He needed to figure out what the hell his brain was doing that his heart didn't know about.

"No problem. I'll have Angela look for a class. I'll text you my email address and you can send me the links to the online stuff. So the worst thing that happens is that I learn CPR and can save a life just like you."

Being called "Honey" wasn't lost on her, but she was on a roll. Terra was sticking it to him, and she'd show him exactly what she could do. He thought of her as a prissy spoiled princess. She would prove him wrong. And at that thought, Terra called up Angela and told her to look for and schedule a local CPR class that started ASAP.

"Cool. Sounds like a..." Jake started then stopped cold, "...a plan."

Jake caught himself before he said 'date'.

"Yup, sounds like a plan. I'll talk with Erik's buddies, who are now my buddies and I'll check on your ride-along," he added.

Jake was relatively sure they could get one done. There might need to be some paperwork on the backend, but actors were always doing things with Fire and EMS around the country. He didn't think L.A. would be a problem.

"So. Now it's my turn to ask a few questions," Jake started. "That text you sent me. That number was from Wisconsin. Is that where you're from originally?"

"Yeah. A little town about an hour outside Milwaukee, called Slinger."

"...and?" Jake prodded, expecting a little more information. He wasn't quite sure how this was supposed to go.

"And what?" Terra asked, taking another bite.

"Oh I don't know... Did you have a childhood? Did you go to college? How'd you get in to acting? You know, the general questions one usually asks. This is what we EMS personnel call *'personal interaction'*."

Terra smirked at the chiding.

"Yes, I know what personal interaction is. It's just different for me talking with someone who doesn't already know everything about me. It's been a while."

"That's what I like about you Terra, your modesty," Jake joked as he smiled back.

He was pretty sure her last statement came out wrong. She didn't mean it in the manner it came out. Jake was slowly changing his mind about her, at least to some degree. She wasn't the arrogant blowhard that he initially thought. He could definitely see how being tailed by people who are constantly photographing every second of your day could make someone at least a little insane.

Jake still wasn't up on all the money and the ideas people seem to have about it out here. It was almost another world. But then, there were certainly parts of Maryland, D.C. and Virginia that seemed to have people living in bubbles of money. He had just never ventured into them, let alone ever been *invited* into one. Picking up old, sick people in a $5 million mansion was one thing, but using it as the pool house to your *big* mansion was another.

"Yeah, that didn't come out right, did it?" Terra tried to backpedal.

"No. No it did not. But I think I know what you're getting at. And I'm sorry, I haven't read up on you. I wasn't exactly expecting to run into any famous people out here, let alone ride with one to the hospital, or have dinner with one. I thought it might be cool to see one, but then I didn't even know you were you, so go figure."

After settling down, Jake didn't once feel uncomfortable with the rest of the conversation that they had throughout the evening, at least not after the initial flashback. It was a strange feeling to him. It was a good feeling, like talking with an old friend. Something he'd only had with Erik, and even then, he was more like a brother than a friend, even if the differences were minor.

As they talked through the evening, nibbling at their food and nursing their glasses of water, neither of them kept track of time. Terra gushed over her acting credentials and had a few secrets she felt she could trust with Jake. After a while, she settled down and stopped talking to Jake like he was a talent agent, and of course Jake loved talking about anything and everything EMS.

The fact that Jake was going out to dinner with a beautiful woman was a distant second to explaining the joys of EMS, at this point in his life anyway. They talked a little more about the requirements and the differences between an EMT and a paramedic and what exactly Erik did up in the chopper. They talked about the cluster of bureaucracy that was Virginia EMS and that the individual counties had their own set of protocols. They also talked about how Terra got into acting and the chance meeting that got her into her current roles.

They had both passed on dessert, and the every now and then, Antonio would refill their water pitcher. At one point, he left the check, which Terra quickly snapped up and opened the black folder containing the bill.

"Hey, buddy! You're a cheap date!" she exclaimed.

Terra grimaced slightly, biting her lower lip, once again not realizing what she was saying at the moment she was saying it. She felt comfortable with Jake. There was no need or desire to put on airs, or try to be someone that people thought her to be. She could be herself. At the same time, she wondered what his reaction would be.

"Well, next time, I promise to get the surf and turf. Maybe

that will change your mind."

Jake caught the reference to this being a date, whether said in jest or not. His reply was automatic and just as puzzling to himself. But he had effectively agreed to see her again without being asked. *Oh Christ! A cat and mouse game. I don't need this right now*, he thought to himself.

"Next time. You're on, and I get to choose the place, a *real* steakhouse." Though she had to admit the food wasn't bad here.

Terra pulled out a credit card and slid it into the folder with the check.

Jake watched her slide the check to the edge of the table, and his Mind-to-Mouth filter failed him again.

"Friends with benefits!" he blurted out.

And with that Jake flinched.

"Sorry! That's not what I meant. Sorry! I meant the bill and dinner and all this," he tried to explain, his hands waiving towards the table.

Terra laughed.

"Yes, I get it. Friends with benefits. But I'll have you know, that I buy men meals all the time, and I mean *all* the time. So don't go thinking you're the one and only. And don't go getting jealous."

They both laughed at the double entendre, and at the awkwardness of it all. Having only met a few days prior, and now they had been talking like they were long lost friends. One trying to *find* himself, one trying to *be* herself.

"I won't tell if you won't," Jake said.

Antonio picked up the check and returned it for her signature. She wrote quickly to make sure that Jake couldn't see how much of a tip she left. Jake thought that was funny. Afterwards, they headed back to the car and drove the 10 miles back to the Ritz talking and joking like friends.

As they pulled in to the driveway, they waved off the valet attendant and said their goodbyes. As Jake opened the door, he reached over and squeezed Terra's hand and looked into her eyes. "Thank you, Terra. Don't forget to drop me your email. If you think you're up for that ride-along." Another squeeze and he got out of the car and closed the door behind him. She smiled as the warmth from his hand slowly ebbed away from hers. She started to drive off slowly, the two exchanging waves. Jake didn't see any 'pap' as they pulled up nor any as he got out of the car. It looks like TJ was good to his word.

Jake waited until Terra had pulled out onto the street and was out of site before he turned and walked into the lobby, extending his arms up and swatting the top of the doorjamb as he entered the hotel. He couldn't remember feeling this good in a long, long time. And there were no real emotional strings attached. At least that was what he told himself.

- TEN -

Jake got back to the room around 11:30 p.m. and, though tired, was in a great mood. The dinner had gone better than he expected and he was looking forward to more trauma in class tomorrow. Jake opened the door slowly, assuming Erik was either asleep or close to, but saw that he wasn't on the couch. He assumed Erik was still out doing whatever it was that Erik did on his own, and opened the door to his bedroom suite.

A loud, shrill scream caused Jake's "embarrassment" instincts to kick in and quickly jump back out of the room and closed the door behind him. Some muffled words and some sheet shuffling later, Erik came out of the room mostly naked, holding a bedsheet wrapped around his waist, somewhat out of breath. He closed the door behind him and leaned on the doorjamb with his free arm as nonchalantly as he could.

"Hey Brother! Sorry, I thought you'd be out later. How was dinner?"

Jake plopped on the couch and ran his fingers through his hair.

"Dinner was fine. Please tell me you were not fucking someone on *my* bed," Jake said, incredulously.

"Sorry, Boss-man. The couch just wasn't cutting it."

Jake started looking at the couch he had just sat on with a new level of disgust.

"Wasn't cutting it? Aw come on man! There's supposed to be a sock on the door or something, man!"

Even though it was disgusting, neither one of them could suppress the smiles or the laughter that followed.

"Dude that's fucking nasty," Jake said, now holding up his

arms, trying not to touch anything by leaning forward and using his momentum to stand up off the couch. "Ugh! That's nasty. I need to shower with a Brillo pad and burn these clothes. God only knows what spooge you've wrought on this thing."

Jake was only partially exaggerating. The door to the bedroom suite opened and a beautiful Latina walked out, clearly irritated, adjusting her clothes, her shoes dangling by their straps in one hand, half talking, half mumbling to herself in Spanish.

"Maria, I'm sorry."

Erik trying unsuccessfully to calm her down. The Spanish got louder and faster and Jake chuckled as he closed the door to the suite and let Erik deal with that drama. Jake picked up the phone, dialed housekeeping services, and requested new sheets. They'd be up in a few minutes. Jake started taking his shirt off and opened the door long enough to see Erik and "Maria" give each other a lite kiss and say their goodbyes. She avoided eye contact with Jake and he looked at the carpet the entire time. She now seemed more irritated with Jake than with Erik. Such was his way with women; Jake just never understood it.

"Alright, Erik, get in here and get the sheets off the bed. I've got housekeeping coming up in a few minutes with a new set. And you're going to have to flip the mattress. Consider this your penance."

"No problem Boss-man. Completely worth it. God she was hot!"

"Yeah, that she was. Please put some clothes by the time housekeeping gets here." Jake was headed into the bathroom to take a shower, hoping there was a Brillo pad in there.

The next morning, the two woke up around the same time.

Jake actually felt refreshed when he'd woke. He couldn't remember the last time he actually felt refreshed after a night's sleep. He grabbed a quick shower and changed into some jeans and a t-shirt. He could hear Erik rustling around in the living room, probably doing the same thing.

"Hey Haus. How'd you sleep?" Jake asked, closing his bedroom door behind him.

"Not too bad, Boss-man. Not too bad at all," Erik replied, the thought of Maria still on his mind. "Do you want to catch some grub on the way?"

"You're my driver, so I guess I have no choice."

Jake was feeling good. Erik noticed.

"I take it last night went well?" Erik asked, the permanent smirk showing again. "Any chance at the details?"

"Not yet. But I may need your help getting Terra a ride along. Do you think you can talk to Darrius or someone and see if it's possible with L.A. County?"

Erik sighed, "Yeah. I guess. Please tell me you're not evangelizing again. Tell me you're not trying to bring someone else into the EMS fold."

"Eh. Maybe. I think she felt challenged is all. She was ready to jump on an ambulance right then and there at dinner last night. She's already looking for a CPR class. That reminds me, I've got to send her the links for the other stuff online."

Jake opened the door for Erik and closed it behind them on the way to the elevator. Jake had a smile on his face. Something Erik hadn't seen in a long time – at least not because of a joke or something, but because his friend actually felt good.

They'd fallen into a routine. Three days was a routine; at least Jake thought it was. They were out the door by 7 a.m. and traffic sucked again. Tuesdays weren't any better than any other day. They grabbed some junk food breakfast at a gas station and Erik dropped Jake off and went to do his thing. Jake assumed Erik was planning more ambushes for him and Terra, but this morning, the thought brought a smile to his face rather than a scowl. Come to think of it, Jake realized he felt a lot better. Better than he had during this trip, anyway.

Jake was a little earlier today and wasn't the last one in the door. The class had a little more buzz to it than the previous day. Jake was anticipating some more trauma. He had a Monster energy drink to go with breakfast, so not only was he feeling good, he was amped to the gills with caffeine. His phone buzzed just before class started and he smiled at the text message.

"CPR Class scheduled for Wednesday night. Bring it on!"

She was a tough one, he thought. *They usually all are in the beginning.*

He had to actively try to clear his thoughts of her so he could focus on the class. He just kept repeating things in his head, *ICP, blood pressure, heart rate, when to or not to hyperventilate the patient, mechanism of injury, threat psychology...* It seemed to work, until of course the next text.

"btw I'm taking you and Erik to dinner on Friday night. No backing out. You promised."

Well, technically, he didn't promise, but he did agree to another dinner with her. Hopefully Erik would be the saving grace. Either way, his morning was screwed. Now all he could think about was getting to Friday, paramedic license be damned! Of course, as the instructor began with trauma scenarios, Jake was in fact able to concentrate on the class at hand. His true love was calling, and she will not be ignored for long.

The class went better and faster on the second day. There was more to learn, and more to engross himself in. There was more about how people learn, and how to keep people in the thought process to react more instead of doubting and thinking.

Reaction was a strange thing to Jake. It was odd when it happened. It was almost like his brain was on auto pilot and he was just along for the ride. His hands flew and the thoughts and measurements and treatments seem to come on their own, effortlessly. He loved those times. But the only way to get there was through practice and the only way to practice was to get on the ambulance and run calls. He was getting rusty, but it was only temporary. His measurements, the conversion from imperial to metric, and the ratios from one dilution level to another – all were spot on.

There were slight differences in the California protocols but nothing too far out. The variants seemed more contrite than anything, just so the EMS Director in this state could say that they had looked at the protocols and made enough variants so as to make it look like his decisions mattered. Most states or regions were all within a degree or two of each other in most aspects, changing only so one could claim this fiefdom or that. *Medical directors were Ego-tripping balls,* Jake thought whimsically.

From time to time, there'd be a new medical director that actually made a difference in his or her state. But the state had to be so far behind the rest of the country for that to happen. Most were getting in-line with each other. There were a few stragglers, but overall, the lagging states would get a more modern director and they'd get straightened out.

The class got out a bit early again, having given the class the option to work through lunch. Getting out into the sunshine, Jake took out his phone and sent a text to Erik letting him know he was out early. It was then that Jake saw Terra's texts again and again, his mind wondered. There was a burger joint across the street and Jake decided to take the chance. Erik pulled up, just as Jake turned around, still chewing a bite of food.

"Hey, Boss-man. You just couldn't wait for me, huh?" Erik said, eyeing Jake as he walked around the car to the passenger door and got in.

"Sorry Haus, I didn't know when you'd be around. Besides, we worked through lunch to get out early. Did Terra get a chance to talk to you about Friday?"

Erik had a quizzical look on his face as he said, "No?"

He drew the word out in question form.

"Well, she said she's taking us out to dinner Friday night and that there's no backing out," Jake said as he showed Erik his phone.

"Okay, but I've got a date with Maria Friday night. That's my last night in town. My last chance to get some... some..." Erik began, acting like he was looking for a specific word, "...to get some. Yeah. My last chance to get some."

"Erik, has anyone ever told you that you have the most eloquent way with words?" Jake asked with a smile on his face.

"Jake, do you realize that when I first saw you this morning, you had a smile on your face, and here it is, approximately 10 hours later and you *still* have a smile on your face?"

Jake's smile faded. "Yeah, well I've been fucked up. I still am, and I will be probably for a while. But I see a little light, you know."

"Yes I do, brother. Yes, I do."

Erik's smile was as infectious as ever, reigniting Jake's.

"Oh, hey! Did you get a chance to talk to Darrius or

whoever about Terra's ride-along?"

"Yeah. He's looking into it. He's not sure if they can do it here in this county, but if not, he knows of another county where she can. He's going to check and get back to us."

"Got it," Jake replied, knowing that there might be some hurdles.

"So what did you do today there, Chuckles?" Jake asked.

"Not too much. Made a few rounds, went and saw a few people I haven't seen in a while. Got to see most of them. I'm trying to set up a shin-dig at the Ritz on Thursday night for the guys. I might move it to that sports bar around the block, but it will be around there somewhere. We should be able to get some answers from Darrius by then."

"Sounds like a date," Jake said, the line reverberating in his mind from when he thought about it last night with Terra.

"In any case, Terra got her CPR class scheduled for tomorrow night, and - damn it! I forgot to send her the links to the online stuff."

"Well, Jake the Snake, it seems like you've got yourself a reason to call her," Erik pointed out wryly.

"Hmph. Yeah. I guess I do. I swear it was innocent. I was going to send them to her earlier during class."

"Hey, you don't have to explain it to me, esse," Erik replied, the comment reeking of sarcasm.

"Uh Huh."

Jake was making a note in his phone to remind himself. Not that it would take much. It was either EMS or her that filled his thoughts for most of the day. When that revelation took hold of him, his mood crashed. He realized that he hadn't talked to or even thought of Meredith all day or most of the week for that matter. Guilt and Shame took their turns running through his head, and he didn't know how to make it stop.

Erik noticed a change in Jake's mood. He'd stopped talking as much. He'd stopped smiling. All within a few streetlights. Erik changed the subject.

"Alright, Broham. What's the deal for tonight? How're we going to *piss* this night away?" Erik placing the emphasis on "piss".

"I don't know. Do you have any friends that are coming off shift?"

Jake liked being in and around the Emergency Services community, preferred it really. The people he had worked with over the previous 15 years there were mostly level headed, at least when it came to everyday happenings. Of course, some were a little touched in the head to begin with, but they tended to stick out like a sore thumb, so they could either be avoided or tended to when needed.

Jake even liked the "fire guys", as much ribbing as he gave them. He knew he needed them as much as they needed him on any given call. They were a family, and it was the same family across the country. Everywhere, held by most of the people doing these jobs – there was a pride in helping people. A pride, he imagined, similar to what a soldier might feel after realizing that they could take the beating and keep going.

They could handle the worst call, take the most foul scene and circumstances and use it for fuel on the next call. Or the next shift. Or the next year. It was a feeling Jake was only just starting to feel again. It was a breath of fresh air. It was just an inkling, but Jake could feel it all the same. The feeling of pride he had putting on the uniform and getting on the ambulance. Even though he was still some ways off from getting his license back, the feeling from the active guys was contagious and he loved it. The feeling pulled him out of his funk.

"Yeah. Darrius gets off in a little while, at 6 p.m. I dropped him a text for Terra's ride along. He never replied, but he might have an answer for us, or know who to talk to at the very least."

"Cool. Is station 20 his regular duty station? If so, we could grab a pizza or two and take it over while we wait."

Jake was itching to get back to a fire house. The class was reigniting his passion.

"You might even get to meet his bad-ass military chief," Jake said.

"Yeah. I guess. I'm not really in the mood for some chickenshit who thinks he's got to prove something. Those guys are always grade-A assholes. We'll see I guess," Erik replied.

Erik was usually a happy-go-lucky kind of guy; it was odd to see him chafe at the thought of someone, even if the guy was an asshole. They hadn't met him yet. Erik started driving in what Jake thought was the general direction of station 20 and with it hopefully towards a pizza joint. The burger just didn't fill him up. Though he did notice he had gotten his appetite back. The thought occurred to him that now he'd have to eat smarter and get more active.

- ELEVEN -

By the time the two got back to station 20 with 5 large pizzas, it was almost 6 o'clock. They weren't sure if Darrius was there or on a call and the pizzas were largely just as a peace offering. The general public – usually, though wrongly called 'civilians' by the department members - weren't allowed in the firehouse unless there was an open house, usually during "fire prevention week" or "EMS appreciation week". That was of course, unless you knew someone working there. But even then, people were limited to the common areas like the TV room or kitchen. Jake was fine with that all the same. He just wanted to get into the firehouse and feel the energy. They could probably squirrel a tour of the apparatus bay and stroke the egos of the firemen there. "Ooh and Ahh" over the big tires and fancy sirens, the LED lights and of course the diamond plating.

The funny thing was that even Jake had to admit that aside from the pressure pumps and the various flow nozzles on the fire engines and trucks and ladders, he too took pride in the LEDs and diamond plate on the ambulances. He did not, however, admit to ever liking parades, an act he would not participate in willingly.

Darrius had just gotten back from a call and was restocking the ambulance when the guys walked up. The bay doors were all open to let in the fresh air. Darrius grinned with the approach of Erik and Jake.

"My brothers!" Darrius exclaimed, stepping down from the side door of the ambulance, letting the others know that these folks were known to him.

Jake was still amazed at the infectious smile and attitude Darrius always seem to have. It was exactly what Jake need right now.

"How're you guys doing? Come on in. We never say 'No' to pizza. Or any free food really," Darrius said as he grabbed the boxes from Jake. "Follow me to the TV room and I'll introduce you to the guys."

A loud cough and clearing of the throat came from behind. It was Stephanie, expressing dismay at being called "one of the guys".

"Aw, Dammit Stephanie, that doesn't count," Darrius protested.

"Besides, you're gay, so samesies," Erik said, leaving Jake standing between the two, exactly where he didn't want to be.

"Hmph. More of a man than you'll ever be, Darrius," she sniped at Darrius, and then quickly changed her tone and held out her hand out to Jake with a smile.

"Hi, I'm Stephanie. It's nice to meet you," Jake said as he shook her hand, "I'm Jake and this is my friend Erik."

Her demeanor changed sharply.

"Yes. I know," she said, curling her lip and pretty much ignoring Erik.

"Well, she's got one thing right there, Darrius. She is more 'man' than you'll ever be," Erik broke in.

Jake looked at him with the standard look of confusion on his face.

Erik turned to Jake, "Stephanie here is one of the best. She is by far the bravest, strongest and most bull headed firefighters I've ever met. She's got Darrius here beat in the cajones department by at least 3."

"Fuck you, Erik," Stephanie replied.

Erik leaned over and whispered to Jake, "I think she's over compensating, if you know what I mean."

Jake was used to the inside threads within the firehouses, but this was all new to him. Erik hadn't been here in 5 years, at least to his knowledge. And things just picked up where they left off, almost like a commercial break.

"Ladies, please. Jake, just so you know, Steph here will kick your ass. She's already kicked Erik's –," Darrius began.

"I was drunk!" Erik protested, cutting Darrius off.

"Which only went to prove that you can take multiple punches and stay somewhat awake if not completely conscious." Darrius corrected Erik, who was flippant to the story.

"But she's one of our best. She just passed the lieutenant's exam, so the promotion should be within the next few months, depending on the attrition rate. She's a true smoke eater. She's good people."

Stephanie gave Jake an affirming nod and sat down at the table in the back of the TV room. It was good to know who the power players were. Darrius brought the pizzas over and placed them on the end of the table.

Then he leaned in to Jake and whispered, "These two don't like each other because Erik is a bit of a man-whore and Stephanie is a bit of a feminist. Personally, I think it's because Erik doesn't like the competition," Darrius joked, and Jake laughed a bit.

It was nearing the shift change and some folks were milling around. No active calls at this point and there were a few early birds showing up. All were happy to see the free pizza. Who turns down friends with pizza? Some were even glad to see Erik. Most, though had no idea who Darrius was talking to.

Jake grabbed a couple of slices of pepperoni before the department scavengers got the last of it. Erik just chuckled at him.

"Well, it looks like you're getting your appetite back."

Darrius approached Jake, looking back at Erik.

"Hey, guys. Let's get out of here. My shift relief is here and I don't want to get any last minute calls. Let me grab my gear. I'll meet you all out back," he said.

"No problem," Erik affirmed.

Jake grabbed another napkin and followed Erik back out to the car while Darrius headed to the bunks to grab his gear.

"Hey Darrius! Don't forget we've got RIT Team refresher training this weekend!" Stephanie yelled.

"Got it!" Darrius yelled back and hustled out to the barracks room.

Darrius met them out back. Jake and Erik were sitting on the back of their car chatting, trying to figure out where to go. Jake hadn't seen any part of the "Hollywood experience", and wanted to at least drive by some of the studios.

"So. I got your text, Erik. And technically, yes, we do ride-alongs for people interested in joining up or junior members and the occasional b-list actor. The issue is you're talking about Terra Dee," Darrius started to get a bit uneasy.

"I talked to our Battalion chief, he sent me over to our HR folks who signed off on it, but they required us to get the public affairs people to accept it. They poo-poo'd it," Darrius said in a low monotone voice. "L.A. County has a long history with Emergency Services. And that is part of the problem. The last thing they want is 'the pap' chasing 'Miss Thang' around out there, invading the privacy of regular people. HIPPA is a big deal, and those dumbasses don't care about anything but snapping a 'good shot'."

"Okay," Jake started, "so where does that leave us?"

"Well, I talked to my battalion chief and he's going to talk to someone further upstate in Tulare or Inyo Counties. You still want to get her some decent call volume, but you also don't want her to draw too much attention. I'll get back to you when I find out more. Probably through Erik here. How much longer are you in class this week?" Darrius asked.

"Tomorrow is my last day. I test out tomorrow. Shouldn't be a big deal though."

Jake was confident in his ability to teach. He already understood the material.

"I'm hoping to get out early," Jake added.

"Okay – and you're headed back to Maryland on Saturday?"

"No," Erik broke into the conversation. "That's just me. Jake will be sticking around another week, right?"

Erik gave Jake the stink-eye. Jake smiled.

"We'll see. I'm feeling pretty good. Make that a maybe."

Jake wasn't ready to give up yet.

"We're meeting Terra for dinner Friday night. I was hoping to have something for her by then," Jake said.

"Okay. Give me your cell number and I'll drop you a text when I hear something. That's the best I can do. I go back on shift Friday night."

Jake shook his head. They exchanged numbers and sent texts so they could add each other to their phonebooks. With the business side of things done, Darrius was looking to have a little fun.

"Where are we off to tonight guys?" he asked.

"I was thinking of running him by the Farmer's Market over in West Hollywood. It's a bit of a shit-show for him and I need to get a few things to get back into shape," Erik said, rubbing his belly. "Plus, we can run him by 'the strip'. We need to *ease* him into the scene. I don't want to scare him off right away."

Darrius smiled, "Sounds good. Who's driving?" as they

walked towards the parking lot. Darrius was game until he took a look at their car.

"Aw hell no! Seriously? You all picked that crap on purpose? Erik, Erik, Erik. We're boys and all, but damn!" Darrius exclaimed.

Jake was laughing the whole time. Erik was taking all the heat for the car when it was Jake who picked it out. Erik could only sit there and take it, while giving Jake dirty looks the whole time.

"Come on guys. Get in. We'll take my car," Darrius said, popping the trunk and dropping his gear in.

They walked over to Darrius's car, a jet black Dodge Charger with blacked out windows, slotted rotors on the front, drilled rotors on the rear with an after-market exhaust. Jake was all smiles at that point. Erik could only roll his eyes.

"Get in the back!" Erik yelled at Jake. "You can ride 'Bitch', your punk-ass got us a damned corolla."

Erik was mumbling at being shown up.

"Don't forget the rainbow air freshener!" Jake yelled back.

"The rainbow what?" Darrius asked. He was smiling if only because Erik was getting irritated.

"Nothing," Erik said. "Just drive."

Erik put the window down and rubbed his eyes.

"Hey Erik, Look! Power windows!" Jake yelled.

Jake wasn't expecting an actual farmer's market. He thought that was just a nick name or something. There was a lot of interesting stuff. Food Jake had never seen before, or seen sold the way it was, crafts and what Jake and Erik both referred to as 'hippie style' clothing. They walked around, sampling things and of course, Erik knew some of the vendors. They stayed until it closed and then they hit the "sunset strip".

Jake was used to odd people and off situations. It came with the job. Most he chalked up to either people being mentally ill or just bad timing. But on "the Strip", insanity was the law. He loved it.

After taking in the sights there, they drove over to Hollywood boulevard and walked the stars a bit. They saw the Capitol Records building. Jake and Darrius had to physically remove Erik from going into Déjà vu. They both knew Erik's propensity for the "adult entertainment" side of things. They came to a burrito joint and picked up something to eat. Erik felt guilty, so he picked up juice smoothie at the joint next door. This place was nothing if not a standing contradiction. After getting the tour, Darrius dropped them back off at the firehouse and they said their goodbyes.

"Dude man, that was awesome. I have no idea what we just witnessed, but that was fun," Jake said, opening the door to the hotel room.

Erik was laughing from Jake's reaction. It was after 1 a.m. and Jake was spent. Erik could party all night, but he knew he had to start living better. They both fell asleep as soon as they hit their respective pillows. And of course both overslept.

About 8am, Jake's phone chirped as he got a message from Terra. He sat up, blearing eyed and checked the phone. He noticed the light from the windows more than anything and freaked out.

"Erik!! Let's go! We've gotta go, man! We're late!" he yelled.

"You mean you're late, Boss-man. I'm just fine," Erik said, sitting up from the couch, still half asleep.

"Come on man, are you going to drive me or what?"

"Naw man. It's time to grow some hair on your sack and drive yourself. You know how to get there. Besides, your name ain't 'Miss Daisy'," Erik said, checking his phone, secretly hoping for something from Maria. He was grumpy and tired.

"True, but you don't look much like an old black man, either," Jake snapped back.

He knew Erik could be a bear in the morning. While one can get used to sleeping on a couch, no one ever liked it.

"Fine. A little more notice would've been nice," Jake whined, throwing on the previous day's clothes. He didn't even take the time to throw on some deodorant, let alone brush his teeth.

Leaving so late caused him to hit a bit of a delay getting his car since the valets were so busy. Overall, T.J. had been working hard to keep 'the pap' away, but this morning he was either late or not on the schedule to work. As the valet pulled the car up and handed Jake the keys, a photographer jumped of out the hedge row and started snapping pictures, while asking a bunch of questions at the same time. Jake had seen and even talked to reporters before, but this guy couldn't figure out what he wanted to be. He just snapped away on his digital SLR, gibbering away asking questions.

"How ya' doing Jake? How'd you sleep? Have you talked to Terra recently?" the man asked.

It seemed he was asking more as a distraction than to actually get answers. Once Jake realized there was really no point to the questions, he got in the car and drove off. He was late and the traffic sucked as much as ever. In the stop and go traffic, he grabbed his phone and texted the class instructor that he'd be a bit late. He wasn't sure when the test was, but he knew the class was at least scheduled until 4 p.m. He received an acknowledgement reply stating he wasn't the only one late which made him feel a little better.

Traffic started moving a bit when he remembered Terra's text. He hadn't had a chance to read it yet. *Thankfully*, he thought, *EMS was still his priority.* Or at least getting to class was. The next time he stopped, he checked his texts. Terra's was second on the list.

"Are we still on for Friday night?" she asked.

"Yes, but Erik was trying to make this girl. He may have to bail," Jake replied if ever so slowly hen-pecking his way through the phone's keypad. He wasn't used to texting so much.

"Nope. Bring her along. He is NOT bailing on us," she replied.

That caught Jake a bit, her referring to "us". In his mind he thought, *There he goes again. Over thinking things again.* Which was true.

He texted back, "I'll tell him. Gotta go. Have class."

And then traffic started moving again.

"Cool. CPR Class tonight!" her last reply before he put his phone away.

He got to class an hour and fifteen minutes late, which all things considered, and how traffic sucked, wasn't too bad at all.

- TWELVE -

Class was a breeze, at least to Jake. He heard a few people complain about what they thought they should have gotten out of the class. Jake and another student helped someone out a bit. It was just a simple issue that needed some tweaking in the mind of the one student, as are most things people are trying to wrap their head around a new subject.

Learning how to teach paramedics isn't that difficult as long as you *are* one. That helps immensely and it's far easier to get their respect and therefore their attention if you've got some 'street cred' or at least some good 'medical chops'. Doctors don't necessarily get the pre-hospital credit, but since they're the ones that treat the patient after the medics are done, it flows more easily if the doctors and paramedics can talk on the same level.

The exam was a little different than Jake had expected. It was a mix of the medical material and the public speaking issues they had addressed. Again, he got an 88 on the exam, but he'd be damned if he'd let Erik know this time. Jake was sure that the instructor, a man this time, didn't have carnal knowledge of Erik. Well, he was mostly sure anyway.

After class, he talked to the instructor and had him send an electronic copy of his certificate back to the Montgomery County Fire and Rescue Services headquarters. Jake gave him Maddie's email and it was a done deal by the end of the day. The instructor also CC'd Jake to make sure he got it as well.

Jake felt some relief knowing he still had a job he loved when he got back. But he also knew there'd be hell to pay. Just the thought of being back in Maryland was hard. It brought back all the memories of Meredith and the time they had. That was something he had steadfastly avoided thinking about the past what – five days? Had it only been 5 days?

Jake was having a great time in L.A. He didn't know how he'd handle heading back to Maryland. He hadn't talked to Meredith in at least a couple of days. Jake couldn't remember when the last time he had. He knew he couldn't continue the way he had been the past few days, with the partying and the site seeing and everything. Jake didn't know *how* it would hit him, just that it would.

He needed time to think. Jake had the car, so he sent Erik a text that he wouldn't be back for a while. He plugged Huntington Beach into the GPS in the car. Jake figured it would be a good place to clear his head. Seal Beach was closer, but was pretty short as beaches go. It was only 3 p.m. "Far From Home" played endlessly from his phone, and when it wasn't playing on his phone, it was playing in his head.

Traffic was pretty bad, at least by his D.C. area standards. He turned in at the Bolsa Chica park entrance and double-backed, passing what he assumed to be the lifeguard station. The parking lot beyond that led to the beach. It took a bit to find his way around.

At about 4 p.m., the sky was as clear as it always was the sun above the horizon still had a few hours of daylight to go. There were a few surfers in the water, just sitting on their boards for the time being. The sun coming off the water was glaring. The ripples were ebbing and peaking and the waves didn't seem to be overly strong. Jake had no idea if the current was coming in or going out. He left his shoes and socks in the car, rolled up the bottom of his pants and headed out for a walk. How far or how long he didn't know and didn't care. He walked across the parking lot and the bike path, both burned his feet. The sand did as well so he walked down to the shoreline passing a few well-tanned and leathery skinned beach-goers. His pale skin and pants might as well have been putting a sign on his back screaming 'Tourist!' That's when he realized that he didn't put on any sun block. *Oh well*, he thought and put the setting sun on his right and started walking.

"What the hell am I doing?" he asked himself aloud. "What am I doing here? What the hell will I do when I get home?"

Jake admitted to himself that he was scared of going back into his house. Scared of the memories. Scared of what he thought Meredith would think. Hell, even he didn't know what he thought about anything anymore.

Thinking to himself he started talking to Meredith. "Talk to me Meredith. What am I supposed to do? I don't know how to do this. How do I go on without you? You were the reason I did anything. Everything. You gave me the strength."

For the past 10 years, a full third of his life, Jake Mitchell had been able to do anything he put his mind to, and he attributed that drive and focus directly to Meredith, his muse. And now it was gone as was the meaning in his life. The goals and dreams, and plans. Gone. Like a bridge holding up a road, being washed away. There seemed to be no way to get to the other side.

Jake stopped walking and stared at some kayakers sliding by – their paddling was a rhythmic distraction. He was close enough to the water line that every other wave would reach him and wash over his feet, splashing up on his pants. Jake felt the wet sand under his feet, and between his toes. Looking down, as the waves rolled back out, they took sand with them, eroding his footing and giving him that dizzying feeling that made him feel as though he might fall. He started walking again, this time, picking up the odd shell to inspect a little more closely or walking around a piece of seaweed. The shells he liked he kept and put in his pocket.

As Jake continued, he started contemplating everything that had gone on in his life for the past 10 years and in the past 5 days. Everything. And in this, he let his mind drift and wander. Sometimes thinking of Meredith, an old memory of his folks, sometimes thinking of Erik, or even Terra. He tried to let go of the guilt. Easier said than done of course, but at least he didn't start crying immediately at the thought of Meredith's accident.

Jake smiled watching some gulls diving into the water for fish – at least, he thought they were seagulls. He didn't know enough about birds to know what they were really. At the beach, every bird was a seagull. The breeze was soft and the beach itself wasn't crowded at all. Of course, it was Wednesday evening so that might have something to do with it. The sound of the waves was intoxicating and hypnotic and allowed him to relax as he thought things through. *Now,* he thought, *I know why people do their yoga stuff out here.*

About 5:30, Jake's phone chirped. He thought he left it in the car, but he fished it out of his pocket, having to pull the car keys out first. Erik had sent a text just checking in. Jake replied with a simple "ok" and turned the phone off. He noticed the time and decided that he'd better turn around. At this rate, Jake should be able to get back to the car with the last of the day light.

Just then a scream came from the water. There was a lot of commotion and splashing from the surfers, most dashing for the shore. One or two paddled their boards to the one screaming though, and slid her onto one of the boards, the water around them turning bright red. There were screams of "Shark!" all around him. Jake ran towards the surfers dragging the woman in and told them where to lay her down.

She was conscious, but not alert. There was a gash that snaked along her right leg about 12 to 18 inches long, starting from behind the knee up to the front of her leg. It cut through the wet suit she had, deep enough to see the bone and musculature. Blood was pouring out of the wound in spurts as her heart was beating, faster and faster. It was bright red and there was no stopping it with pressure.

Jake knew her femoral artery had been severed, and they might have 30-seconds to save her. His first thought was a tourniquet, but he didn't see anything immediately. Jake directed one of the surfers to raise her leg so he could get a better look at the wound. He located the source of the bleeding, pushing the wet suit out of the way. He could actually see where the femoral artery had been sliced but thankfully not completely severed, but it wouldn't take much to do the job. Jake pushed aside some of the hanging skin and muscles, and then used his index finger to plug the hole in the artery, preventing her from bleeding out. Thankfully, it had not been fully severed, or it would have contracted back up into her leg. He had to be careful not to let it slip.

Jake looked up at the girl's face and said, "Hi Honey. My name is Jake. Can you hear me?"

She nodded her head, the pain causing her to take short, shallow breaths. The adrenaline was still having its effect on her. She hadn't started crying yet, either from the pain or the fear.

"Good, can you tell me your name?"

Jake was more worried about her ability to breathe than knowing what her name was.

"J – Jan – Jan….." she said with breathy words.

Again, he wasn't able to tell if it was the pain causing her to breathe like that or something more ominous.

"Jan?" He asked.

"Her name is Janice," someone said from behind him.

"Janice, is it?"

She nodded her head in the affirmative. She was still somewhat conscious, enough to feel the pain, but more importantly she was able to listen to Jake's instructions not to move.

"I need to make sure that you understand me, Janice. Can you wiggle the toes on your left foot?"

She did as asked.

"That's great. Now – I need you to make sure that you don't move your right leg at all for any reason. Got that? If anything we do causes more pain, we need to know that too, okay?"

She nodded.

"Other than your leg, is there anything else that hurts?"

She shook her head slightly, no. She was starting to take deeper breaths, pushing the air out of her lungs as the pain started to get worse.

Jake noted that there were no punctures or tears in the wetsuit above the waist.

"You!" Jake shouted as he pointed the man who dragged her ashore. "Were there any bite marks on her back? Any bleeding?"

"Uh, no. I don't think so," the man replied.

"You don't think so or 'No'?"

"No."

"Slide your hand underneath and check for blood," Jake said.

It wasn't the cleanest of rolls, but he wasn't worried about a spinal injury at this point. He needed to know if she was bleeding from anywhere else.

"No. Nothing. No blood," The surfer replied.

"Good." Now Jake could focus on the femoral artery.

More surfers were starting to gather, some with their phones out to take pictures. Some had called 911 and the beach patrol was on their way. They were within sight of the Huntington Beach Pier, but he hadn't remembered passing it. Actually, Jake had no idea where along the beach he was. There was still an awful lot of bleeding, and Jake couldn't move to do any kind of real assessment. Keeping her legs elevated would have to do for the time being.

Jake was at least able to feel her pulse through the femoral artery, and he was able to see that there were two separate wounds, not one big one as he originally thought. The laceration on the back of the leg had cut the tendons to the back of the inner knee and some of the nerves to the lower leg along with the muscles there. The laceration of more concern was a little further up, starting from the lower, inner thigh where the femoral artery got cut, moving up and across the her quad, slicing and cutting everything up to mid-thigh. Jake tried to go over the names of the muscles in his head, but his last A&P class was forever ago. The Lateral Adductor was the best he could come up with but he knew that wasn't quite right. He'd just stick with "quads" and "adductors".

Jake noticed most of the surfers had a leash attaching their surf boards to their ankles. He looked up at one of the surfers.

"Quick. I need one of those." he said, pointing to the leash. "Let's tie this off some. I can't move unless we do, she'll bleed out."

One of the surfers ripped the leash off his board and handed it to Jake, about 3 feet worth.

"That's perfect, thanks," Jake said handing it back with his one free hand.

"Now I need you to tie it around her thigh right here," he said, pointing to her upper thigh.

Jake looked up at the guy holding her leg up and asked,

"You doing okay there, Boss?"

Jake took a page from Erik's book of names. The man answered his question with a nod, entranced with the injury he was looking at.

"Okay, do you know how to tie a tourniquet? Were you in the boy scouts or anything?" Jake asked.

The surfer shook his head no.

"Okay, someone, anyone, I need a stick, a pen, or a rod of some sort that won't break easily. You!" he said, pointing to a random girl who was caught up in the scene.

"I need you to grab a small towel and place it under the leash. You!" Pointing to another " – I need you to grab another towel and put some pressure on the wound just below my hand."

Jake was pointing to people, making eye contact, and giving them a job to do. So far, he had a team of four people and everyone was doing great. These random people standing around now had jobs to do and action to take instead of standing there, mouths agape at the misfortune of someone else. There was no panic and no one throwing up that he could see. Someone came up with a small towel and a radio antenna and placed the towel under the leash.

"Okay, now tie the leash around her leg there, now place the antenna across the leash and then tie the leash again on top of the antenna. Make sure it's tight. You can wrap it under her leg and tie it again if you want. Now I need you to turn the antenna so it tightens the leash."

The surfer got the hang of it as to what the plan was.

"Keep going. Keep going."

Janice began to scream as the full force of the pain hit her. Then came the tears and the fear. Jake could feel the pressure in the artery drop, as well as the overall bleeding start to slow, though that could have also been the clotting. He still wasn't able to move – or at least didn't feel comfortable taking his finger out of the artery.

Just as the bleeding was stopped, the life guards showed up en masse. They had boats and four wheelers and SUVs. He had no idea what to expect aside from a teenager in red shorts with an orange floaty-thing. The Paramedic chase car – really an SUV – wasn't too far behind, taking it a little slower on the sand than the life guards. They were busy getting information from the surfers as to what had happened and trying to stabilize the patient. Jake was happy they had at least some first aide training. Jake wasn't much help aside from simply showing them why he couldn't move. Most were impressed. The senior paramedic even gave him a compliment, though wasn't as impressed as Jake thought he should have been.

As for the injury, Jake didn't know what happened or how it happened, just that it *did* happen. After some maneuvering, the medic was able to clamp off the femoral artery and Jake was allowed to take his hand out of the wound, if ever so slowly.

Once free of the patient, he headed back down to the water to wash off the blood. He looked like he'd been to a slaughter house. His clothes were ruined. As he finished washing his hands, a young EMT came up behind him and asked for a few details, mainly his name and contact information. The police showed up as well, and he gave them the same information. Janice was conscious and more alert now. Apparently, her pressure was good enough for pain medication, so Jake took that to be a good sign.

They placed her on a back board and walked her to a waiting ambulance that had backed up as close to the sand as they dared.

"Janice?" Jake asked as she tried to focus on him. "Janice, these guys are going to take care of you now. They're good guys, and they haven't dropped anyone all week."

Jake tried to lighten the mood, walking alongside them.

"Well, Mikey here had an incident yesterday," one of the lifeguards chimed in, familiar with the routine.

"Right, like I said, these guys haven't dropped anyone all day," Jake repeated, not missing a beat.

Janice smiled knowing, or at least hoping that they were playing.

"Ah! That's a smile. That's a smile!" Jake said. "You know what that means, right Janice? If you can smile, that means you're going to be alright. Okay?"

Janice nodded and grabbed his arm and mouthed something to him as they lowered the board onto the stretcher.

"You take care of yourself, Janice. You're doing really good," Jake finished as they slid the stretcher into the ambulance.

As Jake turned away, mainly to get out of the way of everyone else, one of the surfers came up to him, "Hey man, are you the dude that saved Terra?"

"Saved who?" Jake asked, still thinking about Janice's injuries.

"You know, Terra Dee. You *are* him! Dude, you're the man."

The man put his hand up as if to give Jake a high five.

Jake squinted with the sun in his eyes and said, "Oh. Yeah, so I can't really talk about that."

He put his hand out to catch the "five".

"Dude, that shit was fire. I've got to run," the surfer said. "It was cool meeting you. Take it easy, man."

Then he headed off without waiting for a reply from Jake, who was simply guessing at the meaning of what the man said. Jake started walking back to the area where they started working on Janice. The trash and wrappers from all the needles and bandages were starting to blow around. Purple nitrile gloves littered the sand as well. Jake approached one of the life guards – who happened to be a Captain and tapped him on the shoulder.

"Excuse me, could you tell me where I'm at exactly. I have no idea."

All he got was a questioning look in reply.

"Well, I'm not from a round here, and I was just taking a walk. I know I parked around Bolsa Chica Park, but I don't know how far away we are from that," Jake explained.

The Captain was kind enough to direct one of the other life guards to drive him back to his car. It was getting late. As they slowly drove on the bike trail, it came out that other surfers in the area had seen a 5-foot Mako shark swimming around in the days prior to the attack. So that was the leading assumption as to what had attacked Janice. Thankfully it had let go. The beach would be closed probably for a day or so, depending on what overhead surveillance came back with as far as sharks in the area. With all the blood in the water, it was hard to tell, especially with the pier so close by.

Jake's nerves had just started calming down by the time he got back to his car. He said "thanks" to the life guard that drove him back and shook his hand. His clothes were still covered in blood. *Well, what else is new?* Jake thought as he got into the car and started the engine. He grabbed his shoes and socks from the trunk and put them on. He pulled his cell phone out of his pocket and turned it on. While it was booting up, Jake plugged the hotel address into the GPS and let it do its thing.

It was a quarter past 6 p.m. at this point. Jake decided to head back to the hotel. He was beat, and he didn't know what all Erik had done that day if anything. As he pulled on to the Pacific Coast Highway, his phone gave a couple of chirps indicating some text messages. Then there were a few more and then it started vibrating from the voicemails. All Jake was aware of was that something big had happened but not knowing his way around, he wasn't about to look at them now. Not in traffic.

He followed the GPS back up to Seal Beach and then to the 405-605 interchange. Jake felt a little more comfortable, but traffic was still a mess. Eventually, he was able to take the 105 exit, but he got hung up at the 710 for a bit, though if there was an accident it was cleaned up before he got there. The 110 was even worse – even though he felt better as this was the highway that drove straight past his hotel. Jake was starting to understand the roads better and know what was going where. Why people would subject themselves to this traffic on a daily basis was beyond him, though.

In any case, he did steal a few moments while waiting to look at some of the texts. Most were congratulating. Jake had couple from Erik. The first making sure he was okay – the one he had replied to earlier. Another asking about dinner on Friday and the third one calling him "Shit-magnet", again. Jake couldn't disagree with him, but didn't quite understand why he'd be calling him that now – and then it hit him…

"No, no, no, no!" Jake screamed.

He checked a text message from Kelly, who was always on the web searching for this or that.

"Dammit!" Jake yelled.

Right there in Kelly's first text was a screenshot of TMZ with the headline "Hero Medic Does It Again!" with a photo of him on the beach, covered in blood, his hand disappearing into the bite wound of a woman – they were at least kind enough to blur *her* face out. The shot was of him pointing – probably directing one of the surfers what to do.

Was there nothing in this place sacred anymore? Did people literally photograph everything that happened? Jake thought. He gave up right then and there. He just wanted to get back to the hotel and not come out. At least he could disappear in the sea of traffic he was sitting in, as much as he despised it.

His cell phone rang. It was Terra.

"What's Shakin' Bacon?" she asked, sounding very perky and energetic.

"Just sitting in traffic. Like always. Is there anything to do around here that doesn't require you to sit in 3 hours of traffic?" Jake grumpily asked.

"Aw poor baby," Terra replied, sounding more like Jake than he wanted to admit.

"Yeah, poor me. What's up?"

He changed the subject.

"Just letting you know I am currently outside the medical center, waiting to start my CPR class. I am going to rock it!"

Her energy level seemed inconsistent with what Jake knew about the class, but he wasn't going to spoil her fun.

"Good girl!"

"Have you heard anything back on the ride along for me?"

"Yes and no. Meaning probably not in L.A. County, but

hopefully somewhere else. Just not sure yet. They're working on it though. I'm hoping to have something for you by Friday."

"Sounds good. I'll let you go. I'll text you when I get out of class tonight."

"Okay. Be safe out there, wild woman."

"Wild woman, huh? Was that sarcasm? That sounded like sarcasm."

"What? No. No sarcasm whatsoever" Jake said, sounding even more sarcastic.

"Okay. We'll see. I may only be getting my CPR card tonight, but soon enough I'll be saving shark bite victims."

And with that, she hung up, not giving Jake a chance to reply. All he could do was chuckle, clench his teeth, and murmur insults under his breath.

- THIRTEEN -

Jake made it home just before 8 p.m. He couldn't get over how ridiculous it was that he took just shy of 2 hours to go 35 miles. Jake was beyond tired. He figured he had walked about 4 miles in the sand. In his mind, that equated 8 miles on the sidewalk. He cringed at what the next day would bring to his calves. His ankles were already feeling tired and weak.

Jake stepped out of the car, still covered in blood, though at this point most of it was dried. The valet attended stopped and starred. Jake tried to hand the keys to him, and he just looked around, unsure of how to handle the situation. Eventually, he covered his hands in some tissues and took the keys.

At this point, there was such a frenzy of "pap" photographers trying to get shots of him, still covered in Janice's blood. Keeping non-paying patrons away from the main entrance was all T.J. could do aside from barring everyone from hotel grounds. Unfortunately, this meant that the sidewalk was still fair game.

It started when he got the tag from the valet attendant. Someone jumped through the hedge just as they'd done earlier in the morning. Another popped out of the lobby itself and still more came from around the side of the hedge. All snapping pictures, their cameras constantly flashing, making the car port look like a dance club. The strobe effect was intense and Jake did what he could to shield his eyes. T.J. ran out to him, threw an jacket around his shoulders and hustled him inside.

"Sorry about that, Jake. These snakes have been getting worse and worse as the week's gone on. And after today, it's only going to get worse," T.J. said, staring at the blood stained clothes, thankful he didn't mess up his own wardrobe.

"Thanks T.J. I know there's only so much you can do. I appreciate it."

Just then, another photographer came around a pillar and snapped a few more photos before security was able to grab him and "escort" him out of the building by his collar. They'd had high profile people here before, so the hotel had plans on how to deal with this type of situation.

"Hey, tell Erik that I'm good for Friday night. I appreciate the offer," T.J. said, as Jake entered the elevator.

As the doors closed, T.J. turned around and straightened his clothes. He was not happy about the intrusion into his territory by "the pap" and he was going to make sure they understood. He grabbed a few more of the security officers and headed outside to have a talk.

Jake opened the door to his room to find Erik sitting there, watching television.

"Hey Boss-man! You've been busy it seems," Erik greeted as he pressed the 'mute' button on the TV remote, showing the same shot that Kelly had texted to him – Jake with one arm in the patient's leg, one bloody arm pointing, his mouth open as if he was saying something.

"Yeah."

Jake didn't have the words, and he just sighed. Erik understood. It was just another day at the office. Jake always seemed to attract the odd calls. He'd seen other medics with the same propensity. It's just that here, the paparazzi found him when they stopped at Terra's accident. Neither Jake nor Erik were particularly special within EMS. They both had people they looked up to and trained with, people who they considered to be better medics.

"So what's the plan now, Boss-man," Erik broke the silence.

"I don't know. Dinner. I need something to eat. I figured I was just going to order some room service. Do they have anything decent down stairs? Someplace where we can go but avoid those guys?"

"I don't think you can go anywhere and avoid them at this point. In fact, at some point, I think you're going to have to actually talk to them."

"Hmph," Jake mumbled, not amused and not in the mood to talk to them. "Well, I'm not talking to anyone on an empty stomach. I'm calling room service."

"Got it."

Erik grabbed the menu from off the desk and handed it to Jake. Jake waved him off.

"Nah. I'll have the same thing we got the other night. I'm not trying to be adventurous tonight. Burger and fries with a water."

Erik picked up the phone and placed the order.

Jake sat on the couch and hit the 'mute' button on the remote. He didn't mind the TV; he just wanted a little silence at the moment. At least something that didn't come from an electronic device.

His phone chirped. Another text.

He stood up long enough to pull his phone out of his pocket and tossed it on the coffee table. He pulled out about a dozen small seashells with it.

Nope. Not right now. I'm not talking to anyone, he thought to himself.

"Dinner is on the way," Erik said as if he'd just accomplished the impossible, then he looked at the seashells as if they were alien to him.

Jake just grunted, staring at the television. Erik sat on the far end of the couch, one leg up on the coffee table.

"So what's going on, man? What happened? I've never seen a shark bite, let alone treated one. How cool was that?" Erik asked.

Erik looked at Jake; he wanted all the details, down the goriest of sinews.

Jake let out another heavy sigh. He wasn't in the mood. Not because of the call or because of Erik, but just because of the entire situation. Erik's expression changed, and he turned towards the TV, not trying to push the issue.

"It was no big deal. I didn't see it happen. I was just walking on the beach and heard the commotion," Jake began. "I got there as they dragged her out of the surf. The wound was no different than any other you've seen. Just the mechanism was different. Trust me, you've treated worse. Call it luck and timing that I was there.

"Most of the surfer guys stayed calm which helped out a lot. They might not have known to look for the arterial bleeding, but all I did was plug a hole with my finger. Half the time I felt like the little Dutch boy. It was one of those calls we always hear about or read about but never see. She wasn't in too much danger once we got the bleeding controlled."

Jake played the whole thing as nonchalantly as he could. On the inside, he was pretty stoked about the call though – as it really was one of those calls they'd only heard about, where putting your finger on the hole saved a life.

"Any shark's teeth stuck in the wound? You know, as a memento?" Erik asked, always on the macabre side of things.

"What? No. Well, I wasn't really looking for any, so I don't know. What the hell kind of question is that?"

Sometimes Erik was odd even to Jake.

"I don't know. Just checking," Erik said, getting up and headed to his bathroom.

Jake sat watching the muted television. The closed captioning on. He was only partly paying attention. Something about heavy bleeding and how the woman was currently in serious but stable condition, which Jake was pleased with.

"Hey, At least she'd have a story to tell her kids and grandkids, thanks to you," Erik said, trying raise Jake's spirits. It worked a little.

A few minutes later, the food arrived. Erik answered the door lest the person delivering the food was another paparazzi. They'd both seen too many movies, but it wasn't out of the realm of possibilities. At least in their ever growing paranoid minds.

Erik brought the cart inside the room and placed the identical trays on the coffee table. Jake moved his phone and saw that the earlier text was from Terra.

"Class was BLAH. It was a video and 3 dummies. The baby part was cool though."

And then a second text, "Call me when you get a chance, kthxbai."

Jake could only assume Terra thought the portion of the class that dealt with choking infants and opening their airway was "cool". He'd give her a call after he finished dinner. Jake was still in a mood and hoped the food would help change that. He and Erik both sat in front of the TV eating their meals. Erik finally reached over and grabbed the remote, turning the sound on.

" - attempts to reach the 'miracle medic' have so far been unsuccessful. Ms. Dee's publicist states that though the two had been in contact earlier this week, neither she or Ms. Dee knew his whereabouts. We do know he's staying at the L.A. Ritz Carlton with his friend, Erik Foerter, who is also a paramedic."

Erik's eyes got huge. He'd finally heard his name on television. He was stoked. In the next moment, Erik had a mouth full of burger, standing on the couch in his boxers, jumping up and down like he was the heavy weight champ. Jake laughed.

"And to think you play it off so well whenever Terra is around. What's up with that?" Jake asked.

He'd caught Erik looking into the stories of what had been going on, but Erik was always "just browsing" as he would say.

"Whatever, Boss-man. You can't tell me you don't like the attention – at least a little bit," Erik protested.

"Eh. Maybe. I just wish it were on my own terms you know? Like I could go to a place and get all the attention I want, and then when I want to leave, I leave and no one follows me. But that's not how it works, I guess."

"No sir. That's not how it works," Erik agreed.

The two talked a bit before Jake turned in for the night. He left Erik with the dishes on the coffee table and the television on. Erik was still watching a movie and texting someone, probably Maria.

"Oh yeah. Terra says she will hunt you down and dismember you if you bail on us Friday night," Jake said, catching himself using the word "us".

"She says that you need to bring Maria along. I don't know about the dismembering part, but I do believe she would hunt you down," Jake warned. "Oh, and T.J. is in, too."

"Copy that. I'll let Maria know she'll be forced to meet and dine with one of Hollywood's top talents, Erik said rolling his eyes in faux resignation.

"Wait. No," Erik said, sitting upright. "I *won't* tell her."

Jake could see the devious thoughts racing through Erik's mind.

"No. I'll just tell her we're going to dinner and if we happen to be going to dinner with you and Terra, so be it."

"Maria is going to wig out man. You know how women are. They're fine with meeting *regular* people but tell them it's someone 'special', and then all of a sudden they need to be dressed right or have their nails done or whatever. She's going to be pissed at you when she finds out you set her up. That seems to be the norm," Jake stated.

"Yeah, but you know I like to sweep the ladies off their feet," Erik responded, repeating one of "his lines".

"Yeah, yeah, and if you can't sweep them off their feet, you can at least keep them on their toes," Jake finished the line.

"I think I've been spending too much time around you when I'm finishing your sentences," Jake chided.

"Uh huh. Hey Boss-man, what did you get on your exam today?" Erik expected a lie.

"A 92. What's it to you?"

Erik started howling in laughter. "That means you got an 88! That's awesome!"

Jake questioned, "And you know this how? Are you batting for the other team now? Because our instructor was a man."

"Ha – No."

Erik's expression changed at the insinuation before he replied, "Because that's the same score you got on the last exam and I know what you really got on that last exam. Two plus two, brother!"

Erik was more than pleased with himself.

"Well congratulations, I guess you'll make 'Detective'

now."

The wind in Jake's sails was shot, so he retreated to the bedroom. Jake called Terra, only to get her voice mail. Then he dropped her a text.

"Sackin' out in the next few. Call me tomorrow and tell me about CPR. I'm done with my class."

She was something, Jake thought. *A 'spark plug' as his dad would call her. She definitely had the go-get-em attitude,* he had to give her that.

The next morning, both Jake and Erik took their time getting up. There was no place to be and no time to be there. About 9 a.m., they were both dressed in their standard casual jeans and t-shirts. They decided to head down to the lobby to see what the hotel had in the way of breakfast.

"Any plans for the day, Boss-man?" Erik asked in the elevator.

"None. You? What did you do yesterday?" Jake asked.

"I hung around here a bit. I missed T.J. though. He was working at some point. I hit the gym, walked around a bit. I found the spa. That was pretty cool. Got the boys waxed. Not much else I could do. You had the car, out saving lives and shit." Erik had mock irritation in his voice.

"Yeah, well next time feel free to drive. The traffic out here freaks me the hell out. It's ridiculous. Wait. Did you just say – Never mind, I don't want to know."

Jake really didn't want to know any of that.

"Hells yeah. Maria likes it like that and I also got a massage, but yeah," Erik said with a Cheshire grin on his face.

"Do the letters T, M and I mean anything to you? You

know it is possible to share too much information, right?"

As soon as the elevator door opened, they saw T.J. patrolling the lobby. They approached him even though he seemed irritated.

"Hey Boss-man, what's up?"

"I can't talk right now fellas, we've got one of those photographer bastards inside somewhere and we can't find him."

Jake felt a bit guilty for that.

"Anything we can do?" Jake asked.

"Aside from leaving the city, no. They'll find you most anywhere you go," came T.J.'s matter of fact reply.

"Okay, well can you point us in the direction of the buffet then, please?" Erik asked.

Erik wasn't going to push the man. Though he did take a moment to see if he had any cigarettes in public view, almost asked to bum one. That he figured was better left for another time.

T.J. pointed in the direction of the buffet and walked off without a word, looking down the hallway, a radio in hand.

The two took it easy for the morning. There was no real desire to do anything but lounge around. During their breakfast, the concierge dropped by their table.

"Excuse me, Gentlemen. My name is Mr. Alexander. I am the senior concierge here at the Ritz-Carlton. Am I correct in saying that you gentlemen are Jake Mitchell and Erik Foerter?"

Jake, not knowing where this was going, replied, "Yes, that's us. Can we help you?"

The concierge smiled and said, "I am sorry to interrupt your dining experience sirs, but the Ritz would like to extend these spa passes to you as a gift for the work you've done. It would be our pleasure to serve you."

Jake and Erik both looked at each other.

"Can I get my money back from yesterday?" Erik broke the silence.

Jake snorted, "Erik, no. Mr. Alexander, Thank you. I appreciate the offer."

The concierge left an envelope on the table and bowed slightly.

"Thank you, again," he said and walked off.

Jake was amazed. He'd never been comped before. He'd only heard that hotels did that from time to time. Mostly in places like Vegas, but none that actually gave a reason other than trying to keep the big-wig traveler happy. He picked up the envelope and saw the tickets inside. They were basically gift certificates but the amount was handwritten "unlimited".

"Holy crap! These are free passes. Unlimited passes to the spa. Anything and everything. Wow!" Jake exclaimed.

Jake was starting to like the attention. At least some of it, anyway.

As Jake and Erik were finishing breakfast, Jake's phone rang. The familiar Wisconsin phone number popped up.

"Hey Lady!" Jake answered the phone. "What's going on? I got your text. What was wrong with the class?"

"Oh my God, what a joke! That class was so sad. And I paid $300 bucks for that class," Terra was not happy.

"$300 bucks? How the hell did you let them charge you that much for the class?" Jake laughed as he asked.

"I paid for Angela to take the class with me. You know us girls. We do everything in groups. I wanted her to take the class too."

"Yeah. Well. Now you know. Did they at least give you a

real representation of what you might encounter? The sights, the sounds and everything?" Jake asked, wanting to make sure she was really ready in case something happens.

"I guess so. The instructor said she was a nurse at a retirement facility," Terra replied.

"Ha! Did she go over how when you start CPR, how the sound of breaking ribs sounds like you're shuffling cards?" At this point, Jake was actively trying to gross her out.

"Ew! What?"

"Yeah, well, you're going to break ribs right? They did tell you that last night, right?" Jake wanted to make sure they at least taught the basics.

"Well, yeah. They mentioned it," Terra said.

"And how sometimes if you don't have the head back enough you can blow air into the stomach and cause the person to vomit back into your mouth?"

Silence.

Jake could sense the growing apprehension.

"...but the dummies didn't have anything like that. Aren't the dummies supposed to be a life-like representation?" Terra questioned, fully expecting that her class was close to reality.

"Oh. Wow." Jake was amazed that the classes everyone thought were so important to know weren't really getting people ready for what they would see in the real world.

"Okay. Well. If they didn't tell you then, I'm telling you now. It sounds like you're shuffling cards. But after you break all the ribs, the chest pumping gets easier. And just make sure you tilt their head back far enough."

"Aw come on!" Terra protested, not wanting to hear it.

"I don't think you're a very good teacher, Mr. Mitchell," she added in a pouty tone.

"I just want you to realize that the adventure that you're embarking on is not as sterile and cut and dry as you seem to think it is. You won't always have a team around, you might not have a protocol that fits your situation, and you'll have to improvise. But you've got a have a clear head and at least have some idea of what to expect."

Jake wanted her to understand that she could do it, but that the mindset is what sets them apart from people that don't rush into the commotion.

"Got it. So anyway," Terra said, changing the subject away from broken ribs and bland classes. "What's your plan for the day?"

"Dodging 'the pap' for one, though T.J. has had a problem with that since yesterday. The hotel just gave Erik and I two gift certificates to the spa here. All day, every day. I need a massage. So I may just take 6 or 8 hours of massage. You know, the relaxing ones, the kind where you wake up in a puddle your own drool."

Jake was looking forward to it already.

"You know you won't be able to hide from them forever," Terra said knowingly. "It's better if you talk to them at some point on your own terms rather than theirs."

There was an inkling of an idea gathering her mind, Jake seemed to hear something in her voice.

"What are you thinking?"

"Well, hear me out on this one. Go to the spa, get yourself and Erik all prettied-up, and I'll set up an interview with Entertainment Tonight. They're much more accommodating than those bastards at TMZ."

"Oh, I don't know about that. I'm not entirely sure I want those guys digging into me like they do you all."

Jake didn't like the idea of talking to anyone in the media

about anything at any time for any reason. In dealing with them in only the past few days, he'd grown to not only distrust them, but seeing how they act, Jake couldn't fathom opening his personal life to these animals.

"You let me deal with that. I'll also call the spa and let them know exactly what you and Erik will need. Trust me."

"Trust you, huh?"

"Yes. Trust me. I trusted you when I didn't know you, didn't I?"

"Yes, but I know you," Jake chuckled. "Okay. I'll do it, but tell them Meredith is off limits. Generalities are okay, EMS is okay, but no questions about Meredith. I get one question about her, I walk. Is that clear?"

Jake was laying down the law for both the interview and for Terra. She knew it, but it wasn't a big deal. Terra knew he'd talk about it in his own time. She wasn't going to push it.

"Deal. No Meredith, or you walk. I think it's too late to get in tonight, but we can do it before dinner tomorrow, if that works for you. Besides, after the spa day, you're going to need some time to bake."

"Bake?" Jake asked.

"Yeah, Bake. Recover."

"Recover?" Jake questioned again, this time a little more concerned.

Terra laughed, "Well, you're going to need some waxing and preening, and that tends to make things red and swollen, at least in the short term, so things should be calmed down by tomorrow afternoon."

"*Should* be?" Jake sighed heavily. "Okay, your call."

"Great! I'll call the spa and set you all up for say 10:30? Does that time work for you?"

"Yeah. It gives us time to get cleaned up a bit. Erik was just there yesterday, so I'm sure they're already somewhat familiar with him."

"Erik? At the spa? For what?"

"You don't want to know."

"Okay well, let me get off the phone here and give those guys a call, get you all polished up a bit."

Jake snorted, "Just like polishing a turd."

"This is Hollywood. If anyone can polish a turd, we can," Terra replied and then she hung up.

Jake put his phone back in his pocket and looked at Erik.

"What's the story, Boss-man?" Erik asked, intrigued at the half of the conversation he heard.

"Looks like we're having a day at the spa," Jake said, getting up from his seat. "Come on, I'll fill you in on the way back up to the room."

***

After cleaning up a bit, Jake and Erik headed down to the 2nd floor, which was where the spa was located.

"Hello! Welcome to the Spa at the Ritz-Carlton. How may we help you two gentlemen today?" a woman behind the counter greeted.

"Hi. My name is Jake Mitchell. I believe Ms. Terra Dee called ahead for us," Jake said, feeling a bit, almost arrogant? Was that the right word? He needed to keep that in check.

"As yes. Well, she didn't call, but her personal assistant did," the woman replied from behind the counter.

"Personal assistant? Okay."

The woman behind the counter smiled. She knew what

was in store for these two. And Jake and Erik looked soft. She looked at them like fresh meat.

"Yes, Sir. We've been expecting you."

All she could do was smile. It was a devilish smile, but a smile all the same.

"If you two would just follow me, we'll get you started and on your way," the woman instructed.

As they were following her, Erik leaned in to Jake and said, "She wasn't here yesterday. I like this one. The one yesterday was a total bitch."

Jake smirked. *Yeah,* he thought, *she seemed nice enough.*

Of course, that was *before* the spa treatments.

After the sessions were over, Jake found himself in a fluffy, white robe, sitting in an oversized lazy-boy recliner off to the side of the registration desk. It was time to call Terra and get an explanation for what had just happened to him. His clothes and personal effects sat in a white plastic Ritz-Carlton bag next to the chair. He dug into the contents, pulled out his phone, and dialed the Wisconsin number.

"Well if it isn't my *personal* paramedic himself," Terra said as she answered the phone.

"A complete body wax?! What the hell were you trying to do to me? Do you know what *complete* means? It means complete! Entire! Whole!" Jake yelled into the phone. "I was lucky to keep my god damned eye brows!"

Terra, trying not to laugh, replied, "Why is it that you men bitch and moan about waxing, yet expect us women to do it? And *we* usually do it every month or two."

Jake continued, "I had to physically stop some of them

from waxing in places I prefer to have hair, or at least places I prefer not to have the skin ripped off. Have you ever seen or heard a grown man weep from pain? I swear I'll never look at Erik the same way again. You're a fucking sadist."

Terra laughed so hard she snorted. Which caused her to laugh more, and Jake to continue. Jake took the chance to ham it up a bit and use some hyperbole for the laughs.

"Yeah. Thanks for enjoying our pain. That helps. That really helps. I know what you meant by 'bake' now. It feels like my whole body is swollen. I damn near lost a nipple. I think poor Erik had a psychotic event. The last I saw of him he was running down the hall naked. Naked, Terra!"

Terra was laughing so hard now that to Jake, it sounded like wheezing. She was hoping that Jake was being facetious, but the thought of Erik running naked and screaming from an old, Asian woman who was chasing him with hot wax was too much.

"I'll call you back when we're back in the room. I'm pretty sure we're done for the day. At least until dinner later tonight."

Terra started to calm down and responded, "Okay. I've got a few meetings this afternoon but I'll be around. Leave a voicemail if I'm not available."

"Alright. I'll talk to you later. Take care," Jake said.

"Bye," replied Terra.

Just then, Erik walked up to Jake

"Jake, my boy, I think I'm in love," Erik said, plopping down on the chair next to him.

"Yeah?" Jake asked somewhat interested, as this was something somewhat unexpected.

"You see that little Asian woman over there? Looks to be the wrong side of 60? Which probably means she's 85, well let me tell you, brother. She's got magic hands. Magic I tell you," Erik said with big smile.

He waved at the woman, who was standing at the registration desk, waving back and returning the smile. Jake rolled his eyes, not wanting any more details. They both grabbed their belongings and headed back to the room to recover a bit.

A few hours later, after Jake and Erik had calmed down a bit, and their skin had stopped screaming from their so-called relaxing day at the spa, it was time for dinner and a little more soul searching.

"Hey, man. I thought you said you had some sort of shindig set up for tonight. What happened to that? Are your guys coming here or are we headed out?" Jake asked.

"Yeah – about that. Seems that half of the guys didn't want to be around the mess that's going to be following you, and half of them did – being the firefighter glory-hounds some of them can be. I figured it was better to call it off. Especially since we'd have to explain to them that we spent the day at the spa and just had our man parts waxed," Erik replied.

Jake gave Erik a glare, "You had them waxed, *again*?"

Erik responded with an impish grin.

Jake didn't quite know why they'd have to tell anyone, but at the same time, he knew it would come up.

"Eh, I just figured we'd keep the day going by chilling out for the rest of the night. Besides, tomorrow is a big day. We don't want to have to worry about any hangovers or beer farts on national television," Erik replied with his frat boy wisdom.

As was becoming the habit, Jake and Erik decided once again to stay nearby the hotel. There were a ton of restaurants they hadn't been to yet and one was even a steakhouse – and one with a very good reputation, too. About 8 p.m., after the swelling had gone down some, they headed down to Fleming's

Steakhouse.

Jake and Erik started talking about everything that had happened in the last week. It was only Thursday night and the EMS class that he had originally come out for had been the least of his concerns really. As their plates arrived at the table, Erik had a huge smile on his face.

"What are you up to, Erik?"

"Nothing, man. Nothing at all," Erik said, trying to play it off.

"No. No. It's something. Let's hear it."

"Well, it feels like I'm starting to get you back. It seems like this little vacation has worked. I can see you coming out of your shell again. You're not all the way there, but I can see you again."

"Yeah. Maybe a little."

Jake was a bit uncomfortable about that subject. So he decided to change it.

"How're things going with Maria?"

"Oh man! I haven't told her about today," Erik said as he checked his phone. "Nope. Good. No messages from her."

"She is going to flip out when she meets Terra tomorrow night," Erik added, getting excited.

"Have you told her anything about tomorrow night? Anything at all?"

"Nope. Just that we were going to dinner since it was my last night here."

"Yeah, well, do me a favor and get your own room. Is she going to be okay with me there?"

Erik laughed, "She'll be fine. I hope anyway. I'm thinking that she won't care that you're there since Terra will be."

"So she's not okay with me?" Jake asked, concerned.

"You? No. She's still pretty sore about you walking in on

her in the throes of an orgasm," Erik recalled with a smirk.

"Yeah, well whose fault was that?" Jake asked, trying to defend himself.

"Guilty as charged, Mofo!" Erik said with a laugh. "I tore that ass *up*!"

Jake, realizing his mistake, interrupted him, "Alright, alright. Settle down. I wasn't trying to get you on an ego trip."

"Hey Boss-man, let me ask you a question."

"Shoot."

"Are you going to be okay with the interview tomorrow, man?" Erik questions, the concern in his voice heavy.

"That my good man," Jake answered as he raised his Whiskey Sour up, "is the question. So here is a toast you to, my friend. I wouldn't have made it this far if not for you. To answer a question as deep as that wouldn't have been possible without you, brother."

"To friends," Erik joined him in the toast before taking a drink of his beer. "You are my brother. Don't forget that."

- FOURTEEN -

Friday morning came bright and early. Terra had called but didn't leave a message. Jake didn't know what the schedule was for the day. He had no clue what lay in store for him.

Erik had a fitful night of sleep. There were more bad dreams on top of the fact that he was concerned about the interview. He always wanted to look good for the cameras. He was known to mug for the reporters who would show up on scene or at the hospitals. But more, he was concerned about Jake. He had finally gotten his friend back, to some degree, and he didn't want the interview to snuff that out.

On the way down to breakfast, Jake called Terra again and this time she picked up.

"Hey you. Did you sleep well last night?" she asked, very cheerfully.

"Yeah. I guess so."

"Sorry I didn't get back to you last night. I was in meetings all day and most of the night. You know, all that showbiz stuff."

"Yeah, I know all about that stuff," Jake replied sarcastically while rolling his eyes. "So what's the plan for today?"

Jake wanted to get the interview over with. He couldn't wait to see Terra again, but he had to get through the interview to get to dinner.

"Well, I've set up the interview for 3 p.m. That way it won't be live; they'll have time to edit it and make you look as good as possible. Worst case scenario, we should be out of there no later than 6 p.m. so its in time for the late night stuff on the east coast, depending on how long it takes to do the final cut. Hopefully a lot sooner than that, but that's worst case scenario."

"Okay."

"Well, you're the hero this week, darling," Terra said, pronouncing it "dah-ling" as if she were back in the vaudeville days. "They love to build people up, out here."

"Yeah, and then they tear them down in ways more vicious than car accidents. I know about that one. That's what I'm afraid of." Jake was back to thinking too much.

"Oh, don't worry about them. I've got them on a leash. They've already started the commercials for the interview, and we've got final edit approval."

Terra was trying to calm Jake down. He was obviously scared and it came out more as irritation than anything else.

"I figure I'll pick you guys up around noon and we can go grab some lunch if you want to before the interview. Otherwise they said they could send a car for you around 2 p.m. and I'll meet you at the studio. It's up to you," Terra added.

"I wouldn't mind lunch, but honestly I'm not sure eating right before the interview would be the best thing to do. I'm not sure how well I'm going to keep breakfast down as it is."

"That's fine. I'll let them know you'd prefer the car at 2 p.m. in the lobby. I'll text you any details. Sound good?" she asked with more pep in her voice.

"Yeah. I guess so. This whole thing still wigs me out."

"Relax. You'll do fine or they'll just reshoot the question. Trust me, would you?"

Terra was doing her best to reassure him, but in the end it was up to him to be okay with everything. She wasn't sure if it was still too soon. She knew they'd push the boundaries with questions about his wife or at the very least the call. But, that's why she insisted on the final edit. They said their goodbyes and hung up.

By the time the conversation was over, Erik was already seated. Jake had stayed back to finish the conversation without all the ambient noise in the restaurant. Both ordered a generic breakfast and Jake picked up a Mimosa to go with it. It wasn't that he liked them, but he figured it was a "breakfast drink" and he needed something to settle his nerves, and if he got sick, he could blame the drink.

"So what's the deal, Boss-man?" Erik asked.

"The studio is sending a car to pick us up at 2 p.m.," Jake answered.

"Oooh, fancy! Maybe I should order an appletini and keep the 'fancy wagon' rolling," Erik said.

Jake wasn't entirely sure Erik was sober at this point, but that didn't mean much.

"That reminds me, Erik. Make sure Maria doesn't drink tonight. Terra is still recovering," Jake said, hoping that this breach of HIPAA wasn't without merit.

"Bummer. But that's cool. I understand. I'll let her know."

After breakfast, the two walked out to the lobby, Erik making a b-line for the front door to grab a smoke. Jake followed him.

"I haven't seen T.J. lately. Have you?" Erik asked. He was looking for another smoke buddy, but also wanted to verify his suspicions about T.J.'s cigarettes.

"Not since yesterday morning when some photographer had gotten into the building and he was working with security to find them."

Just then T.J. walked out, shoes polished to a high gleam and a cigarette behind his ear. He seemed rushed but not as irritated as he was the last time Jake saw him.

"Speak of the Devil," Jake said.

"Hey fellas! How's it going?" T.J. replied.

He had a big smile and was definitely in a better mood.

"Hey T.J.! My man! Where the hell have you been? I haven't seen you for a bit," Erik greeted him.

Erik only casually glanced over, tapping his ashes on to the sidewalk. He didn't see the cigarette behind T.J.'s ear.

"Man you just would not believe what these clowns are doing. Thank God y'all are going on TV tonight. I was about to have to kill a bitch."

Jake smiled. Erik chuckled. T.J. fished in his pockets and found his lighter. The moment of truth for Erik. He perked up. Erik knew he was smoking Virginia Slims. T.J. saw him looking at him intently.

"Something on your mind, Erik?" T.J. said with a smirk, knowing what Erik was looking for.

"Nope," Erik said, taking another puff on his cigarette, knowing that T.J. knew, and still trying to play it off.

"Um hmph. So Jake, have you decided if you're staying or leaving tomorrow?" T.J. asked, putting his lighter back in his pocket, not giving Erik the satisfaction.

"I still don't know. I'd like to stay, but I don't know what benefit that would give me other than relieving me of more money. Right now I think I'm good to go home. The interview tonight is all I'm really worried about."

T.J. turned his attention towards Erik.

"And you," T.J. said, pointing at Erik, "you cracker-ass white boy. Here's your damn cigarettes."

T.J. then tossed a pack at Erik. Erik started laughing and caught the pack of cigarettes.

"Cracker-ass white boy," Erik repeated, enunciating each word in his most Caucasian of voices.

"I told you! I told you, bamma!" Erik started yelling at T.J.

He had flipped the pack of cigarettes over to see the Virginia Slims logo.

"Yeah, yeah, whatever. You bastard. I'm a laughing stock now, asshole. I have to hide when I smoke now."

"Well, maybe this is how you stop smoking, then," Jake added.

"I might have to," T.J. replied. "I can't let the ladies see me smoking these. It's embarrassing."

"Are you kidding me? You're a trend setter, now man! A trend setter. It goes with your style. The clothes, the look. Everything," Erik said, trying to make him feel better.

"So what, I get my trends from some no-style, country-ass white boy from the east coast?"

"Hey," Erik whined and started to sulk. "I have style."

"We'll see. Come on guys. I have orders from the 'princess' to get you two ready for the show, and not much time to do it in."

"The princess?" Erik asked, looking at Jake. Jake had no idea what he was talking about.

"Wow you two are clueless. Terra's the princess. Terra asked me to take you two to get some clothes. At least *someone* around here appreciates my style."

"I have style!" Erik repeated.

"Uh huh," T.J. said looking at the two in their jeans and t-shirts. Erik had a salsa stain on his shirt from the eggs. "You're lucky I already gave them your sizes. I hope you all don't mind."

Jake and Erik were still taken aback by the whole idea, still not 100% on what that idea was, but obviously were all for it.

"Are you gentlemen ready to go now, or do I need to hold your purses while you get yourselves together?"

Erik laughed.

Jake nodded his head and replied, "I'm good. I think I've got everything. We can take the Corolla."

"No. No Corolla. We'll take the hotel van," T.J. said and rolled his eyes. He hated that damned car. "We've got to get going then. I'll call ahead so they're waiting for us."

A half hour drive later, Jake and Erik piled out of the black van and onto the sidewalk.

"A parking garage? You brought us out here to a parking garage?" Erik asked sarcastically. "Is this where you bring the hotel guests to 'off' them?"

They were parked outside a store called "Johnathan Behr". Jake had never heard of it. Erik was unimpressed, as of course he thought he already had style. Still the store window did have some fine threads, though some uncomfortable looking chairs.

"Gentlemen. I give you the finest suit clothier in all of Los Angeles, within our budget, of course," T.J. announced, pointing to the corner of the building.

"Now, these guys only do custom, so I gave them your general measurements last Tuesday. They're doing a favor for Ms. Dee. They'll be taking the final measurements and doing the final alterations on the spot. They busted their asses to get this far. I get all my suits here. Custom, of course," T.J. said with a hint of arrogance, if only to irritate Erik.

"Should I ask how you know our general measurements?" Erik asked, somewhat concerned.

"It's part of the job. I work very closely with the concierge desk, and with my own attention to detail, I know ballpark measurements. Enough at least for Mr. Jung over at Danil, next door. We do a little more work with those guys, though it's been a pleasure working with Behr."

"You've been planning this since last Tuesday?" Jake asked.

"No, Ms. Dee has been. I guess you made plans for tonight and she wanted you all to look good. I can't say that I blame her," T.J. said, looking Erik up and down with pursed lips.

"What?" Erik protested, really getting irritated.

Jake laughed, hit Erik on the shoulder, and said, "Damn, man, relax. He's just busting your chops. Get over it. Imagine what Maria will think when she sees you all decked out. Besides, T.J. is more of a pimp than you are, and if Terra trusts his style, I think we can."

A few hours later, and a few pin pricks on Erik, the guys walked out with 2 new suits apiece for Jake and Erik, complete with shirts, per T.J. They'd have ties, handkerchiefs, shoes and socks waiting for them back at the hotel. Jake was afraid to ask how much they cost. T.J. simply put it on a Ritz-Carlton credit card. *Hopefully,* Jake thought, *these would be the last suits he would ever need, maybe even the one he'd be buried in. Assuming they came back in style at some point.* Jake smiled at the thought. Erik on the other hand was beaming. He really wanted to wear one of the suits out of the store like a kid with a new pair of shoes. Jake knew he'd be changing into one as soon as they got back to the room.

It was just after 1 p.m. and they had to high-tail it back to the hotel anyway. Jake was starting to feel ill. His nerves finally caught up with him.

"You doing alright back there, Jake?" T.J. asked, noticing the green hue Jake had turned.

"Yeah. Just nerves. Now all I have to do is get through the interview and then I can throw up," Jake answered.

"Yeah. Do that *after* the interview. It tends to look bad if you puke during," Erik consoled him, as if he was a pro at going on national television.

Thankfully, the drive back was quick and uneventful. They got back to the hotel about 1:30 p.m. and headed upstairs to get changed. Erik walked a little faster with more excitement than Jake, who didn't feel the need to rush. He was the interview. Technically they both were, but they weren't going to start without him. The car would pick them up at 2 p.m.

The car came exactly on time, and the phone call to the room was almost instantaneous. Erik had already been ready for 15 minutes, but Jake was having a hard time with his tie. The Windsor knot wasn't his favorite; Jake instead usually just tied a hatchet knot on the premise that it should take a hatchet to undo the damn things. Erik was trying to hurry him along, obviously more excited about the whole process than he was. Finally, Jake got tired of trying to tie the knot and just let the tie hang loose around his neck. Granted, it didn't really fit with the suit, or so he thought, but all in all they both had cleaned up nicely.

Jake and Erik walked out of the elevator and into the lobby. T.J. was standing at the lobby doors and shook their hands as they left.

"Good luck, you two. Hey, Erik. *Now* you've got style, baby!" T.J. teased. This time it didn't faze Erik.

Hopefully, Jake thought, *it was because he finally felt that he did have style.*

The car, a Lincoln Navigator with blacked out windows, was waiting beneath the overhang in front of the hotel. The driver, in his own dark suit and sunglasses, held the door for them as they exited the hotel. Then he closed the doors and walked over to the driver's side to get in. He checked some of his paperwork, noting the time, sent a text message to his dispatch office, and pulled out on to West Olympic Drive.

"So, you gentlemen are off to Studio City. Let's see if we can get you there in time," the driver started to make conversation.

Erik obliged him, trying to fill the void that Jake and his nerves had created.

"Yeah. How far is it? Will there be any famous people along the way?" Erik asked.

The driver was amused. He thought that simply meeting Terra Dee, let alone spending any amount of time with her would be enough for most people.

"It's not too far. Only about 10 miles. It's the traffic that we need to be concerned with. Its 2 p.m. on a Friday. That's going to be a bit rough. As for famous people, we might see one or two. You guys haven't had your fill of that stuff, yet?"

The driver had either known who he was driving beforehand or had recognized them.

Erik looked at Jake who was looking out the window, feeding his sick fascination with the amount of traffic or trying not to think about the interview, he wasn't sure.

"Nah," Erik continued. "It hasn't been too bad, actually. I'm not really the one everyone is after, and I know my way around the area pretty well. I used to be a paramedic out here a while back. My buddy here on the other hand seems to attract the vultures."

Erik speaking both in reality and metaphorically.

As they drove on to the 101 freeway, the traffic was even worse than the driver had imagined. It was a veritable parking lot.

"10 miles, huh?" Erik said. "So it will take us how long to get there?"

"Oh, I guess probably 45 minutes, maybe an hour, give or take," the driver said, gauging the traffic, and checking his watch.

At first Erik thought he was joking, until he saw the look on his face. After that, he just sat back and tried to distract Jake. Overall the drive wasn't horrible, as long as they didn't think about how far they were actually going. An hour in the car in the Washington, D.C. area wasn't much different, but at least you moved further than 10 miles, even if you had to take side roads. Los Angeles was on a whole different level.

As they pulled up to the guard station outside the studios, Jake was more alert, almost anxious. Erik kept his eye on him. He was no psychologist, but he didn't want his best friend being emotionally ripped open again. Certainly not for the entertainment of the masses.

The guards checked their paperwork, made a phone call, and verified that there were in fact only two people in the back of the vehicle, and then let them through. The car parked off to the right after coming through the check point and soon someone drove up in a golf cart to take them to the actual studio where the taping would be done.

"Mr. Foerter and Mr. Mitchell, I presume?" the guy asked.

Jake and Erik both nodded, not knowing how to respond.

"My name is Terry, I'll be driving you around this evening. Ms. Dee is already here," the golf cart driver added.

Jake was visibly relaxed at that. He had no idea what they were walking into and he was placing a lot of trust in Terra. He was starting to second guess himself now and was pretty sure this whole thing had been a mistake. Jake was sweating just from the thought of the interview. He didn't know what to expect, which in his line of work is normal, but he knew how to handle trauma patients and medical emergencies. Jake didn't know how to handle whatever it was he expected to find behind those doors.

As they pulled up to the doors of one of the massive buildings, Terra walked out to greet them, and Jake relaxed even more. Without Erik, he didn't think he would have done the interview, let alone be in L.A. Without Terra, he wouldn't be able to do the interview. But somehow, seeing her gave him more strength. He was no longer on the verge of tears. Terra hugged them both, grabbed Jake's hand, and gave it a squeeze.

"Wow! You guys look great!" she gushed over them.

"Yeah we do!" Erik agreed.

Terra immediately started tying Jake's tie.

"How is it that it always seems to be the women who know how to tie these damned things?" Jake asked as Terra was finishing the knot.

"Something we all seem to pick up along the way. Men almost never want to get dressed up to go anywhere, so we do it for them," Terra said. "It's like playing with life-sized dolls."

Both Jake and Erik shrugged in agreement. Neither one of them liked getting dressed up to go anywhere. Terra straightened Jake's tie and smoothed out his lapel. She turned towards Erik who backed away, holding his hand over his tie.

"Nope. I'm good," Erik said.

Terra smiled at him, turning back to Jake. She looked Jake straight in the eyes and asked, "Are you ready to do this?"

"As ready as I'll ever be," Jake replied with a sigh.

"Oh, and everyone needs to mute your phones," Terra reminded them

Jake looked down at his phone to see a text message from Kelly.

"Good Luck. I love you," it said.

Right then, Jake missed Kelly, missed home and

everything he had left behind. He started tearing up. Right then he wanted to go home. He wanted to be a kid again, protected by his parents and immune to the cares of the outside world. Terra saw his expression and grabbed his arm as he turned his phone off and slid it into his pocket. Jake stood up a little straighter and cleared his throat.

"If you need to stop, tell them to stop, Jake. You're in control here," Terra reassured him.

"Yeah. Got it," Jake said, still clearing his throat, trying to get his composure back.

"You two will be in there, it's a small room, but cozy. Comfortable. That's where the interview will be done. I'll be in the sound booth with the producer and the technicians. Okay? Where is the producer?" Terra asked.

A man burst through the swinging doors.

"Sorry! Sorry. I'm so far behind today," he said extending the 'S' in each word. "My name is Gerald. I'll be producing the show tonight."

He held his hand out towards Erik with his wrist up and palm down, like a woman expecting her hand kissed. Erik, a bit uncomfortable with the situation, tried not to laugh out of nervousness and just shook his hand. Seeing Erik shaken cheered Jake up some. He was used to the more flamboyant gay men, so it didn't bother him in the slightest.

"Nancy will be doing the interview. I guessed that she might make you a little more comfortable," Gerald said, looking at Erik.

"Besides, putting you two in with Kevin would be too much for *me* to handle," Gerald added, giving Terra a wink, who returned a smile.

Jake had no idea who "Kevin" was, but Erik chuckled with

uneasy nerves, which gave Jake even more reason to laugh. The producer showed them into the room where there was a couch and what looked to be a bar stool with a coffee table between them. Jake took a seat on the couch, on the end closest to the bar stool. Erik, still feeling slightly embarrassed, sat at the other end of the couch, not wanting to get near Jake and possibly give Gerald any ideas, or so the thought went in Erik's head. Terra saw it from the control room and chuckled while rolling her eyes.

Someone walked into the room with a makeup kit and dabbed some powder on both of them, putting a little more on Jake as he was sweating more. The makeup artist looked up to the control room as if looking for an answer and apparently got what she was looking for and left. A few moments later, Nancy O'Dell walked into the room, a script of some sort in her hand. A former beauty pageant winner, she stood taller than Erik by a solid two inches, which was amusing to Jake and somewhat intimidating to Erik.

As she introduced herself, in walked two men behind her with headsets on. They put lapel mics on all of them, clipping the battery packs to their waistbands. A few sound checks later and everything was ready to go. Overall, it wasn't as bad as Jake had imagined. He was definitely more comfortable than he imagined. One of the sound guys brought in some cups of water for everyone, setting them on the coffee table. Jake instantly snatched his up and downed it.

"I just want to let you know, guys, that if you need to stop, just tell me to stop," Nancy said, laying the ground rules for the interview. "I will do my best to stay away from the sensitive topics, but at the same time, people want to know what happened and how you're doing. So, I will stay out of the details, but I might tip-toe on the line, okay? If I cross the line, just tell me to stop and we can move on to something else, okay?"

"Yeah," Jake replied quietly. Erik just nodded his acknowledgement.

"Are we ready in the control room?" Nancy asked, receiving a thumbs up.

"Are you two ready?" she asked Jake and Erik, who both nodded "yes".

Jake looked at the clock on the wall. It was only 3:15 p.m.

"Well, Jake, Erik, It seems you two have had quite the busy week here in L.A. How're you two holding up?"

Nancy's first question caught them off guard. They weren't sure if this was part of the interview or just her making polite conversation. They looked up at the production room and saw one of the guys making "rolling" motion with his hand. It looked like they were on.

"Hi Nancy. We're hanging in there," Erik chimed in.

Jake smiled and nodded.

"Let's see, first there was the car accident with Terra Dee and then the shark attack that Jake was there for," she continued.

"Yeah, so we can't really talk about any of that stuff. We can talk about what we did, but we can't mention names or anything that identifies people – and seeing how the press has made everything public, I'm not sure where we stand on talking about them," Jake said, both in relief and in stating the facts.

"Well, Jake, we have a written release from both Terra and Janice allowing us to ask you about their situations," Nancy replied, raising a few sheets of paper.

She handed two of them over, and Erik and Jake reviewed them both.

"Looks legit to me," Erik said, handing the papers back to Nancy. Jake shook his head in agreement.

"Now, Jake," Nancy continued, "We have a letter here from Janice. She was the girl you saved last Wednesday, she had something she wanted to say to you. She just started her senior year in high school. Do you mind if I read the letter to you?"

Jake felt a bit set up. He wasn't expecting anything like this and he wasn't sure how he'd handle the letter. He had met a few patients after their ordeals. Some came by the firehouse to say "Thanks"; some had approached him while he was at the store near the firehouse. No matter how they approached him, Jake never knew what to say in reply. It always made him feel uncomfortable. The one difference was though that in all the others instances, he always had an "out"; either a call would come in at the station or he could tell them he had to go. Here though, Jake was a bit of the prisoner, with nowhere to run or hide. There were no excuses that he could give to get away.

Jake nodded to the affirmative, unsure of what else he could have done.

Nancy started reading, "To the man that helped me yesterday on the beach. My name is Janice Miller and I am 17 years old. I was the one bitten by a shark. My friends told me that you saved my life. I may be in the hospital for a while, but I wanted to thank you before you went home."

Jake sat quietly listening, not quite resting his head on his hand, his fingers across his lips.

"That's got to feel pretty good, Jake. You saved that little girl's life. Without you, her family would be planning for her funeral instead of a graduation party," Nancy said.

"Yeah," Jake responded contemplatively.

He didn't really know what to say or how to react. He was choked up for sure.

"Now you two have been part of the emergency medical services or EMS for some time - about 10 years each? Why do you do this? What do you get out of it?" Nancy asked.

"I get a charge out of it," Erik started.

"Call it a rush. There you are, with a patient who needs help and you have the ability to help them. Not only the ability, but the duty as well. The duty to serve runs deep," Erik said, putting a softer touch to what some would call a god-complex.

"Yeah. It was the excitement that drew me in, too," Jake added. "Add to that the sense of accomplishment - the immediate satisfaction of getting results. It's the fact that what we do in EMS has an immediate impact on people."

"They need help now," Jake explained, snapped his fingers to demonstrate the immediacy, "and they get help 'now'. There is very little time between treatment and reaction."

"What's your favorite part of being in EMS? What keeps you going?" Nancy asked.

"Trauma," Erik said almost before she finished the question, being somewhat facetious.

Jake smirked.

Nancy just raised her eyebrows.

"Not really, but most of us are trauma junkies," Erik continued. "So for me, it's a mix between helping people like trauma victims and watching drugs work their magic. Narcan is the coolest thing I've ever seen."

Jake shook his head in agreement, though his favorite drug was Amiodarone.

"So, basically just the idea that you're helping people, right?" Nancy clarified.

"In a nutshell," Erik said with a smile.

"Now, Jake, how about you - what keeps you getting on that ambulance?" Nancy asked.

"A 3-year-old girl," Jake said. There were other stories of course, this was just the one that he parroted whenever someone asked the question.

Nancy tried not to show her surprise before she questioned, "Can you explain a little?"

Jake went on to tell the story about his first on-scene car accident when was 17. The same one he told Terra at dinner. The issue was that this time, under the lights, cameras, the pressure of the interview and the fear of having to deal with Meredith's accident in front of everyone, the tears came. His expression never changed, just the tears dropping down his cheeks.

As he told the story, he wasn't aware that he was crying. It looked to them as if he was in complete control of his physical body, but his eyes and tears betrayed him. This of course only endeared him even more to the people in the production office and they hoped to the people watching it.

It would of course; they could all but guarantee it. To them, this was pure ratings gold. Regardless of whether it was building someone up or tearing someone down, it was gold. This time, the story was about the humble and modest paramedic, crushed by personal providence, continuing to slog on because of it and in spite of the ongoing horrors of the lives of others. And the side note, which seems just as interesting, if more hidden and maybe more provocative, is the story of his best friend. How could people not like these guys?

A few minutes later, after encouraging people to join their local volunteer fire departments, Jake stepped off his proverbial soapbox. He was on cruise control, and as long as it wasn't about certain subjects, he was the EMS "fan boy" to beat them all.

Jake eventually grabbed the handkerchief out of his front jacket pocket and dabbed at his eyes.

"So, back to Janice. Tell us what your thought process was," Nancy prodded.

Jake smirked, "My thought process? Well, the first thought was that I didn't know what was happening, just that there was lot of commotion. Then when they brought her out of the water, it was apparent what the issue was. She was bleeding out, I simply plugged the hole and added a tourniquet. I'll tell you what really helped out was that no one panicked; everyone did what needed to be done. I wasn't the only one there.

"Panic is what gets people in trouble, and no one panicked, so that was awesome. We're trained to handle situations like that. Those other people there, they were the real heroes. Other than that though, there wasn't much more. Find the hole and stop the bleeding. I asked her a few questions and made sure she was conscious and breathing, but there wasn't much more I could do until the big boys got there that had the equipment to get her to more definitive care. I never saw the shark or the attack."

"Well, as the letter said, she's doing well and the doctors said she'll make a full recovery," Nancy finished the topic of Janice and the shark attack.

"Yeah, this guy's a real shit-magnet," Erik blurted out, a smile beaming with pride in his friend.

Jake's eyes got big, and he and Nancy just looked at each other unsure of what to say. Terra blinked hard in the control room, then started laughing.

"This guy is nuts. He has no filter whatsoever," the producer chuckled.

"Yeah, that's great. No deficit is always a good thing. It's good to see her awake and getting along," Jake said, trying not to laugh.

"Yes, we'll make sure you get her contact information. She's been asking for yours. Can we get that to her?" Nancy asked.

"Sure. That'd be fine," Jake said with a smile.

"Now Jake, I have to ask," Nancy started. Those words almost sent Jake into a panic attack. "How have things been the last few months?"

Terra held her breath.

It wasn't the worst question she could have asked, but it was all connected, so emotionally it was the same as "How do you feel about not being able to save your dead wife and son?"

"It's..." Jake hesitated. "It's been hard, for sure." The tears came again.

"But I've had a strong support base. My friends and family. This S.O.B. right here," he said, slapping Erik on the chest.

Taking a hard sigh, he continued, "I miss her for sure. But she'd expect me to keep going. I can't let her down again."

It was the "again" that made Nancy stop. She knew she was pushing his limit. Nancy was already getting the emotion that she was aiming to see, but this very well may have been his limit.

As Jake dabbed at his eyes again, Nancy turned to Erik and asked, "So Erik, I've been told you moved in with Jake. How's that going?"

"It's been going fine as long as Jake doesn't take all the hot water," Erik made light. "I give him his space until he needs me. He's my brother, might as well be anyway. He's not getting rid of me and nothing he can say or do with get me to leave until I'm satisfied that he's good to go. He's getting there. He's getting on his feet. They were together for 10 years. That's not something you quit overnight."

Jake got up, walked out of the camera's view, and broke down. The cameras stayed trained on Erik.

"Erik, I also understand that you were an L.A. County paramedic. How did that come to be?" Nancy asked, keeping the flow going while Jake composed himself.

Terra walked down to meet Jake while the producer was working to keep the sobbing out of the soundtrack. Jake saw Terra through the window in the door and put his hand up to tell her that he was okay. He dabbed his eyes again, cleared his throat, and sat back down on the couch.

The cameras didn't pan back to him until his color had returned to normal, even if his eyes were still bleary, and Nancy made sure not to go near that subject again. When Jake was fully recovered, Nancy went about asking him how he liked the L.A. area and how the emergency services in the county compared to that of his native Maryland. Nancy's last question was on the bright side, at least comparatively.

"So, how have you and Terra been getting along?"

That brought a smile to Jake's face. What he didn't realize was that all the people in that studio watched his eyes light up. It even managed to make Terra smile and blush a bit. Without even answering the question, they saw it. Erik saw it and smiled too.

"She's a good friend," Jake answered. It was the safest thing he could come up with. "She's treated Erik and me very well."

Nancy and Erik shared a look; Erik's smirk highlighted his dimples.

"Is that all we're going to get out of you?" Nancy asked.

"Yeah, that's pretty much it," Jake said, breaking a smile.

"Okay, gentleman. I think we've got everything we need."

Nancy looked up at the producer who nodded at her through the window and flashed the "okay" sign. At that, she thanked them for their time, and shook their hands. That effectively ended the interview. The two guys with headsets on came back in and removed their lapel mics and battery packs.

As the three walked out of the sound room, the producer thanked them, shook their hands, and went straight back to the editing room with Nancy. Terra was waiting for them and again hugged them both. Jake's eyes were red, and he looked exhausted. Terra grabbed a hand from each of them and pulled towards the door. Jake still had his handkerchief in his hand.

"That was fantastic!" she said. "You guys are going to be the love of the country by this evening. There won't need to be much editing at all, except when Erik made the 'shit magnet' statement, but it fits his personality, so hopefully they'll just bleep it out."

Terra looked at Jake and grabbed his other hand before continuing, "Thank you, Jake. That took a lot of courage. I promise that's all. You'll never have to answer another question if you don't want to."

"Hmph," Jake grunted. "I'll believe it when I see it."

"Well, let me go check on a few things with the producer and all the editing and then we can go grab some dinner. If you all want to wait in the lobby, we can take my car. Erik, go ahead and give Maria a call and tell her to meet us at Nick and Stef's Steak House. It's off South Hope."

"Nick and Stef's, South Hope. Got it," Erik replied as he pulled out his phone and started texting as Terra walked through one of the doors.

Jake sat on a bench in the lobby and found he hadn't really stopped crying.

- FIFTEEN -

T.J. and his girlfriend, Lonnie, were waiting for the three as they pulled up to the restaurant. Lonnie had no idea who they were going to meet. Maria was there waiting as well, again, with the idea that it was going to be a quiet night with T.J. and some friends Erik had mentioned.

A silver Mercedes with blacked out windows pulled up. It was nothing special to see one. There was lots of money in this town, and lots of people who wanted to look like they had money. Lonnie didn't pay any attention to it, but T.J. saw it, turned the car off, and started getting his things together. Lonnie took the cue and started getting out as well. As Erik got out of the car, Maria saw him and got out of her car. They all met up in the lobby before the six of them were seated.

The first 20 minutes were spent with Maria and Lonnie gushing over Terra and how they were huge fans, asking about certain other actors and what it was like to do what she did. Lonnie also showered her displeasure with T.J. for not telling her who they were meeting. Jake, Erik and T.J. sat watching the women chatter back and forth. The ladies were also somewhat surprised to meet the "Miracle Medic", as the press had taken to calling Jake. That phrase made Jake really uncomfortable. Terra was used to the attention, but she was also somewhat expecting it, and giving a little leeway for friends of friends.

Drinks of tea and water were ordered and Jake was again surprised by the quality of the filet. The conversation over dinner bordered on polite chitchat, with no one really bringing up the interview. While Terra had heard a bit about Jake's introduction into EMS, she had heard hardly anything about Erik's background at all.

"So, Erik. Tell us how you got in with the State Police out there. How is it that they have paramedics?" Terra asked, wanting to know a little more about Erik and his background.

"All helicopter EMS transport in Maryland is run by the Maryland State Police," Erik replied.

"Yeah, there's a reason it's called the People's Socialist Republic of Maryland," Jake chimed in.

"Yeah, and it's also one of the best in the country, jackass. "We're used for a whole bunch of other stuff too, like search and rescue, certain investigations, locating suspects. Things like that," Erik said.

"No. I meant how did being a paramedic get you get a job as a police officer? That was a requirement right? That you were a paramedic first?" Terra asked.

"Oh, so that story. Let me tell you about that story," Jake cut in.

"Yeah, I think you tell that story better than I do," Erik conceded.

"So, at the time, Erik and I were both ground-pounders. Riding in a normal ambulance like every other paramedic in the country. Then one night, Erik and I are working our shift out of Company 1, in downtown Rockville," Jake began, feeling funny saying "Rockville" and "downtown" in the same sentence, considering they were in Los Angeles, a city a hundred times larger. "This call comes in for the police. There were some street racers blasting up route 355, one of the main roads that pass through Rockville and past our station. So anyway, the cops start headed over towards the area, but they've got their sirens on, so everyone hears them and takes off.

"Well, one of the racers takes off straight up 355. He blows a tire, starts losing control of the car and sideswipes a guy walking his dog. He just so happened to be next to a mailbox – you know, those big blue ones on the side of the road? So basically, this guy gets pinched up against the mailbox. The car winds up flipping across the middle of the road and then we get the call, maybe a quarter mile down from the firehouse. Erik was driving – as usual."

"Screw you!" Erik fired back with a smile.

Maria hugged his arm, listening intently. Erik liked hearing the story as much as Jake liked telling it.

"Anyway, so we pull up to the car, because we don't know the guy walking his dog got hit. So I get out of the ambulance and start working the driver. He's hung up in his seatbelt, had a probable concussion and some dings, no big deal, right? This guy," Jake points to Erik with is thumb, "this guy sees a puppy that's freaked out and trying to get away from something, but can't because its owner has the leash, right?

"So Erik goes over to see what the deal was, maybe 50 yards away or so, and sees this guy literally ripped open. He had no other problems aside from this hole in his chest where his ribs had been ripped away. It was the damnedest thing. The guy is just lying there, in shock, having a hard time breathing."

"He didn't have a left lung, anymore," Erik added.

"Right. Well, once Erik gets over there, he starts yelling for the trauma bag and the airway kit and a bunch of expletives."

"Erik yelling expletives? I don't believe it," Terra said sarcastically.

That got a laugh from everyone. Maria was getting a kick out the whole thing, listening in awe how "her man" dealt with some of the most horrific things imaginable.

T.J. and Lonnie however were not used to the subject matter. They were used to the general questions like "What do you do? How did you get into that?" But to them, EMS was mostly gore and heartbreak. EMS was there to clean up the mess. As far as they were concerned, this conversation was going downhill fast.

Lonnie abruptly stood up and excused herself, partially out of her desire to leave the conversation, partly her way of expressing her displeasure with the topic while eating dinner. She asked if either of the other ladies wanted to join her, but to her surprise, they declined. Lonnie walked away in a huff. Terra and Maria just looked at each other, Maria rolling her eyes, Terra giggling. T.J. dropped his napkin in his lap and covered his nose and mouth with his hands, knowing he'd have to deal with that later in the evening.

Jake continued, "So, anyway, Erik is over there yelling, but I've got my own patient to worry about and I can't just leave him. Finally, the engine rolls up, from the firehouse, just down the street, mind you. So my patient is BLS all the way – that means he's a basic, routine patient with no big issues. I grab an EMT off the engine, hand my patient over to him, grab the airway bag and go help Erik. I get there and Erik is looking in the trauma bag for some forceps.

"Meanwhile, I'm losing my mind. This guy is spitting up so much blood and froth, gasping when he can. I've never seen anything like this before. The man is missing most of the skin on his left side, and pieces of 6 ribs from his side and chest, I can see – I can literally see this guy's heart beating inside his chest. I can see the muscles and part of the spleen, everything except the lung. There was no lung. At all!"

"Well, pieces of it were still there, you could see pieces," Erik corrected.

Jake looked at Erik with a smirk and responded, "The whole area was larger than a dinner plate. So then the guy starts to come out of the initial shock and he's not breathing right and he's starting to fight us, mainly because he couldn't breathe. So Erik, finally grabs a set of forceps, and simply pinches off the left bronchial tube – the big one, or what was left of it. That's it. That's all he does.

"Erik RSI'd him, tubed him just in case he spasmed or puked, but even that was probably an overreaction. And the guy starts breathing a little more regularly after that, we get him on some oxygen, his heart started slowing down, his O2 'sats' improved and everything. The only injury this guy had was that his chest wall and lung were literally pinched off. If I hadn't seen it, I'd have said there had to have been other injuries involved. Other more major injuries, a crush, a head injury, something. But nope. Erik, as calm as he is now sitting across the table simply grabbed a set of forceps and clamped onto his bronchial tube."

"Now what exactly is RSI?" Terra asked unfazed by the gory details.

"Ah, well," Jake started, in some cases we have to tube people who are still conscious. so we have to effectively paralyze them, insert the tube, and then bag them for a few minutes until the drugs wear off," Jake hoped his simplistic explanation would be enough.

"paralyze people? On purpose?" Maria chimed in.

"Yeah. Paralyze them. It's only temporary. It's either that and we breathe for them or they suffocate or drown in their own fluids. It really is that simple sometimes," Jake said.

"Well there was some other stuff, too," Erik tried to

protest, getting back to the story. He wasn't as keen on teaching who he thought of as 'civilians' the intricate details of 'Succs'.

"My ass there was. We collared him, boarded him and put a moist towellette on the guy and that was it. Hell, even the ER staff were calling other doctors and nurses in to take a look."

"No, I meant the guy had recovery issues," Erik again protested.

"Whatever. That guy lived and that's what shoed you in for the State Police job," Jake reminded Erik of the point of the story.

He leaned over to Terra and said, "I've never seen this guy flustered. Not once. He always keeps his head on straight and always knows what to do."

"Unless confronted by a flamboyant gay man," Terra returned.

Jake choked on his water. Everyone at the table was looking at Erik, and all he could do was give everyone his famous smirk, and the dimples were out in force.

With the pressure of the interview off, and surrounded by friends, both old and new, Jake let go of his angst, if only for the evening. The rest of the night was spent talking about EMS and training and when that got old, Terra starting dishing about the entertainment industry and who was the real deal and who wasn't.

"Do you guys *really* have to leave tomorrow?" Terra half asked, half whined.

Erik and Jake shared a look.

"Yeah, I've got a shift on Sunday," Erik said. "I've been trying to get this guy to stick around, but I know he's itching to get home."

"Yeah, sorry," Jake said, looking at Erik, with Maria hanging on his neck. "At this point, I'm going to head home too, I think. There are a few things I want to see before heading off though."

"So maybe an extra day or two?" Terra asked with a glint of hope in her voice.

Jake chuckled, "Yeah, maybe an extra day."

Jake and Erik shared another look. Erik chuckled.

"You really want to go that bad, huh?" Erik asked.

"Hell yes, I want to go," Jake replied, the others at the table not knowing what they were talking about.

"Go where?" Terra asked.

"Jake and I grew up watching re-runs of *Emergency!* and *Trauma Center*," Erik explained. "*Emergency!* was a 70's sitcom based on the very first EMS department. The firehouse where they shot the show is out in Carson. I never really looked too far into *Trauma Center*, aside from the fact that it had Lou Ferrigno in it, and that one episode with the maintenance elevator – that to this day gives me chills."

"Yeah! I even met one of the nurses that consulted on *Emergency!*. I think she was the basis for Julie London's character," Jake said, getting excited. "The show used Company 51 as the unit, but there they didn't have a Company 51 at the time. They shot the show at Company 127. I was hoping that Darrius would help me out some and let me take a tour over there."

Jake could see Terra's face light up.

"Julie London? Finally, something I can understand. When are you going to head over there?" Terra asked.

"Well I was hoping tomorrow, but it depends on if Darrius can help me out," Jake replied.

"I've already put in a call to him for you," Erik said giving his trademark smile "and I'll drop you his number. I'm sure he won't have a problem with it."

As the servers started closing the surrounding tables and upending chairs so they could sweep, it was apparent that they were the last party in the restaurant. Erik had been watching the interaction between Jake and Terra and decided it was time to take his leave.

They all stood, Terra looking for the server to get the check.

"Hey brother, I'm not working the next few days. With you all leaving, I need a break myself," T.J. said with a smile.

"Well good luck my man," Erik replied. "Look us up if you're ever in the DC area. You've got my contact info, right?"

"Yeah, I got it," T.J. said

"Cool, well, if any of you need anything before then, my flight leaves at noon, and I will be incommunicado for most of the night," Erik smirked at Maria, who smiled back, getting in a quick squeeze of Erik's butt.

"I'll be back to get my gear and I still need a ride to the airport though," Erik added, looking at Jake.

T.J. smiled and said, "I got you. Well either way, if I don't see you before then, it was good knowing you two. If you're ever out this way again, warn us first."

T.J. put his hand out towards Erik and Jake and they took their turns, shaking his hand, finalizing their "Good-Byes". The ladies exchanged contact information and made their promises to call each other. This was the part that Terra hated the most, knowing they probably wouldn't see each other again, yet having to act as if they would. She gave them the number for her assistant, Angela.

With that, Erik and Maria and T.J. and Lonnie took their leave. Jake and Terra sat back down, still waiting for the check. An easy silence lingered between the two, which was strange to Jake. He didn't feel the need to fill in the silence with aimless banter.

Finally, Terra broke the silence and said, "So, when are we headed out to this firehouse of yours?"

"I'd like to go tomorrow. It depends on when I hear back from Darrius. Hopefully after I take Erik to the airport."

"Okay, well let me know. Give me a call. I'd like to go with you, if that's alright."

Terra was taking a bit of a chance, giving Jake the option this time to decide if he wanted her around instead of her making the plans and expecting him to show up. She didn't know how he'd react, but guessed his answer at this point would either be the nail in the coffin, or the key to open the door to a friendship or maybe a "friendship".

"Yeah, sure," Jake said with a smile, really thinking nothing of it.

He was more concerned about actually getting to see the firehouse that partially inspired him to get into EMS and helping people and saving lives. If there was anything going on in his subconscious, he wasn't aware of it. Jake really liked Terra, daydreamed about her even, but he knew he needed to control the distance between the two. It was just too much for him to deal with to go any further than friends. He'd just as soon drop all contact at this point than to get into anything more serious than a friendship – at least that what his mind said. His heart and his emotions had planned something else entirely.

Jake's phone chirped and the screen lit up. Erik had texted Darrius' number with a message that he'd left a voicemail with him. The waiter brought the check, and Terra took care of the bill.

A few minutes later, they were back in her car on the way back to the hotel, making friendly chatter about the day's events, the suits, and the interview. So much had happened in the past week, it was hard to digest everything. Where he was simply two weeks prior was even more unfathomable to him.

"Looks like Erik set us up with Darrius. We should be good to go tomorrow afternoon. I'll give you a call?" Jake asked.

"Sounds like a plan," Terra said.

Jake smiled at her use of the line.

As the car pulled up to the valet in the hotel, they said their goodbyes. It was still early in the evening yet, at least as far as Jake was concerned, but he was tired all the same.

- SIXTEEN -

Morning came with the sun shining through Jake's window. He looked over at the clock and saw that it was 8:30. It took him a second to realize he was allowed to sleep in. Normally Jake didn't like to sleep in, but there was nothing he could do at this point. It wasn't like he had anywhere to be at the moment. He just laid there staring at the ceiling. Eventually, Jake reached over and grabbed the TV remote off his nightstand and flipped on the news. It was the same old non-event static he'd come to hope for. A slow news day was a good news day as far as he was concerned. Especially if it kept his name out of things.

Jake grabbed his phone and checked the text messages. There was a text from Kelly asking about his return trip and the logistics behind it. He didn't have an answer for her right now – wasn't sure when he'd have one either. There was also one from Terra last night letting him know that she'd gotten home okay. Jake thought it a bit odd, but he did tell her to be safe on the drive home. He guessed that was her way of letting him know she was thinking about him.

About that time, he heard Erik walk through the door. Apparently, having had a good night, he walked into the suite very loud and energized.

"Jake? Where are you, Boss-man? It's 9am. We need to get downstairs and get some of that free breakfast before I bounce out of this Motherfucker!" Erik yelled.

He was definitely in a good mood this morning. Jake shuffled out of the bedroom in just his boxers.

"Hey buddy," Erik said, trying to look behind him to see if anyone else was in the room.

Jake got the hint and threw the door open so he could get a better look at the empty bedroom.

"Satisfied, Erik?" Jake said, still a bit bleary.

"Yes I am, Boss-man, even if I'm the only one," Erik joked, pushing his luck. "Come on man, we got to get down stairs and grab some grub before you take me to the airport. Throw on some digs and let's go."

He must be caffeinated, Jake thought. He grabbed the suit pants from the previous day and slipped back into his loafers. Jake then grabbed the shirt as they left the room. He'd have to come back for a shave and a shower later. His phone chirped as he slid it into his pocket. A few minutes later they were ordering breakfast and it was only 9:15.

"So Boss-man, how'd last night go after we left?" Erik asked.

Jake, not quite knowing what or where this line was going replied, "It was fine, I guess. We just talked a bit more. Nothing unusual. No one came upstairs if that's what you're asking."

Jake was now getting annoyed so Erik backed off for the moment.

"Hey man, I'm just asking. A brother's got to ask, right? I mean, I was in he... he... heaven last night. God damn! That was a hot night last night. Definitely one for the 'Spank Bank' later on." Erik was on a roll, on *something* at the very least.

"Wow. What's got you all riled up this morning? Usually I'm the one waking you up, now it's revered. I haven't seen you like this in a while," Jake asked.

"Well, hot sex with a hot woman will do that to you. And she didn't let me sleep much, so don't ask. I've had two Monsters already and some B-12, so I'm about as charged as I need to be for the flight home. I'll have to get one more before the trip to the airport."

Jake was always curious about Erik's escapades. They always seemed more outrageous than what Jake had experienced. But then again, Erik usually picked the wild and crazy women (with emphasis on *crazy*) that were always nice to look at, but you never brought home to mom. Jake was usually able to weed out the crazies, which he guessed meant that they weren't as crazy in the sack too. Not that it mattered to him at this point. Over the past two months or so, he'd been amassing an "Erik-esque" porn collection to deal with any "distractions" that popped up.

"I'll tell you what, Boss-man. Those El Salvadoran chicks are fucking crazy. But I like crazy, if you know what I mean," Erik continued going on about Maria.

"Well, if you like her so much, why don't you bring her out the east coast?"

That stopped Erik cold. He was forced to put his food down.

"No. No no no no no. You see Boss-man, that would be counter-intuitive. She's hot as fuck partly because I haven't seen her in a few years. And partly because, well, she's just hot as fuck. I would get nothing done back home with her ass walking around the house all day," Erik explained as only Erik could.

"Well, sure," Jake tried to understand. "There is the 'bunny stage' – a few days, or weeks where you're just going at it like rabbits, but eventually you come up for air, right?"

"Exactly," Erik said. "That's exactly my point. I don't want to get to the stage after that. I'm good with staying in the 'bunny stage', or whatever you call it."

Jake didn't quite understand it. He did to a degree, but he was always the emotionally stable one of the two. He had always been in a relationship with Meredith as long as he'd known Erik.

That realization hit him pretty hard. He was starting to get tired of these epiphanies, though his reaction to them at this point was getting easier to control.

At 10 o'clock, they headed back up to the room to finish getting Erik's things. They called down to the valet to have their car ready when they got back down stairs.

T.J. was not on-duty so there was no one else for Erik to say his goodbyes to. They piled his bags into the Corolla and Jake plugged L.A.X into the GPS. He was still learning his way around. Erik had managed to grab another Monster from somewhere.

"So the 110 it is," Jake said, looking at the GPS. The trip to the hospital on the way in had Jake a little turned around. "Yeah, it's the 110 to the 105 to PCH. It seems everything in this town happens between the 405 and the 110."

"Well, that's just what everyone wants to see. There are some things down south that are pretty cool, your beach in particular. But yeah, the touristy areas are there in central L.A," Erik replied.

"Hey man, how come you never really talk about your time out here? All these people you know, your time with L.A. County? Maria?" Jake finally asked.

"Nothing really to talk about, Boss-man. I did four years in the Corp as a corpsman, a combat medic. I was discharged out of 29 Palms, and decided to follow my medical training. You know the story. Do you really want to hash this out again? I just want to get home," Erik said with a bit of exasperation, trying to change the subject.

"I don't know man. It's just that my entire life has been laid out for you, but I'm starting to realize that I want to know more about what makes you, you," Jake began to wax sentimental.

Erik took this to be a good sign. It meant his friend was seeing a lot more clearly about his life, the people in it, and what it could be in the future. That his friend knew he *had* a future.

"I'll tell you what, Boss-man. When you get back, and get settled, I'll let you take me out drinking one night and you can ask all the damn questions you want. But, you're buying; that's not an option," Erik relented, thinking at least it would buy him some time.

"Fine. I'll take what I can get at this point," Jake said.

"What about you, Boss-man?" Erik started, adding his dimpled smirk to the question. "I already know the answer, but has this little trip helped you as much as I know it has?"

Jake laughed, "Yes. Is that what you wanted to hear? Yes. This trip has helped me a lot. I'm sure as hell not staying out here another week, though. I don't like places where the ground moves. It's not natural."

Erik gave him the stink eye for the comment, but he also laughed at the joke. At least it was a better reaction to the line than what he got from Terra.

"I know I'm still dealing with things, but at least I'm actually dealing with them now. And I have you to thank for that. So, thank you," Jake said.

"Fuck you, jackass," Erik replied at the inference that he expected any thanks.

Jake laughed again.

"This. All this..." Erik pointing his fingers in the air at nothing and everything. "This was all for selfish reasons. I wanted my friend back. And I also wanted to get laid."

"This trip was all about me. That's it," Erik protested as much as Jake knew he was being facetious.

"So," Erik started back in with the previous topic. "What's

the story with you and Terra. How late did you get home last night?"

Jake rolled his eyes.

"Oh, god. Don't start that stuff. There is no story. We're friends..."

"But she's hot, right?" Erik cut him off.

Jake sighed, "Yes, she's very attractive. But she's out of my..."

"So you like her, right?" Erik cut him off again.

Jake was getting frustrated.

"Yes. I like her. She's a friend. We are friends. That is all."

Erik let him finish, staring at and swishing the last of his Monster around in the can.

"Do you know how difficult it is, I mean, at least for me, to be 'friends' with a hot chick? I mean, maybe not for you, but I'm the type of guy who likes to look at my hot friends. I mean, you. Look at you. You look like someone shaved a monkey's ass. That's why I hang out with you. You're like the rusty, busted-up car parked next to the Ferrari," Erik said.

That got a smile out of Jake. He knew where this was going and couldn't stop it.

"But a hot chick," Erik continued.

"A hot chick is not something I can't be around on a regular basis and *not* think about," Erik finished, never taking his eyes off his can, trying to remain nonchalant the entire time he was making the case.

"You asshole," Jake responded. "What do you want to know? What? Have I thought about her? Yes. Have I thought about sleeping with her? Absolutely, each and every which way a man can. Hell, *you've* probably thought about all that too.

"But I'm also thinking about Meredith and how I've only

talked to her once, just before the shark attack. Just once this whole week, and it was interrupted by that damn fish. I don't know how to feel about that, other than being afraid to start talking to her again. I don't know if that makes me a bad husband. I don't know if that makes me... I just... I just need time. I know you want me to move on. We've had that discussion. I'm just not ready right now. Not yet, okay?"

Erik could tell Jake was making progress; it just wasn't on the expedited schedule he wanted. The last few minutes of the ride were quiet. Erik wanted to talk more but he knew Jake had already shut down with the mention of Meredith. Erik missed her too. Jake just stared at the road, eyes bouncing between the cars and the GPS making sure he was taking the right exit.

Jake pulled in under the airport overhang and found a spot along the curb to stop. The duo hopped out, and Jake popped the trunk with Erik's bag. They shook hands, gave each other a shoulder hug, and said their goodbyes.

"Do you want to know something that scares the hell out of me?" Jake asked.

Erik lifted his eyebrows.

"I haven't had any nightmares all week. Ever since meeting Terra, not one nightmare. No more screaming howls or creepy eyes staring at me. I've been able to sleep all week. I can sleep."

"What I wouldn't give for one week free of nightmares," Erik said quietly.

"And," Jake continued, "I haven't used Ambien for 4 days now."

"Ooh, goodie. More for me," Erik said, only somewhat joking. "Hell, I've *named* my walrus."

"I'll text Kelly and tell her you're on the way. Does she

know what time you're supposed to get in?" Jake asked.

"I hope so. She's picking me up."

And with that, Erik flashed his dimpled smile and walked through the doors of the airport.

***

Jake did his due diligence in both texting Kelly and trying to call her. Erik was due to get into BWI about 9 p.m., and Kelly was giving him a ride back to Frederick. After making sure Erik would be set up back east, Jake gave Darrius a call to set up the time for the station 127 walk-through.

"Hey Darrius, what's up man? It's Jake. Is this a good time?"

"Hey, man. Hey we are all set up for the walk-through. I told the guys it would only take about a half-hour or so, is that okay?" Darrius replied.

"Yeah, that's fine. Hey, Terra wanted to go as well, is that going to be a problem?"

Darrius sighed, "No, but we'll take my car. The guys are going to be star struck as it is; we don't need them gawking any more than they will be. Can you meet me back at station 20?"

"Yeah, sure. Whatever makes it easier for you. You're doing me the favor. I'll have Terra meet me at the hotel so we'll drive over in the Corolla. Is that fine?" Jake asked.

"Yeah, that's fine," Darrius agreed.

Jake, looking at his watch. It was just past noon.

"I'll see you at Station 20 at 3 p.m.? Hoes does that jive?"

"Even better," Darrius approved. He figured they could get in, get out, lickety-split.

"Okay. Sounds good. Let me get Terra lined up and we'll

see you there. Take care."

"Yeah, you too."

And they hung up.

Jake punched in the number for Terra. There was no answer, so he left a voice mail telling her to meet him at the hotel and then they'd ride over in the Corolla. All this as he was pulling out of LAX. He figured he'd be able to make it back to the hotel by 1 p.m. and grab a shower and some lunch. He still had yesterday's suit pants and button down on.

Jake got back to the hotel a clean 20 minutes later. There was almost no traffic. It was bizarre enough for him to notice while he was driving. He needed a shower badly before seeing Terra – or heading out to the firehouse – he corrected himself.

Jake ran up to his room to grab a quick shower. As luck would have it, Terra called while he was in the shower. The voicemail she left said she was on her way over. So he threw some clothes on and headed down stairs to grab a bite to eat. He wanted to leave out about 2 p.m. to meet Darrius at station 20.

As Jake came out of the elevator into the lobby, Terra had just given her keys to the valet. They exchanged looks and Jake gave her a heads-up nod and then realized he hadn't shaved since the previous day, so he had a couple of days of growth on his face. He walked out to the valet and handed him the ticket for the Corolla. Some of the valets were still staring at Terra.

"What's shakin', Bacon?" she asked with her hands in her pockets, swinging her shoulders and purse around.

Jake raised his shoulders and put his hands in his pockets, squinting into the sky.

"Same stuff, different day. Did you sleep okay?"

"Yeah, pretty good. I take it you got Erik to the airport in time?" Terra countered.

Jake grunted and replied, "Sometimes that S.O.B. just pushes buttons so he can push buttons."

Terra smiled. She had talked a while with Erik while Jake was in class. She knew Erik was a big teddy bear when it came to Jake, and guessed they probably had a conversation about her. She wasn't quite sure what to do with Jake. She liked him, sure. He was cute, and the paparazzi loved him. They seemed to have backed off a little since the interview, but it had been less than 24 hours. Erik was her go between, as odd as it was. It was almost like high school all over again. The only thing missing was the note with the check boxes with "I like you, do you like me?"

Granted she had a full schedule otherwise; the movie promotions were still going on. This week was an anomaly. Terra used the car accident to take a break as well as to keep in touch with Jake and Erik. She caught herself wondering about him more and more, checking her phone for texts or missed calls. The few meetings she'd had that week were torture.

She couldn't figure out what it was. Terra simply liked being next to him; having him around made her feel more... was 'normal' the right word? 'safe', maybe? 'At ease' for sure. She just couldn't put her finger on it. At first she chalked it up to him being a paramedic – and paramedics save lives all the time, right? What reason is there *not* to feel safe around a paramedic? Maybe it was the "wounded puppy" thing? She couldn't believe she'd be that shallow, but she couldn't rule it out. Maybe it was just one of the factors. Jake wasn't a "fanboy" and that alone was a breath of fresh air. In any case, Terra felt better when she was near him, and for the moment, that was enough for her.

"How about after we get the tour, we grab a bite, are you up for it?" The valet pulled the corolla up and still had a smirk on his face as he watched one of Hollywood's most famous actresses get in as the door was opened for her.

Jake thanked the valet and got in to the driver's seat and they were off.

"I love this car," Terra smiled, looking over the lack of amenities within. "I haven't seen manual windows in years. I didn't know they still made them."

"Some people just don't appreciate the art of 'mechanical design' anymore," Jake said with no lack of sarcasm.

"So, how far away is this place?" Terra asked.

"Well, we've got to drive over to station 20 to pick up Darrius, and then over to 127. It takes about a half hour to get to station 20, and from there another 15 miles give or take. The issue there is that it's closer to the beach and its Saturday, so I figure 30-45 minutes, going by the L.A. definition of 'traffic'."

Terra laughed and rolled her eyes.

The drive over to station 20 was a little more tedious than Jake had wanted. He found himself worrying that his Corolla wasn't up to Terra's standards, though she said nothing of it. The chit chat made the trip shorter. Darrius was waiting for them in the back parking lot at the station. After locking the car doors, Jake introduced Terra to Darrius and vice-versa. Darrius, who claimed to never be star-struck, had the charm turned to 'eleven' today. And he was laying it on thick and heavy. Jake tried not to get jealous.

"Please, allow me." Darrius said opening the passenger door of his car and extending his hand. Terra obliged him with her red-carpet smile pretending not to notice Jake gritting his teeth.

The whole way to station 127, Darrius was talking it up to Terra who he gave front-seat privileges. Jake, while used to the back seat at this point was slightly irritated. One because it was his idea to tour the station, and two, Terra was *his* guest, not Darrius'. Try as Jake did, he just couldn't get a word in edgewise. The two in the front seats just yapped away, with Darrius answering all of her questions. It put a damper on his spirits to say the least. Towards the end of the drive, Jake had simply taken to staring out the window. It was the first time all week he'd felt alone.

***

As they pulled into the station, the driveway led around the right side of the building to the rear. Sandwiched between two auto parts stores, it was as non-descript a firehouse as there could be. They walked around front, Jake snapping pictures left and right.

"The Robert A. Cinader Memorial Fire Station. I've never seen a memorial firehouse before," Jake said, taking the time to say the entire name.

Jake had never heard of the man. Maybe he just hadn't paid attention to all the firehouses he'd been to in the last 15 years, but he honestly couldn't remember a single one named after a specific person. They were always named after their districts, like "Kensington", or "Germantown". Sometimes they'd be named something a little more descriptive like "Independent" or "Citizens". Not that it was odd, it was just different to him. It even had a full plaque dedicated to the man.

Terra however loved it from the start. A firehouse dedicated to a producer. She had never imagined that a *producer* would have made an impact so far as to get a firehouse named after him. Most of the producers she knew were not exactly service-minded. At least, not in regards of service to "others".

"...it showed public officials across the nation that lives could be saved by local paramedic programs," Terra was reading aloud, but softly as Jake came over beside her.

Darrius had been here a few times before, but had no attachment to the *Emergency* show. They rang the doorbell, and a young firefighter greeted them.

"Hi," Darrius said. "We're here to see Lieutenant Sloan. We're here for a quick walkthrough."

The fire fighter just started at Terra, who smiled as politely as she could. It was her first time at a firehouse and she had no idea what to expect.

"Hey Probie! Let 'em in! I told you they were coming," Lieutenant Brian Sloan came to the door, smacking the young probie in the back of the head, and out of his trance.

The probie walked back into the firehouse with a sheepish smile on his face. He was in love.

"Hey Darrius," the lieutenant said, shaking his hand.

"L.T.," Darrius replied. "These are the two I was telling you about, Jake and Terra."

"Jake," he said, shaking hands.

"Ms. Dee. It is my pleasure," the lieutenant said with a hint of what he considered charm.

He took Terra by the hand and led her into the firehouse, leaving Jake and Darrius there at the door. They exchange exasperated looks and both rolled their eyes.

Walking around the interior, it was a pretty basic firehouse, at least as far as Jake and Darrius were concerned. It still had the old wood paneling from the early 70s or 80s, but at this point, it had been so long, it was back in style, at least according to some. There were folded American flags in their respective frames and framed newspaper articles on the walls.

Firefighter figurines and model fire engines adorned most of the shelf space where protocol or log books didn't sit.

"Well, this is home. Feel free to walk around. If the door is locked, that means you're not allowed in there. If you want to see the radio room, come get me and I'll let you take a gander, and stay out of the apparatus bay. At least without me or Darrius here," Lieutenant Sloan said.

And at that he let them be. He kept an eye on them, especially Terra, but other than that, he and Darrius just stood by the television and talked.

It was then that Terra realized that all these things in the firehouse were toys. Even the fire trucks out in the apparatus bay were just toys for grown children. She'd never really thought of it that way before. Not that she had cared before.

Terra and Jake were both looking at all the pictures on the walls. Mostly of the ladder trucks and engines that were there or had been at one time. The TV room was also the workout room, so the chairs and recliners had free weights around them or nearby. There were a couple of stabilizer balls in one corner. There were beds in the back of the room; two were neatly made, the other two were bare mattresses. The door beyond led to the shower rooms, and presumably the toilets. Terra wasn't inclined to verify.

It was a small firehouse compared to what generally got built out these days. It really was bare bones. And considering there were two businesses on either side of the firehouse, there wasn't any room to expand. There was a single wide and elongated bay, wide enough for two trucks or engines, side-by-side. The tiller truck took up one whole side of the bay. The other side was an engine; both were fire engine red. *As if there was any other kind,* Jake thought. Jake wasn't sure what was supposed to be in front of the engine as it was not there.

Probably on a call, he thought. For the time being it was just Lieutenant Sloan and the probie manning the station.

"Dammit, son! I didn't see any 'red light oil' in that engine out there, did you go over to station 83 and ask them if they had any?" L.T. yelled to the probie.

Darrius had a serious look on his face.

"What? You let the engine run out of 'red light oil'?" he chimed in.

"Yes, Sir. Sorry, Sir. I called over there and they said they were out too, so they told me to call station 118, and they said *they* were out, too. I called almost a dozen stations and no one seems to have any. I had a couple ask me for some too, when I find it. And the strange thing is I don't remember seeing it in the protocols."

"Probie!" L.T. yelled at the mention of protocols.

"Sir!" the young firefighter snapped his head up.

"Get your ass back on that phone and find me some 'red light oil'!"

"Yes, Sir."

And off he went to the radio room to finish calling what L.T. and Darrius both thought would be about 150 fire stations looking for "red light oil". Both waited until he left the room before cracking a smile.

"What's 'red light oil'?" Terra asked.

Instantly, Jake said, "Oh, it makes the red lights work. It's *really* complicated. It gets into fluid dynamics and hydro-analysis and all that. I'll tell you about it later. You may need to know this if you're serious about EMS."

"You know I am," Terra said, feeling like she was learning stuff already.

"Yeah, well, we'll see," Jake replied, cutting a look at the other two guys.

You can never be out of character around the newbies. Fire and EMS was still a brotherhood. Jake put his arm around Terra's shoulders and turned a corner to leave the room.

"'Red light oil'?" Darrius asked. "I haven't heard that one."

"Yeah, well 'Hose Stretcher' was too played out, and with HR breathing down our necks, we have to keep it mostly clean, at least until we know the guy," L.T. Said.

Darrius shook his head in agreement.

As Jake and Terra turned a corner, they saw what they had been seeking on their quest – photos and memorabilia from the show. The cast and crew, and some of the actual people that inspired the show; the folks the show was based on. There were pictures of the scenes and drawings of the trucks. Paramedics didn't respond to calls in an ambulance during that time period. In the show, they were riding around in an old Brush Truck that was retrofitted to hold the crude items in use at the time.

Jake was in heaven. He *loved* looking at the old equipment. Trying to figure out how it worked and the protocols and bullshit they had to put up with. The arrogance of the doctors back then. *As if that's changed much,* he thought. He couldn't help that much. He actually liked his current medical director, but considering the crap that the docs at MIEMSS had put him through, he wasn't in a position to give them any slack, the bastards.

- SEVENTEEN -

All things done, the whole tour took about 45 minutes. That included touring the firehouse, walking around and through the tiller and engine, and looking at the training equipment they had out back. Jake had so many pictures; his phone was full.

Jake and Terra said their goodbyes and Darrius and Brian agreed to meet up "some time" for drinks. Terra thought it was their version of "Have your people call my people" kind of thing that rarely ever led to anything other than their "people" networking and gossiping.

After driving back to Station 20, Jake shook Darrius' hand, and Terra gave him a hug goodbye, if only for the attempts of flattery. Jake just gave a look of irritation. From the angle he was at, he didn't think Terra saw it. They walked over to, and got into the Corolla. That's when the real question was asked.

"So," Terra started.

"Buttons," Jake said, trying to be funny.

It took her a second to figure out what he was doing, and then Terra replied, "Ah. So buttons, sew buttons. Funny."

"Yeah?"

"No," Terra said, shaking her head, eyes closed in a long blink. "I was going to ask what your plan was. Are you going home or are you going to stay another week?"

"Eh."

Jake hadn't really made up his mind. He wanted to go home, but the thought of the house still scared him. He wanted to stay a bit longer but had no money, and every day here with the car was more money.

"I have to get home. I can start work almost immediately,

maybe even Monday. I get to teach EMS, and I'm pretty much broke."

Terra tried not to show her disappointment.

"Okay. Well..." Terra said

"Water."

Terra rolled her eyes at Jake before asking, "It's a quarter 'til 5. Do you want to grab one last dinner?"

"Sure. But only if I can pick *and* I can buy," Jake insisted, and Terra agreed on the condition that it wasn't a steak house.

Jake took a second on his phone to find the nearest address and plugged it into the GPS, still suction cupped to the dashboard. It was almost a straight shot up Norwalk Boulevard. He was starting to get the hang of driving L.A. now.

15 minutes later, standing outside the Corolla, Terra looked a bit bewildered. She wasn't expecting a Michelin Star restaurant, but this was on the other end of the scale.

"Tummy Stuffer? I've never heard of it," she said.

"You, my fair lady, are in for a treat. This is real food. *This* will make you stand up and slap your momma!" Jake said, getting almost as excited as Erik had on his first trip a few days ago.

"Right. Well, I'm sure she would appreciate that," Terra said with no small amount of doubt..

"You've been telling me to trust you all week. Now I'm telling you to trust *me*."

Terra shook her head in acknowledgement.

"But I trusted you first," she said, having to have the last word.

"Just trust me," Jake answered, not realizing that he had just stolen the last words back.

"Okay," Terra dragged the word out, still unsure and not giving in.

Finally getting to look at the menu without Erik making him feel rushed, Jake ordered a number 42 – steak, no chips – this time. *Ha! Meredith didn't say I couldn't have a steak sandwich.* He thought. His blood ran cold. Even his thoughts betrayed him. Jake tried not to think of it. He corrected himself immediately, even though it had all happened inside his head. What did it mean? Jake had no idea and the confusion came back to him. Terra was still in front of him looking at the menu. She had no idea the battle going on in his head. Jake did his best to hide his fear.

Terra went with a number 101 – avocado roast beef and turkey – and a bag of chips. They grabbed their food and had a seat near the door. Jake didn't like having his back to the door, lest someone threatening come in, and Terra didn't like facing the door, lest people see her and become hysterical. It was a natural fit.

Terra realized something as she was eating. She knew Jake didn't care what she looked like eating this thing, and there really is no sexy way to eat an oversized sub sandwich. But she didn't have to put on pretenses around him. Jake saw her as a regular person and he didn't have any unrealistic expectations of her. Then the taste hit her and she was in heaven.

"Oh. Oh my god this is good," Terra said, eyes wide, still with a mouth full of food, the lettuce and fixings dripping from her mouth and chin. Jake smiled and handed her a napkin. The rest of the evening was polite banter. Him telling her about his childhood, Terra telling him about hers. It wouldn't hit either of them until much later that this really was their first "date". For the moment though, they were friends catching up on each other's lives, and after a while, it felt more and more natural.

They got back to the Ritz about 9 p.m. They said their goodbyes, and Jake was supposed to let Terra know when he was leaving and what airline. It had been a long day and he would have agreed to anything just to go to sleep. He hadn't had a nightmare all week. Looking back at everything, the experiences, the people, it really was a fantastic week.

And as he fell into bed, staring at the ceiling, he told Meredith that he loved her, as a tear rolled out of each eye. He hugged his pillow, inhaling deeply, trying to imagine the smell of her again. This time though, he smelled nothing. Jake had done everything he could. He had given her all of his love. Something inside of him had changed, and just like that, it was time to forgive himself. His last thought as he fell asleep was how he had proposed to Meredith, on one knee with that tiny rock gleaming as bright as it could. Then he turned on his side and slept the deep sleep of self-forgiveness.

***

The next morning Jake woke up early. It was 4am. He hadn't been up this early in months. Again, there were no nightmares. No horrors of previous calls. It was 4 a.m. and he was as refreshed as someone could be this early. He rolled over and called in some room service for breakfast. After shaking out the cobwebs, Jake grabbed a shower, during which he made the decision to head home today assuming he could get a ticket. The open ended tickets always deferred you to the end of the line. While waiting for his breakfast to come up, he called in to see when the earliest flight back to the DC area was. He didn't really care which airport at this point. He had amped himself up to head home.

To his surprise, American Airlines did have a non-stop 8:30 a.m. flight available. He snatched it up immediately. After finalizing all the flight arrangements and speaking with the rental car company, Jake texted Terra the details.

The breakfast came and went with no reply, even though Jake found himself pining for the reply. He busied himself by packing up and making sure the hotel knew he would be checking out soon. Jake wanted to be at the airport early. Leaving the hotel at 6 a.m. gave him time to return the car and take the shuttle over to the terminal. He checked his bags and got a paper ticket printed out. Jake was a bit old fashioned still and liked paper tickets and real books that he could hold.

At the airport, Jake headed over to the security line, when his phone buzzed from a text message.

He hurried to grab it so fast he almost dropped it. In the process of catching it, he looked up and saw Terra walking towards him, a few star-struck fans walking behind her.

"Now, I *know* you weren't going anywhere without saying goodbye," Terra said with a perturbed look on her face.

Jake stuttered a bit. He was waiting and hoping he'd see her more than he thought he should, but at the same time he didn't really know what to do besides hang around the airport.

"Well, I never got a reply from you. I didn't know if you were going to come see me off."

"Hmph," Terra rebelled, wrapping her arm around his and walking him over to one of the plate glass windows overlooking the tarmac.

Walking arm in arm with her felt good, Jake thought. Once they reached the window, she turned closely to face him. Her arms around his, his arms under hers, wrapped around her waist. Terra fit in his arms like a glove. She gave him a hug, which he returned, bending down a bit and nuzzling his nose into her shoulder. To him though, it was more than a hug. He was holding her, but it was over in an instant. She pulled away, grabbing his hands.

"I did get you something though," Terra said with a hit on excitement.

A curious look came across his face. Terra reached into her pocket and pulled out a small velvet box and handed it to him.

"You didn't have to get me anything. You've already done so much, really," Jake said with a smirk, though accepting the box.

Opening the box, he found a small teardrop shaped silver pendant, about an inch long, attached to a silver chain. There were two small stones, one of red coral and one of blue turquoise with a snake slithering between them. He flipped it over to see the mark, "Effie C Zuni".

"She's one of my favorite artists, and with the snake, I thought it was a perfect fit. You know, with the EMS symbol and everything?" Terra thought she needed to explain.

"You need some bling, but something understated," she added.

Jake smiled. He understood the reference instantly, and it really was a pretty cool pendant, even for a guy. He unhinged the clasp and put it around his neck, making sure it was outside of his shirt so Terra could see it.

"I knew it. It looks great on you. Something to remember me by," Terra said, taking a step back.

"Trying to get rid of me, now huh?" Jake asked.

"I didn't get you anything to remember me by. I figure just every time you see an ambulance you'll think of me and how I saved your life," Jake said looking at his fingernails, trying to look and sound arrogant.

Jake knew this was going to be the hard part. He didn't know how to say goodbye; he didn't *want* to say goodbye, but he had to. Terra was just as nervous. She didn't want this to be the last time she saw him. The silence between them grew palpable, and then uncomfortable. They both knew there were things being left unsaid.

"So," Terra started. "Do you think you'll be back out this way again?"

"Absolutely, if only for 'Tummy Stuffer'," Jake said with a smirk, trying to bring some humor to the situation.

When he saw it didn't work, his smirk faded and he looked down. Jake slid his hand down her arm and grabbed her hand.

"Yes," he said, more seriously this time. "I will be back."

Terra's face brightened a little before she responded, "Well, if it's any easier I can..."

Jake cut her off, pulling on her hands and bringing her closer to him, gently kissing her forehead. She wrapped her arms around him, burying her face in his chest; Jake, resting his chin on her head, looked out at the airplanes. Still in her embrace, he allowed himself to breathe. Something he never thought he'd be able to do.

"Just give me some time, okay?" Jake whispered.

Terra just nodded her head, still holding on to him.

"I know you're going through a lot. And if you want me to back off, I will. Completely if that's what you want. I just don't want you to feel awkward around me, because I'm so sick of people feeling awkward around me, but mostly because I feel so comfortable around you. Pretty selfish, huh?" Terra said then smiled at the relief that came over Jake's face.

"It may get a bit awkward at times, but as long as we know it ahead of time, then that takes the edge off, right? Don't you think?" Terra asked hopefully.

"Well, if there is one thing I am, it's 'awkward'," Jake joked back.

After a few more moments, Jake broke the embrace and said, "So, you know all about my plans for the next few months; what are you going to be up to?"

Terra pulled herself together.

"I'm supposed to be doing more tours and more appearances and interviews overseas for the movie. I took the week off after the accident. I've got to get back at some point," she said, somewhat reluctantly.

Terra liked the *idea* of the glamour and lights more than the actual glamour and lights. She looked over towards the security line, where as usual, people were staring at her, whispering and taking pictures. Jake took the hint and started walking with her in the opposite direction, this time holding hands. They walked around the airport a bit, grabbing an overpriced bottle of water.

Eventually, Terra walked Jake back to the security line. The last goodbye was a little rough on them both, but they knew *something* was happening, so it wasn't the worst goodbye. With their promises to call and text done and over, Jake walked down the jetway. A few more minutes and he was in his seat, buckled in, waiting for the rest of his life. A strange calm and a wry smile came over him. He couldn't see Terra watching his plane taxi away from the gate, but she did.

She didn't know how she could be sad and exhilarated at

the same time, but she was. Her thoughts were interrupted by a little girl.

"Excuse me Ms. Dee, can I take a picture with you?"

Terra, back in character, smiled and cleared a tear from her eye. The little girl was maybe 10 years old.

"Absolutely!" she said, squatting down to be at eye level with her.

The little girl's mother, who was almost embarrassed, snapped a picture or two with her phone. Terra pulled hers out, too, snapping a selfie of her with the little girl. Then it hit her that she hadn't taken any pictures of Jake. The only pictures she had of him were from the paparazzi. *Eh, maybe they're good for something after all*, she thought, walking out of the airport.

- EIGHTEEN -

Jake's plane landed at BWI about 6 hours later; nine hours if you include the time difference. He filled his time watching the video screen in the back of the seat in front of him, reading old magazines, and trying not to obsess over Terra, which of course only made things worse.

As soon as they landed, Jake turned his phone on, and it took time for all the texts and voicemail alerts to stop. This time it didn't bother him. He looked first for the message from his sister, Kelly. And of course, it had a paparazzi picture of him kissing Terra on the forehead. It was a good picture actually. He liked it. There were no messages from Terra, but he let her know he'd landed safely. The text was returned with a smiley face.

To Jake's surprise, it was Erik who was waiting for him at the baggage claim. Jake saw him, walked over, and gave him a hug. Not a hand shake, not a shoulder bump, but a hug one gives to their brother.

"Thanks, man," Jake said. "I thought you had a shift?"

"Meh, scheduling quirks are scheduling quirks," Erik replied.

Erik was about to make a smart-ass remark, but he saw Jake's smile and decided to keep it to himself. He had his friend back. Erik had seen the LAX scene on TV; he'd watched all week how Jake was handling things. He knew the next big challenge lay 50 miles to the west. Erik hadn't really touched anything in the house, though he desperately wanted to. He didn't know if it would help Jake or hurt him to start the process of reclaiming Jake's home, so at Kelly's behest, he just changed the sheets in the bedroom and removed Meredith's things from the shower, but he left the rest of it alone.

"Damn Boss-man, you're in a good mood. Did that sweet little goodbye at LAX have something to do with it?" Erik asked, knowing the answer.

Jake just smiled and replied, "Maybe."

Then he headed over to the conveyor belt to wait for his luggage. This also gave him time to think about the answers he would give to Erik for the inevitable questions. After they grabbed Jake's bag, they headed out to the parking garage, with the usual cursing and ribbing: "How was your flight? Fine, how was yours?" The two didn't really get into the meat of the conversation at hand until they were half way down Route 70.

"So," Erik started, "so, I take it that the one day I was gone was productive?"

Erik noted a bit of déjà vu driving home on this same stretch of road, the subject matter differed, but there was still talk of a woman involved.

Jake chuckled, "Yeah. I guess you could say that."

"One day? I was gone *one day*, and look what happens," Erik complained with a smile.

Jake started to blush a bit, but driving into the sun, Erik never saw it.

"Yeah, well I don't know, man. I had a short talk with Meredith, or maybe she had one with me. I don't know. I'm still working things out, for sure. But I have a starting point and things are looking up some."

The closer they got to home, the more uneasy Jake got. He knew going back to the house would be a test. He accepted it, knew it would be rough, but was determined to get past it. Jake just didn't know how.

His phone chirped, and he saw that Kelly had dropped

him a text asking how his flight was and making sure he was okay. She finished it with a wink. What was it with women and emoticons? The rest of the trip was quiet.

After picking up a bite to eat, they got home around 7:30 p.m. Erik made sure to keep an eye on him. The initial entrance was pretty normal. Something Jake and Erik had done countless times before the trip. This time, Jake was just tired. He was tired of thinking, tired of worrying, and tired from the damn time difference. Erik headed down stairs to get some sleep before his next shift.

Jake dropped his bags in the foyer and sighed heavily. He had a great time in L.A. almost a vacation of sorts. But now the realities of being home were starting to hit him. He had to start taking some inventory of his life. There was family to deal with, everything that had happened over the last 8 or 9 days, and of course he still hadn't completely dealt with Meredith, but at least now he could see that it was possible. All of the events of the last three-plus months that had led up to this point were a whirlwind. Jake was exhausted from the trip, but he was now more hopeful of the future. He'd completed his ACLS class, and Maddie had made it clear his job with the county was secure, which meant that for the time being his finances were at least stable. All these thoughts and he hadn't even made it to the kitchen.

Jake glanced into the living room as he passed. When Meredith's urn caught his eye, it was yet another shot to his psyche. He had hoped he was done with those. After all these months, he didn't know why he kept it. Jake had told himself he was going to sprinkle her ashes near the rapids in the river at Great Falls, Virginia. It was her favorite place to hike and take photographs.

She hadn't left any actual wishes per se, but that's where he thought her final resting place should be. Up to now though, he just couldn't bring himself to do it. He made a resolution then and there to make sure he took care of her in that manner. It was time to suck it up and deal with the questions and issues that had been hounding him these last few months. Now that he was clean and sober, and both Erik and Terra had thrown him a lifeline of possibilities and hope, he could think more clearly to be able to move on.

He left a note for Erik, in case he wanted to come along. He knew Erik wasn't the kind to go to funerals. Jake wanted Erik there for Meredith, but also for his own benefit. He'd call one or two of Meredith's friends to see if they wanted to be there. He wanted her to be surrounded by the people who undoubtedly loved her, and who would've given their lives for hers had they had the chance. Folks like that don't come into your life very often, though the Fire and EMS community was a bit different.

Jake was bushed. He grabbed a quick shower and checked his voice mails and messages before heading off to sleep. Among a few other messages, Maddie had called and wanted to see him the day after he got back. She sounded chipper, so he was happy. He wouldn't bother setting an appointment or calling. He wanted to drop by unannounced. After all, she wanted to talk to him. He decided to grab some sleep. He see her the next day.

***

"Jake! My boy!" Captain "Maddie" Jostler threw her arms around Jake as he walked into her office. "My! You're looking a helluva lot better than the last time I saw you. Feeling better I hope?"

Jake smiled at the gushing of attention and replied, "Yeah, I'm feeling a lot better. And this time I really am completely sober."

"Well, I can't ask for perfection, but that'll do."

Jake sat in the stiff armchair in front of her desk before he asked, "You said in the voicemail that you wanted to see me?"

"It seems your actions out west have garnered a lot of attention. Apparently MIEMSS has been hounded non-stop about your suspension, so it looks as though you can start back at your station as soon as you feel ready, and as soon as you can pass the physical and psych evals."

Jake was floored. He was resigned to spending the next few months teaching trauma evaluations and protocols regarding increased ICP and grading practicals.

"Uh, yeah. Yes. Sure. Absolutely. What do I have to do?" Jake stuttered.

Maddie giggled a little, and then replied, "All you have to do is meet with Dr. Murphy, the county chief psychologist, and if he clears you for duty, you're all good. But understand, he will dig into what happened with Meredith. He *will* cross any lines you may have to make sure you're stable enough to serve in public."

"Yes, ma'am," Jake said, back in medic-mode.

"I'll have a talk with him and get back to you about the scheduling. In the meantime, try to relax a little."

He knew that was going to suck, but Jake thought he'd already been through the worst of it, at least mentally.

"No problem, I'm available all week," Jake said, walking out, trying to sound confident though also wanting to make sure he took care of Meredith.

He was determined to get straight again. He had started eating somewhat better, and he still had a gym membership that he never used. Discipline was going to be the next step to getting his life put back in order.

On his way out, his phone buzzed. *Finally something from Terra,* Jake thought.

"What's shakin' bacon?" He smiled at her usual greeting.

Jake decided to give her a call. He missed her voice more than he was willing to admit. At least he admitted it, he thought.

"Hey Chica! How're you doing?" he asked as soon as Terra answered the phone.

"Hey!" she replied. "Good. I'm doing real good. How about yourself?"

"Good news, I may be able to get back on the ambulance by next week. It seems all the publicity last week put enough pressure on the docs out here to get me my license back a little quicker."

"You're welcome," Terra said with a bit of sarcasm in her voice.

"Yeah. Thanks. So, has your schedule firmed up any? Do you have to head back on the road soon?"

"Uh hmm. I'm leaving this evening for Seoul, so I may be out of contact for a bit. I'll text you when I get there."

"Seoul? As in South Korea? For the movie?" Jake asked, knowing the answer, just trying to keep her on the line.

"For the movie," Terra said somewhat regretfully. "Angela said she could get me all set up for the ambulance ride along while I'm away. I just have to make sure my return date is solid. I'll let you know how all that goes."

Jake had pretty much forgotten about her ride-along.

"Are you going to be okay? You don't sound too happy to be flying out there."

"No, I love Seoul. I've been there before; I just hate the

flight. It's a 13-hour flight if it's non-stop, and then add the time difference, and it just gets worse from there."

Jake thought she was being a little melodramatic, but if EMS had taught him one thing it was not to minimize people's situations – or at least how they viewed their own situation.

"I'm sure you'll make it through. Give me a call if you can't handle it. I'll talk you down from the ledge."

"I will," Terra said, the smile evident in her voice. They said their goodbyes and hung up. He hadn't been home 24 hours and he thought about her more and more. Jake hoped the same of her.

Jake got home later that afternoon and was walking in the door as Maddie called. Together they made the appointment to see Dr. Murphy on the following Friday. If all the stars fell into place, he could be back in rotation on an ambulance in a week.

After Jake got off the phone with Maddie, he called the relevant people in Meredith's life and it was decided that Wednesday afternoon was to be the day that everyone could get away from their respective responsibilities to say their last goodbyes to her.

***

The day began as a very dreary and overcast day. It was mid-September and though the temperature was nice, the weather had not cooperated most of the day. It was supposed to clear up in the afternoon, which was one reason he chose that day. During the drive, Jake's mood started to wane, thinking the weather was just another thing he couldn't get right. Thankfully, the rain had slowed to a drizzle as they pulled into the parking lot.

There were four of them that showed up. Himself, Erik, Kelly and Terra's mother, Jane. It was a somber moment. Jake silently said a few words with the others looking on, saying their own. The wind had kicked up a bit as Jake walked to the river's shoreline, the sound of the rapids a distant cacophony broken only by the gulls and the ducks. He knew why this place was her favorite. The sun started to break through some clouds across the river, shining rays of light across the light drizzle that remained. Jake took a moment to watch the ducks shaking the water off their backs and thought it was a fitting metaphor. He watched the sun rays spread across the river, shining brightly on the rapids and the grass and finally reaching them.

Jake closed his eyes and turned his head to the sun, feeling its warmth, drying what mist and tears remained on his face. Opening his eyes and seeing the beauty of the park in front of him, he opened the urn.

"I love you Meredith. I did from the moment I met you. Jonathon, buddy. I love you too. From the very beginning. Take care of your mother," Jake's voice trembling, the tears followed.

With that, he tilted the urn, releasing Meredith's and Jonathon's ashes to be where Meredith always loved to be. The wind kicked up, taking the ashes at first into a cloud, and then to the distant parts of the park. She was now part of it all. The sun made the carbon shine and sparkle like glitter in the wind. Jake and the others followed it as long as they could, watching where it landed, both on shore, in the rapids, and even across the river where the ducks and geese were sunning themselves. There, high above the water, Jake saw the sun rays shining on what rain and mist remained giving them a rainbow to beat them all. It was then that Jake knew without a doubt that Meredith had spoken to him, in her own way, and finally, the storm had broken.

- NINETEEN -

When he wasn't thinking about Meredith or Terra or EMS, Jake spent his week trying to get into a new routine of eating right and going to the gym. He had never known his gym was open 24 hours, 7 days a week. He and Terra exchanged a few texts, and from there, a few e-mails for the longer discussions.

Friday was there before Jake knew it. He didn't really have time to get nervous about seeing the doctor. That was until the morning of the appointment. In the shower that morning, he finally realized that all of Meredith's things had been removed. They were still in the bathroom, just not the shower. Leaving the bathroom, Jake focused on the sheets and realized they'd been changed too. In fact, he realized he hadn't thought about Meredith since he let her ashes go. Jake wasn't sure how to take it. Up until now he hadn't thought the meeting would be an issue. Now he wasn't so sure. Jake had the physical to take care of that morning, so no eating, less it screw-up the blood tests. He'd have to have a talk with Erik later.

The medical offices were on the second floor of the county fire and rescue headquarters. The physical went as well as could be expected; the blood draw and urinalysis was first. He wasn't expecting to be on the treadmill with a monitor hooked up to him, but he ate an apple while doing it anyway. Over the course of the previous 14 weeks, he'd dropped 63 pounds, or almost 5 pounds a week. Jake was down to 212 pounds. Normally losing weight that fast would be of notable concern, but considering the medical staff knew that there were good reasons for the dramatic weight loss, they didn't say a word. His pressure was up a bit; Jake guessed it had to do with him being a little freaked over the upcoming psych eval.

He was finished and dressed by 10:30 a.m. His appoint with the shrink was at 11, so he killed some time chatting with Maddie. She had a way of calming him down. It was the motherly instinct, and she knew he was a little scared. Jake was definitely "clock-watching".

"Good morning, Jake. How're you doing today?" Dr. Murphy started out, still sitting behind his desk.

Jake was expecting a couch, or some type of stereotypical setting. Instead, he found himself in an office exactly like Maddie's, sitting in the same type of chair he sat in at her office.

"Good. I'm doing good."

"Good. So," the doctor began, leaning back in his chair, "tell me what's been going on with you lately."

Jake chuckled, trying to be nonchalant, "Not a whole lot. I'm just trying to figure out if I still have a job or not."

Again, trying to inject humor into a tough situation. Dr. Murphy was not amused with the tone of the answer.

"Look Jake, my job is to make sure you're stable enough to deal with the streets again. The last thing anyone needs is you losing your head because you have an episode. We don't have time to sit here and dissect your whole life history. This is one session. I need to know what's going on in your head right now."

The doctor wasn't quite telling the truth, but if it shocked Jake into being more truthful, more open, and more straightforward, then so be it.

"Okay, where do you want to start?" Jake said, a little more sheepishly, a bit surprised with such a frank manner from someone whose job is to be more gentle – if somewhat stereotypically.

"Meredith, the accident. Let's start there. I want to know where you're at with that," the doctor replied.

"What do you mean?"

"I mean how are you dealing with it? Do you blame yourself? I have the police report, I have witness statements and letters of concern here, and of course I have the notes from your weekly psych sessions," Dr. Murphy said, flipping towards the back of the folder. "It says here that you're having trouble sleeping? Are you still taking medication for that?"

"No."

"When did that stop?"

"The last pill I took was last week in Los Angeles," Jake said, getting tired of the aggressive approach.

"Okay. Are you still having problems sleeping?"

"No."

"What kind of problems were you having?"

Jake sighed heavily, slouched down in his chair, and replied, "Nightmares".

"About the accident?"

Jake just nodded his head and responded, "Among other things. Mostly the eyes. I kept seeing her eyes and hearing her gasp for breath. The gasps would turn to shrieks."

Dr. Murphy softened his tactics now that he was through the tough-guy exterior that most first responders seem to have.

"Can you tell me about them? Is it the same dream every time?" Dr. Murphy asked.

Jake shook his head no. He didn't like talking about them; he hadn't had them in so long – over a week - that he'd actually started to forget about them.

"It's usually different every time. Generally, it will be a

scene I've been on, but she'll be there somehow, and I can't help her. But I haven't had anything like that in over a week, almost two," Jake said defensively.

"So you're dreaming of other calls? Did those calls end with poor patient outcomes?"

Jake bit his tongue.

"Poor patient outcome? You mean did the patient die? Yes, the dreams I had were all scenes where the patients died, okay? Blood, alcohol, brain matter and screams and gasping and gurgling. Imagine the worst level of hell and that's what my nightmares of made of. People begging for their life, begging for me to help them, begging for me not to let them die," Jake said forcefully, fidgeting with a chip on his thumbnail.

"You can always tell when their brain stem is controlling their breathing. The grunting, the muscles trying to help, and the last sounds of death catching up to them. Only it's not the patient that died. It was always Meredith's voice or the last noise I heard her make. Sometimes it was her; she'd have an umbilical cord hanging down on the ground, dragging..." Jake stopped, staring off into the corner of the office.

Dr. Murphy was getting into the thick of it.

"So, what's changed? Why don't you think you're having these dreams anymore?" the doctor asked, very matter-of-fact like.

Jake smiled as he thought of Terra.

"I met *her*. That's the best answer I can come up with. I met Terra."

"So, things are going well with you two?"

"We're just friends," Jake said, still unable to wipe the smile off his face.

"And I take it she knows your... situation?"

The smile faded before Jake replied, "Yeah. She knows. And she's okay with it. I got her to take a CPR class, and… and I helped get her set up for a ride-along when she gets back," Jake said with a slight smile.

Dr. Murphy returned the smile with a smirk of his own, and took some time to write some things on his notepad. It was time to make sure he was stable enough to return to work. He'd hoped it would only take one session, but it doesn't always work that way with people who are usually further out from their trauma in terms of time. Most of the time the county tries to be pretty quick with the stress debriefings. The sooner the better for all parties involved.

"Jake," he paused more for effect than anything else, "why do you still want to be a paramedic? After everything you've seen, and been through? After being unable to save your wife? The daily tragedies you see on a regular basis. Why go back?"

He asked these questions not in a specific order, but in a specific way. He needed to gauge how Jake handled losing patients while evoking the most painful loss he'd hopefully ever have.

Jake sat there for a few seconds, soaking in the question. Trying to put into words how he felt. How does someone explain a "calling"? He'd only ever heard of such things until he'd felt it.

"Selfishness," Jake said.

This surprised Dr. Murphy. He hadn't heard this line of reasoning before, though it seemed to at least start out honestly.

"Oh?"

"On the outside, people see us and what we do and a lot of them are amazed because we run towards the trouble. Well, not if it's on fire. I say let those things burn."

The doctor knew this attempt at humor was a bit of

deflection, and gave the requisite smile.

"Most people love us. Everywhere we go. We're more loved than the cops or the UPS man. And it feels good to put on a uniform that means something. It means something that's free and clear of any and all political bullshit."

Jake pointed to the Star of Life emblem on the wall before continuing, "The *only* meaning that symbol has is that we are here to help. That we will always help people. Come hell or high water, we will do whatever we have to do to help people."

"So you like being a paramedic because you want attention? To be adored by people?" Dr. Murphy asked cautiously.

Jake shrugged and replied, "I love helping people; I love actually taking a shitty situation and within five minutes it's a complete 180-degree difference. It's the instant gratification of helping someone, who just minutes before was on the edge of death, and being able to draw them back from the edge or who simply thinks they're worse off than they are, and being able to calm them down to see and understand that they are going to make it through whatever the situation is. *That* is what gets me, that I can make a difference. That I *do* make a difference and *that* makes me feel better about myself. Sometimes when I can get into a groove, it's like being inside a positive feedback loop. It's a bit of a high."

"Sounds like arrogance."

"Maybe. I'm sure I have my days. They didn't invent the term 'ParaGod' for nothing, but I'm old enough and experienced and have had calls that have humbled me enough to know it isn't all rainbows and unicorn farts. I think I got dealt a fucked up hand and there's not one god damned thing I can do about it. I know now that I did everything I could have to help Meredith, even going outside of my protocols, and it still wasn't enough. But helping people helps me. It returns to me exponentially. Call it whatever you want; call it karma. I do it because it makes me feel good. So, call me selfish. For me, EMS is... life."

"Then *why* do you 'love EMS' so much? What got you to this point?" the doctor pushed.

"Why do I love EMS?" Jake repeated the question, absentmindedly, looking for the words. "Why, why, why? Hey doc, have you ever ridden in an ambulance? I mean, other than being a patient?"

"I've had some practical hours for my degree, but nothing since."

"So, what? Five hours maybe?"

"Five to ten, I'd say. I spent more time in the emergency room" Dr. Murphy replied, trying to make himself sound more medically adept than he was.

"Okay, so let's say 10 hours," Jake began. "That's less than a full shift for anyone really. I mean, even the volunteers usually do 12-hour shifts. Hell, let's mark it up to a full shift. You did a full shift and either nothing special happened, or you were just doing your time. No big deal. I got into EMS initially because I loved fire trucks and I loved the thought of being in the thick of it all. Rescuing people from fires and kittens from trees. I wanted to be one of the guys I looked up to.

"Some kids look up to their favorite sports hero, Lebron James, Alex Ovechkin, Tom Brady and they want to do what they did. I mean, as far as sports went, I wanted to be like Eddie Murray. But, when I was 4 years old, I remember telling my mom I wanted to be a fire truck. Not a 'fireman', I wanted to be the actual truck. I guess it was the way my 4-year-old brain worked. As I grew up, I realized that I wasn't going to be the next switch-hitting Hall of Fame First-Baseman with bitchin' porkchop sideburns, but I really could be riding on the fire trucks. I could be one the people I saw as heroes. I had no idea what they did aside from putting fires out, but I knew I could walk into a firehouse, ask for a membership form and just show up. 90% of success is just showing up."

"I like not just being able to make a difference, but being in the mix of things, actually *doing* it. There are always going to be days where you get shit on, literally and figuratively. You're going to have the bullshit calls, the frequent fliers, and the druggies that we all complain about. But every so often, you get that call, maybe only a couple times a year or maybe a few times in a *career* that changes you, challenges you, where you can actually make a difference in someone's life. It's tangible, and it's almost immediate.

"You can see results by the time you pull up to the hospital. Whether it's getting a hard tube to keep someone breathing, or just holding a little old man's hand because he's scared. I can't tell you how many times I've sat in that ambulance and prayed with people because they were so scared. I'm not overly religious. I've got my doubts and God and I are rarely on speaking terms, but helping people who are hanging by threads," Jake had stopped focusing on Dr. Murphy.

"Helping people either because they're hurt, or scared or incapable of helping themselves," Jake paused, "feels good. Hell, just being in the station *waiting* to help someone feels good. So, yes, its selfish. I do it because I'm selfish, and I get paid to feel good."

Jake blinked out of his trance to see the doctor staring at him, biting on the end of his pen. Jake didn't realize the doctor didn't care what his answer was, but more so how he explained it, and what kinds of emotions were involved.

"Have you ever felt like that at the end of the day, doc?" Jake asked.

The doctor scribbled something down and looked up, giving one of those quick uneasy smiles before replying, "No. At least not the way you described it."

He finished writing some things down and told Jake that his review was complete.

"I'll make my final notes, and pass them on to Maddie. She should be in touch," he said, holding his hand out to Jake.

"That's it? No other questions? You don't want to hear about Terra or Los Angeles?" Jake asked.

"Is there something I need to know about you and Terra or what happened in Los Angeles?"

"No," Jake said quickly, not trying to give the good doctor any more information than he had to, aside from the fact that he himself didn't know what was going on between the two.

"I wish we had more like you, Jake. I see way too much pain come through here and not enough hope."

Jake walked out of the county medical offices and headed over to the burrito stand to grab some lunch. It just so happened that it was next to the movie theatre, and *Moonlight Storm* was playing in the matinee.

He texted Terra for the first time that day.

"Just passed my medical eval with flying colors. I should be back on the rig soon."

He didn't think she needed to know that it was mostly a psych evaluation.

"That's great!" Terra replied after Jake had eaten about half of his burrito.

"*Moonlight Storm* is playing here; I'm going to catch the matinee because I'm a cheap bastard," Jake typed.

Jake didn't know what the time difference was between Washington, D.C. and Seoul but he wondered if she was up later than he thought she should have been. The movie started at 1 p.m., so at worst it was, what? 2 a.m. there? He wasn't sure.

Terra responded with a blushing smiley face. At least that's what Jake thought it was.

"Blushing? Really?" Jake replied.

A few minutes went by, long enough for Jake to stroll over and buy a ticket. His phone chirped with Terra's reply.

"I miss you."

It caught him off guard, but it was also a relief. He'd been thinking about her as well. It was good to see someone else admit it first. It was always easier to tell someone how they felt by text. No real contact involved. But he still had to "play it cool".

"Why do you think I'm going to see your movie? I'll text you later. Get some sleep."

And at that, he turned his phone off and lost himself in the movie, and in seeing her again. Jake could have cared less about the plot. It hadn't even been a week since he'd last seen her.

***

The call from Maddie came just after 5 p.m. that evening. Jake picked it up on the first ring.

"Congratulations, my boy! You're back in," Maddie said. "We've got you back down in Kensington if that's okay, but the shifts don't open up until the end of next week at the earliest. Until then, we can set you on the bench in case someone calls in sick and you know that's pretty much a given any and every day."

Jake was ecstatic. He was going to be back at his old firehouse in Kensington, hopefully by next week, and he'd be back on an ambulance maybe as soon as tomorrow as there hadn't been a day in the whole history of Montgomery County where someone didn't call in sick.

- TWENTY -

"You've got to be kidding me! Un-fucking real!" Jake said in exasperation on Tuesday morning – a second day after no one called in sick throughout the entire county.

"I know," Maddie said. "It's the damnedest thing I've ever seen. I can't complain, but I know you want to get into the mix. Just sit tight and enjoy these last few days of rest. Being the 'shit-magnet' you are, you're going to need it. Your first official day back will be Thursday. No actual EMS work, but there will be a lot of paperwork."

The call Jake was hoping for, came late Friday afternoon. His first shift back as an actual paramedic would be that evening. In emotions very ubiquitous within the rest of EMS, he didn't want people to get sick or injured, but if they did, he wanted the call.

His first working shift was a fill-in at the Washington-Grove fire department in Gaithersburg by Lake Forest Mall off Montgomery Village Avenue. They were generally one of the busiest departments in the county. They were also a split volunteer and career house that had volunteers at night and county manned during the day. This evening was a bit unusual though as they needed county crew to cover for them due to their annual awards banquet.

Jake showed up just before 6 p.m. and met with the watch officer, was given a quick tour, and was on the clock just like that. Driscoll "Dris" Linwood was Jake's partner this evening. He hadn't worked with him before, but he seemed pretty smart.

"Hey Jake, can I ask you a personal question?" Dris started off the evening on the wrong foot.

Jake didn't want any bullshit about what happened with MIEMSS or his wife.

"It depends on how personal," Jake said cautiously.

"It's about Ms. Dee," Dris said. "Is she a normal person like you and me?"

Jake smiled and replied, "Yes, she's a normal person. Now as far as you and me being normal, that's a question that is open to debate."

Dris chuckled.

"Now, if it hadn't been for her car wreck, I can't say she'd have let me see her 'normal' side," Jake continued, putting up air quotes as he spoke. "She's pretty reclusive when she wants to be. But she can also turn on 'the diva' in a heartbeat. It was interesting to see her deal with people she either didn't know or didn't want to know."

Jake was starting to reminisce and it hadn't been but a couple of weeks.

"Do you still talk to her?" Dris pushed.

Jake smirked, "Wow, you're pretty infatuated with her, eh?"

Dris just smiled bashfully and hung his head in slight embarrassment.

"Yeah, I guess so. She's just hot. I wondered if her personality was cool or if she was, well, you know..."

Jake knew.

"Yeah, she's cool. We've talked a bit since I came back, nothing too detailed though."

Jake was hiding the fact that their phone calls were getting longer and longer. She was still in Seoul, but she was bouncing around East Asia for the next six weeks.

"She's over in Asia somewhere, so it's not like we have the opportunity to talk much. Mostly texts, if anything."

He liked Dris for his bashfulness. He was a good kid. Turns out he was pretty young, too, just 22. He'd only been with the county for about a year or so, but had been with the volunteer squad in Germantown before getting a job with the county. It seemed to Jake that the local volunteer squads were just farming out all the first responders as fast as the municipalities could snatch them up. It was too bad they were all forced into the union as a condition of employment. But, there was nothing he could do about it. Hell, he was *part* of the union.

The places his mind wondered when it wasn't preoccupied with EMS or Terra. Jake's phone rang. It was Erik.

"What's up Boss-man? How's your first shift back going?"

"Good, it's going real good. I met a few new folks out here at Washington-Grove. It's a nice station, though probably not as nice as those cushy state barracks you get to stay in," Jake replied with the hint of sarcasm.

"Ha! You need to come out here once in a while then. I'll show you how nice it is. Most of the time we're lucky to be fully stocked on toilet paper. Oh, and one more thing, Jake."

"What's that, Erik?"

"I hope you have a *quiet* night." Uttering one of the words feared most by most any medical professional.

Erik was laughing as he hung up.

"God Dammit!" Jake said, and before he could put his phone back in his pocket, the tones went off in the station.

"Fuck you, Erik. Wherever you are, fuck you!" Jake said.

Dris and the guys started rolling out of the bunks or the recliners or where ever they had happened to be lying.

"Rescue 708, Engine 708, Medic 708 Charlie response for a two car MVA, Southbound 270, closest exit is Montgomery Village Avenue. 2353."

Dris ran over to the ambulance and hopped in the driver's seat. He seemed eager, if nothing else. Jake grabbed a copy of the run sheet off the printer and got in on the other side, just as the engine had cleared the bay door.

"Hmph. They're feeling a bit froggy tonight," Dris noted as he pulled out behind them.

"I think Jonesy and Sarah were doing an engine check, going over the inventory and making sure the batteries were all working," Jake replied.

Jake had to find the ambulance number before he mic'd up. Finding it, he keyed the mic, "Medic 708 en route."

"Engine 708, same traffic."

"Copy that, Medic 708, Engine 708 en route, 2355," came the reply from communications.

Jake noted the en route time on the run sheet. The county had started moving to laptops and iPads to replace the paperwork, but Jake still thought it easier to use the paper forms. One more thing he'd have to learn. It had been just over four months since his last proper EMS call. His heart rate jumped as soon as the tones went off and he was feeling the adrenaline rush he'd come to miss.

The engine got there ahead of them for a change.

"County, Medic 708 on scene. 2 cars and debris across 3 lanes. Looks like we've got some starring on a windshield. Can we get a bird on stand-by?"

"Medic 708 on scene, 2359," came the response from communications.

The accident didn't look too bad, but that was just part of

the scene size-up. Bystanders were pointing and telling Jake what they thought the problems were and so on. The one thing Jake wanted to know is what cars were travelling in what direction, and at what speed, etc. The intersection, if you wanted to call it that, was an unlit on-ramp to the interstate, so there was nothing really to slow anyone down.

One car, a yellow Chevrolet Impala, was driving south on 270 approximately the speed limit, some said faster, so Jake assumed 65-ish. A smaller red car, a Nissan Sentra, had pulled out onto 270 from Montgomery Village Avenue. No speeding up to match traffic, just pulled right out, apparently. The driver of the Sentra, an older woman of 67, having not seen the Impala, hit the car on the passenger side. The accident sent the Impala spinning 720° across four lanes and into the Jersey barrier that separates the north and southbound lanes. Thankfully, there were no other cars in the immediate vicinity.

All in all, it wasn't that bad a wreck – especially for what could have happened. The Impala had such a low center of gravity – lower than the Sentra - that it spun instead of rolling. In any event, the impala hit the barrier at an angle, which helped dissipate more energy throughout the car instead of through the driver. The driver of the Sentra was out walking around, talking normally aside from being shook up and concerned about the other driver.

The patient that was worse off was the 27-year-old male, unrestrained driver of the Impala. The car that got side-swiped at 65+ miles an hour. He was still in the car, somewhat dazed when Jake approached. All the windows were shattered save for the rear. The driver's side door opened without an issue and Jake was able to begin his assessment.

"What happened?" the driver asked.

Jake was thankful that the man was able to speak and move air.

"You were just in a car wreck, man. My name is Jake; I'll be checking you out for a few minutes. What's your name?"

"It's Anthony. Oh man, my head hurts; where's my girlfriend? Can you call my parents?"

"Was your girlfriend in the car with you?" Jake asked, somewhat nervously.

They didn't sweep the area for anyone who might have been ejected, not knowing his partner, Dris was in the process as he was assessing the little old lady.

"No, but she's expecting me. Can you call my parents?"

"We'll let the right people know. You just try to relax and tell me what hurts and what hurts the most," Jake replied.

Jake checked his pupils, sluggish but very unequal. There was some starring on the inside of the windshield. Jake noted no ligature marks, indicating his seatbelt was used. No medical alert jewelry; he had some busted knuckles, a busted nose and there was blood on his collar. Jake grabbed a 4x4, folded it over twice, and dipped the corner of it into the blood coming from his patient's ear. Then, he unfolded it and let it sit flat while he continued his assessment and grabbed his glucometer. After he was done, he looked down at the 4x4.

"Oh shit!" Jake said aloud, and then grabbed his radio. The halo had formed as clear as day. It was a crude test, but one he couldn't ignore. The blood on the bandage formed the center of the circle was used to test for cerebral spinal fluid – or CSF. If there was any CSF in the blood, it would separate itself to the outside, forming what looked like a halo. Jake took a glucose reading of the patient's finger and it was a respectable 123. He took another test of the blood coming from the ear and it registered 68. Not good. It simply confirmed his concerns about the halo test.

"County, Medic 708, we're going to need a bird out here ASAP. Head trauma, with possible CSF. Can we get a status on Trooper-8?" Jake un-keyed the mic cutting off part of his transmission and swinging around to grab his oxygen bottle and a non-rebreather.

"Copy Medic 708, Trooper 8 is spinning up. ETA approximately 10 minutes. Rescue 708 should be on scene within the next minute or so," the operator responded.

Jake looked behind him and could see the lights of the heavy rescue vehicle coming up the road. The engine didn't carry the helicopter landing equipment. It was all on the recue, which thankfully had been dispatched.

Hearing the conversation on his radio, Dris left his patient with one of the EMTs on the engine for the time being and came over to Jake as he was sliding the oxygen mask over Anthony's head.

"Looks like just these two. She may want to go get checked out, but she's walking wounded. How about this guy, what do you need?" Dris asked.

"We've got a pretty serious head trauma here," Jake replied.

Jake was checking breath sounds. He pushed Anthony's left ear forward, showing Dris the halo on the dressing.

"Good air movement, equal both sides," Jake stated, taking the stethoscope out of his ears. "I'm going to set up a couple of lines for access, can you grab the monitor and a long board? And get one of those firefighters over here to hold c-spine."

Jake grabbed some IV kits and a couple of saline locks.

"Hey, what happened, why does my head hurt?" Anthony

asked again.

"Hey Anthony, you were in a car accident," Jake replied, wrapping the blood pressure cuff around his left arm, the stethoscope already draped back around his neck.

"Oh. Why does my head hurt? Where's my girlfriend? Can you call my parents?"

"Sure, sure. Just hold on. You hit your head. I don't know where your girlfriend is. She wasn't in the car with you. We're still checking you out. Does anything hurt more than usual? Do you have any medical issues we need to know about?"

"No. no. I'm fine. What happened?"

The good part was that he was an easy head-trauma in that he wasn't combative. There was definitely head trauma. Signs this early was not good. A broken nose and "battle signs" made it difficult to see where one innocuous injury ended and the other more ominous one began. Jake made sure to keep an eye on his breathing, and his pressure, though there was not much he could do if his brain started to herniate into his spinal column, cutting off the autonomic nerve signals that forced his body to breathe. If that happened, he'd be bagging an organ donor. For now, the patient was awake and talking so that was always a good thing.

A firefighter showed up and got into the back seat behind Anthony. Holding c-spine, Jake showed him the same thing he showed Dris – the blood from the ear, careful to put his finger to his lips to show him that he wasn't supposed to say anything – mainly out of practice to keep patients calm – though Jake doubted Anthony would be much of an issue. The firefighter fought the urge to check the right side as well, something Jake hadn't done.

"Chopper's on channel 6. They're about three minutes out," Dris said, turning both his and Jake's radio to channel 6.

Dris had placed the monitor on the ground between Jake and the car, and started connecting the added leads to the monitor port. Jake cut the shirt off of Anthony, and started placing the 12-leads, while Dris took the blood pressure cuff off and replaced it with the one from the monitor. Jake had decided to leave Anthony in his current position since he was stable.

They could see the lights; the helicopter and the fire crew had set up the reflectors, and flares, and had moved the trucks, facing their headlights into the wind. There was also a windsock on top of the rescue that Jake had never noticed before. As the helicopter approached, Jake and Dris could hear the radio traffic between the helicopter pilot and the fire lieutenant. The team rotated Anthony and slid him out onto the board.

"Hey, what happened?" Anthony repeated.

"You were in a car accident; you hit your head. I don't know where your girlfriend is," Jake tried to answer all his questions before he asked them again, but couldn't remember the last one.

"Oh. Can someone call my parents?"

"Dammit," Jake uttered so only Dris heard, and he chuckled at the attempt.

They slid Anthony onto the board and brought him up to the stretcher. Thankfully, he was only about 180 pounds so it only took the two of them. They brought the stretcher up to its full height and wheeled him over into the ambulance for the time being. They could see and hear the chopper coming in. They had gotten a couple of rounds of vitals when the flight medic and flight nurse opened the back of the ambulance and stepped up and into the ambulance.

"Hey ya' Bastard!"

It was Erik.

"What kind of mamby-pamby shit you got for me today?" Erik yelled the question over the noise of the accident scene.

"Aw, how cute! A little head trauma?" Erik said, sticking out his lower lip as if to pout, closing the back doors of the ambulance.

Jake, quite surprised by Erik being the flight medic, started giving his report out of habit.

"26-year-old male, unrestrained driver of the yellow car. He bounced around inside a bit, no trauma to the extremities, lungs equal bilaterally, and pupils sluggish and unequal. Active bleeding noticed coming from his left ear. Halo test was positive as was the glucose test."

Fuck. He didn't check the right ear for blood, let alone a halo. But either way, it's bad enough.

"His pressure has been elevated, but steady, the pulse-ox shows him at 97% on 12 liters Oh-2," Jake finished reporting.

Erik took it all in, looking mostly at the monitor, staring at the 12-lead interpretations. The flight nurse, Betty, started talking to Anthony to get a sense of his level of consciousness, saying things such as: Hi Anthony, I'm Betty and this is Erik – we're the flight crew taking you to Fairfax.

"Fairfax? Why not just jump over to Suburban?" Jake asked

"Because this week, their entire neuro team is in San Diego for a conference – well, all the good docs, anyway. The Fairfax team took the hit this year. All serious head wounds go to Fairfax for the week," Erik replied, not taking his eyes off the monitor.

"Hi. What happened?" Anthony replied.

"You were in a car accident, you hit your head. I don't know where your girlfriend is; I'm sure she's safe, and yes, someone has called your parents," Jake cut in, proud that he remembered all the questions.

Anthony looked irritated that someone had answered all of his questions before he even asked. Betty too seemed a bit perturbed as she had a reason to ask the questions.

"Sorry, he's just repeating the same questions over and over. I thought I would get all the answers out of the way," Jake told the nurse.

The back of the ambulance opened up and the ambient noise from all the trucks and helicopter was immense,

"Hey Anthony!" Jake was yelling now. "These two are going with you in the helicopter. It's really loud up there, so make sure you ask your questions very loudly!"

Dris laughed out loud, and Betty mouthed a sarcastic "Thanks."

Erik, still tied to the monitor, gave the okay to unhook everything and move the patient. Erik printed off the tape from the monitor to make notes of his blood pressure and stats. If it was a bad head trauma playing possum, he didn't want it sneaking up on him and having the patient herniate en route. The helicopter crew had their own stretcher that Anthony had to be transferred to and hooked back up to everything on the helicopter's equipment.

"No problem, Boss-man!" Erik yelled in Jake's ear as the turbine on the helicopter started up.

Jake grabbed Erik's sleeve and said, "Nurse *Betty*? Seriously?"

Erik winked and smirked, giving that mischievous look he was known for, and turned to secure the patient.

"Lucy, you've got some splainin' to do," Jake said in his best Ricky Riccardo voice.

Jake ducked out of the down draft and headed back over

to the ambulance. Erik turned around and flashed his dimpled smile before stepping into the helicopter. And just like that, the chopper and her crew were gone. Jake had to admit Erik had style after all; he just needed a flight suit, a major trauma and a brand new 15-million dollar AgustaWestland helicopter.

After all the commotion, Jake had completely forgotten about his second patient. The "little old lady" that Dris had done the initial assessment on. She was standing just outside the ambulance the whole time – though Dris was keeping an eye on her when not focusing on Anthony.

Dris convinced her to get checked out. Considering she'd just been a decent car wreck, she initially wanted sign the release form and go about her day however that would have ended. They decided to take her to Shady Grove Hospital, though the euphemism most of the EMS community used was "Shady Grave", more so because of the name of hospital than the quality of treatment. It was all part of the gallows humor of EMS.

Still, all in all it was a good call. Dris was busy with his patient. The little old lady was starting to feel the effects of the seatbelt and subsequent crash. The adrenalin was wearing off for everyone involved. The guys on the rescue engine were busy dropping kitty litter on the spilled fluids and the police officers were busy directing traffic, calling in wreckers to move the cars and writing reports.

Dris' patient probably could've walked into the ambulance, but they cleaned up the stretcher, threw some fresh sheets on it and let her ride that back into the ambulance. She was so worried about the other driver, as well she should be. But Jake thought it a sweet thing for some reason, even if the accident was her fault. While Dris was in the back starting a new round of assessments, Jake jumped into the driver's seat and radioed

Comms.

"Medic 708, County. We've got a single female patient headed to Shady Grove."

Jake almost slipped and said 'grave'. He'd have to watch that.

"Starting mileage when you're ready," Jake said.

"Go ahead Medic 708," Comms replied.

"Starting mileage is 13,687."

"Copy Medic 708, starting mileage 13,687. Zero-zero-38."

Jake banged on the window to the patient compartment and got a muffled "Go ahead" from Dris. And they were off to the hospital.

Waiting at "the grave" wasn't too shabby. Like most hospitals, they had some refreshments for the EMS crews. Usually Gatorade or bottled water and usually some peanut butter and graham crackers to go with it. All too often there were shifts where that was all they'd get to eat in a good 10 or 12-hour stretch and everyone who'd ever had one of those shifts was thankful for it. Jake wasn't as familiar with the crew at "Shady Grave", so he'd didn't joke around with them as much. They were pretty busy with the walk-ins, though they were the only ambulance there at the time.

Dris finished his paperwork on the computer, got his release forms signed and handed his patient the obligatory HIPPA forms. Some of it was nonsense, but it had to be done per state and federal requirements. He dropped off a copy of the patient care report to the charge nurse and his one call for the night was done.

"One call. In the one of the busiest if not *the* busiest station in the county and I got one call," Jake said into the phone as soon as his shift ended at 6 a.m.

It was 9 p.m. in Seoul and Terra was just coming off her public relations movie tour for the country.

"That is so cool!" Terra exclaimed, excited for him. "So, how was he?"

"He who?"

"The guy driving the car. The guy Erik took. Are you even listening to yourself? You had a guy that was leaking brains out of his ears and you're asking 'who'?"

She had a point, Jake thought.

"Well, he wasn't leaking brains out of his head, just the CSF, the fluid around his brain."

"And that doesn't freak you out at all?" Terra asked incredulously.

"Well, I was a bit shocked at the time, but all I can do is call for a bird, and keep him as stable as possible."

Jake realized that he did sound a bit jaded, at least to someone who didn't run into these things on a semi-regular basis.

"So how was your day?"

He almost said "Hon". Jake knew he was tired and his brain-to-mouth filter faltered when he was tired.

"It was good. Mickey, the tour manager, is running things like a drill sergeant. It might be a good thing too, but I haven't had a chance to get out and see much. This is my second time to Seoul and I haven't gotten to see much either time," Terra lamented.

"I'm sorry," Jake said, again almost adding "baby". He really needed some sleep. "So what's your next stop?"

"Taipei. I haven't been there before, and I've talked to Mickey, so I'm hoping she's scheduled some down time for all of us to be able to actually see and experience the countries we're trying to sell."

"Cool. Are you still going to go on your ride-along when you get back?"

"Yes!" Terra said indignantly. "I told you I would. You still seem to think what I do isn't difficult."

"I don't remember ever saying that," Jake responded. "I was just wondering if it was a phase. Some people gets these wild hairs and take off in a direction and don't stick with it."

He knew it was a stretch, but he was testing the waters. Terra, with her penchant for reading into things, saw it.

"No. It isn't a phase. I think it's fucking cool. I just never knew it was as easy to get into as it has been. If only my schedule would allow it. And no, 'this' is not a phase for me. You are not a phase for me. Got that?"

Jake was suddenly very uncomfortable. Terra was a strong willed woman and she was just as straightforward with him as he tried to be with others. She was definitely an "alpha".

"Thanks, Terra. Just don't give up on me," Jake said with a smirk in his voice.

His filter had failed him completely.

"Never," she said.

Terra decided to let him get some sleep, "Well, look, I'll let you go. Do you want me to send you a text when I get to Taipei?"

"Yeah. I should be back at my regular station on Monday. I've got to verify a few things, but yeah. Drop me a line when you get there. You have a safe flight. Take care."

"You too, Goodnight," she said, not connecting that it was morning on the East coast.

Jake smiled, "You too."

And they hung up. Jake hopped in his car and drove the 40 minutes back to his house. Along the way Terra sent him a text, which he didn't get until he got home. "You haven't given up on me, so I won't give up on you." It meant a lot to him. Erik wasn't back from his shift yet, wherever the hell he came from last night.

Jake made sure to close all the curtains in his bedroom and crashed into his bed, a smile on his face. His next 'real' shift was Monday back at his old Station 5 in Kensington. As much as Jake said he hated the Kaiser Permanente building, he couldn't wait to wheel the stretcher back in there.

- TWENTY-ONE -

It felt good to be back in his old stomping grounds at the Kensington Fire Department. He and Dris hit it off so well that the county shuffled around some other medics and made Dris his new regular partner. The morning drive in wasn't too bad. There were the standard issues on the way in with broken down cars, fender benders and the like, but nothing he wasn't used to. All in all he was in a good mood looking forward to the day and days ahead. Something he hadn't done in a while. The tones for his first call went off about 90 minutes after the shift began.

The call came in at 7:27 a.m. County Communications chimed in on the speakers that the MVA was on the inner-loop, just past the Connecticut Avenue exit. Calling out companies 705 to cover the inner loop and 719 to cover the outer loop in case whoever called it in didn't know exactly where they were. Apparently there were several cars involved, mostly dent and scratch. These are usually the sign and release types. Maybe someone who wants to go get checked out in order to bring a lawsuit later. Exactly the kind of call that gets people in trouble. There was one patient said to need treatment. Something about contact with the airbag.

Jake jumped into the passenger side of the rig, leaving Dris to do the driving. Whether Jake liked him or not, the greenhorn drives. Dris didn't say anything. He just grabbed the run sheet off the printer and handed it to Jake as he got inside behind the wheel, and turned the master switch on. Dris keyed the ignition and the battery minder ejected as the ambulance fired up.

Jake grabbed the mic and keyed, "Montgomery, Medic 705 en route."

"Copy Medic 705 en route, 0728." Comms replied. Jake heard 719 mark up as well.

The ambulance radio connected to Jake's phone by Bluetooth automatically had started playing "Far From Home." Jake smiled because it no longer had the same effect on him. He grabbed his phone and picked the next song. He needed something with an up-tempo feeling and heavy guitar riffs. The next song just so happened to be "Highway to Hell" by AC/DC. Jake reached over and turned it up. No one had hit the switch for the street light, so cars didn't see or hear the ambulance coming out of the station at first; they had to wait to clear the intersection. Once through, they blazed down the last mile or two at 50 miles an hour where they could, dodging traffic where they couldn't. Dris spun the wheel hard to the left to take the turn to get on to the inner loop where we could see traffic was already more fucked than usual. Thankfully, the wrecked cars were all on the right side shoulder, letting the people from routes 495, 270 and 355 merge without a blockage other than rubber-neckers who've never seen a wreck before, or a flat tire, or a police car or anything sitting on the side of the road, really.

As they pulled up, they made sure to block the merge lane, forcing cars to get over sooner. There were several cars aligned on the shoulder, with a flatbed truck being at the front of the line. Jake grabbed the jump bag from the back of the rig while Dris called the particulars into Comms for the rest of the responding units. Station 19 has called to respond on the outer loop, in case the caller didn't know exactly where they were.

"Medic 705 on-scene, inner-loop, right shoulder, approximately 100 yards passed Connecticut Avenue," Jake un-keyed and then re-keyed the mic. "Looks like we got 4 cars and a flatbed, most are out and walking around, no fluids visible.

Starting our assessments, Company 19 can go back in service at their discretion."

"Medic 705 on-scene, 5 vehicles. Medic 719 back in service, 0732."

"Copy that, Medic 719 back in service," came the reply from the released crew.

The folks standing next to their cars were all on their cell phones with who-ever as Jake and Dris asked who needed help. To the letter, they all waved them off, and pointed to the front of the line – most not even stopping their phone conversations. Apparently, there was an injured lady up front. One woman was crying as she pointed. All of these were walking wounded, if that. The truck driver was kneeling down at the open driver side door of the car the car that had rear-ended him. As they approached, he stood up and walked over. He was anxious and sweaty. Worry covered his face.

"I.... I don't know what happened. Some asshole cut me off, I had to hit the brakes. Michelle – that's her name, she didn't stop fast enough," the truck driver stated.

Jake peered over the truck driver's shoulder. He could see the front part of the car was crumbled up, but wasn't wedged under the truck. It didn't seem that bad of a wreck. Jake saw part of the airbag, and a lady's arm come down, some blood dripping onto it.

"You got these guys?" Jake asked Dris.

Dris just nodded his head in the affirmative. Dris guessed they were mostly refusals, if not, far less serious than Michelle. When Jake got to the front of the car, the door was open, airbag deployed, some starring from the outside, but nothing major – nothing from inside had hit the windshield. She was leaning back, wearing her seatbelt. But as he turned to better face her, his stomach squealed. Goddammit, he *hated* these types of injuries. This or anything to do with the eyes.

Jake put the jump bag down, and started his assessment. Introducing himself and getting her talking was a better way to gauge her airway. She was on the verge of all out panic. The pain was excruciating; anytime she tried to look or focus on anything, pain would shoot through her skull like lightning. There were some abrasions on her cheek and forehead, probably from the airbag and the powder. She was conscious and alert as far as he could tell. She hadn't hit the windshield or steering wheel. It was just a regular chain reaction wreck. She had forgotten her mascara that morning and was applying it in traffic when someone cut off the driver of the flatbed, causing that driver slam on the brakes, causing her to hit the truck, causing the airbag to drive the mascara brush into her right eye. All 352 nylon bristles tearing through the cornea and then the iris, pushing through the globe of the eye, spilling the aqueous fluid, and severing the optic nerve – all within the fraction of a second.

Her heart rate and pressure was a bit high but considering she'd just been in a car wreck and had her eye impaled, it wasn't anything to worry about, yet. Her tidal volume was good, and she was moving air with no problems. Her lungs we clear. The truck driver helped her a lot in telling her to keep both eyes closed for the time being.

Jake started getting her past history, grabbing some 4x4 bandages out of his bag. Did she have asthma, diabetes or current medical issues to be concerned about? Did she wear contacts? Was there a possibility of pregnancy? The basics. He noted there were no medic-alert bracelets or necklaces. Getting all the answers verbally while he patched both eyes, he could fill out the paperwork in the rig.

Finally, after the initial assessment, Jake moved to the eyes. 10 on 10 pain to say the least. Jake had to force himself to look at the injury, even though his stomach revolted. By then the engine was there and a young firefighter was in the backseat, behind Michelle. He was bright-eyed and bushy tailed and ready to help. He must have been a probie. Either way, the help was appreciated. The young fire fighter helped Jake get Michelle collared up; they still weren't allowed to clear the cervical spine on scene, yet, though it was in the works, much to the chagrin of a lot of doctors who felt more threatened than anything. The guys had brought a long board and some head blocks too.

While still in her car, Jake used a couple of 4x4s to cover the left eye that was still in-tact. Covering the good eye would reduce the movement of the injured eye. Then he set about securing the mascara brush as it was still embedded. This caused a *lot* more pain than either of them had expected, and Michelle went into full hysterics. Jake hadn't even thought about pain meds until now. He handed the job of securing the brush to the EMTs on the engine and started a line in her left arm. A standard 18-gauge line with a saline lock. He didn't have a saline bag with him but he'd add that in the rig. Jake cut the zip ties off the med box in the bag and found the Fentanyl. Thankfully Michelle didn't have any allergies – which she knew of.

"Hey Michelle, I've got meds coming to help you feel better. I need to know how much you weigh," Jake said.

"I don't know. One.... one-forty-three, I think," Michelle responded.

"One hundred and forty-three pounds. That's very specific for someone that doesn't know how much she weighs."

Jake tried to wedge some humor into the situation. If he stayed calm, hopefully, she would calm down.

"Doing the math, that came down to about 65 kilograms, so we're looking at 65 mikes of Fentanyl.... Well, your vitals are up a bit, so let's start with 50 mikes – just to be on the safe side, take the edge off."

Marking the time, dose and route, Jake pushed the meds into her blood stream and felt Michelle instantly loosen up.

"How're we doin' Michelle?"

"Hmmm. Better. Still hurts though, like fire. Now down to a dull ache. As long as I don't move. Or blink. Or breathe."

In actuality, Michelle found herself not really caring about much. Obviously she was concerned about her eyes, but the fentanyl gave her a very "easy come, easy go" feeling.

"Good. That's what I like to hear. Though we're going to have to move you, Hon. We're going to slide a board under your butt, and slowly spin you to your left and slide you out on to the board head first. We've got to keep your neck and back straight though, okay? You let us do all the moving for you, and if something starts to feel funny or something hurts, tell us right away, okay?"

"Okay. But everything hurts."

Jake smiled and replied, "Yeah, some things are going to, but if anything new, comes up, tell us."

He took off the blood pressure cuff and put back in the trauma bag.

Dris had brought over the stretcher and was holding it in place.

"Okay, on three. New guy, you have the head, we turn her on your word," Jake said.

It was a smooth transition. All the folks involved have been doing this for years – even the new guy had it drilled into his head for months – probably 500 times before he got out of the academy – and probably countless times before then at a vollie house. The spin motion and transfer to the cot was very fluid and there were no issues. Michelle was secured to the board, head blocks in place and the spider straps put on. Jake hated spider straps. He'd lobbied for the speed clips. God, how he hated spider straps.

Shit! I didn't ask about any previous addictions, Jake thought to himself. That might be an issue as she rehabs. Well, she didn't mention anything when he asked about meds or previous medical history – that should be enough he surmised. Though the thought did bring up question about how morphine and fentanyl metabolized in the body. Some knowledge he'd have to refresh after the call. He was thinking way too much again.

It's been said that the capital beltway is a parking lot that drives at 80 miles per hour – that is until something happens. Anyone who's driven it during rush hour would understand. Jake hoped that Dris knew how to drive in a mess like this. Jake's priority was Michelle. He was pretty sure she'd lose the eye, but legally he couldn't tell her that. She was stable other than that. After the patient was loaded, Dris went back to get the last of the refusals from most of the other drivers.

The other firefighters helped Jake load Michelle up into the ambulance. Jake turned on the heart monitor, wrapped the blood pressure cuff around her right arm, and placed a 4-four lead on her to monitor her heart with the Fentanyl. He grabbed a bag of saline off the bag warmer and spiked it, ran the line out to get all the air out of the line, and twisted the connector to set the drip roller to roughly half way for the time being. Dris finished up with the other drivers and a couple of the passengers; all had signed refusals. If anyone else needed help, there were still firefighter/EMTs on scene.

Dris keyed the mic, "Medic 705, en route to Holy Cross, one patient, starting mileage 2,766."

"Medic 705, en route to Holy Cross, starting mileage 2,766, 0752," repeated Comms.

Probably the best hospital for the situation was Suburban Trauma Center. The problem was that there was no place to exit the beltway or even turn around before Georgia Avenue, and at that point Holy Cross Hospital was right there. "The Cross" as everyone called it to shorten the names, was a pretty good hospital for what it was. The Emergency Department was mostly dependable, depending on who was on duty.

With a 5-minute ETA, Jake grabbed the mic, turned the radio frequency to match the Emergency Department of "The Cross", and keyed the mic.

"Holy Cross, this is medic 705," Jake began, then waited for a response. Nothing. "Holy Cross Hospital, this is Medic 705."

"This is Holy Cross, go ahead."

"Holy Cross, this is Medic 705 inbound with a 42-year-old female patient involved in a chain reaction MVA, patient was a restrained driver, however the airbag impaled an object into her right eye," he un-keyed, then re-keyed the mic.

"Patient is stable, object is secured, both eyes covered. All vitals within normal limits. GCS is 15. Patient is immobilized, received 50 mikes of Fentanyl on-scene on standing orders. Our ETA is approximately 3 to 5 minutes," Jake added.

Holy Cross replies, "How long ago did the patient receive the Fentanyl?"

"Medic 705, Holy Cross, I pushed 50 mikes, that's five-zero mikes at zero-nine-forty-eight. Patient stated her weight was 65 kilos."

"Copy that, room assignment on arrival, Holy Cross

clear."

"Received, Medic 705 clear."

This morning the charge nurse was Becca, or "Brutus" – depending on her mood. She didn't take grief from anyone. It was inspiring – as long as you weren't on the wrong side of things. She had over 30 years' experience as a trauma nurse, and had come to be considered understatedly jaded. She also did some teaching for the community college on the side. The frequent fliers feared her, the attending physicians feared her, and the medics simply irritated her. Jake took it to be a game, as he'd seen her soft side before once, what seemed to be a long, *long* time ago. He knew it was there, anyway. She would never admit it publically, let alone show it. She needed her reputation to keep order in the place. One seemingly odd thing she hated was when medics came in with their stethoscope around their neck. So, naturally Jake took this to be a required part of his uniform when visiting "The Cross." He did it all the time anyway, but he made sure the stethoscope was more prominent and shiny when he knew Becca was working, if only to annoy her.

As Dris backed the ambulance up to the ED, Jake was busy taking down the last of Michelle's vitals and unstrapping her from the various pieces of equipment. He transmitted the EKG feed to the hospital, and then printed out the tape of her four-lead for the paperwork and hopped outside to unload her from the ambulance. Dris badged the door open and the two wheeled Michelle into the ED as gently as possible where Becca met them.

"Put her in Trauma-One," Becca said, pointing to Dris' left.

It was the first room just inside the door. They'd already called the various specialists in to start looking into treatment. Jake only recognized the ER Tech and a few of the nurses. Apparently one of the unknown ladies there was an oculoplastic surgeon. The thought of what they did sent a new round of chills through his skin.

They rolled the stretcher up to the bed and transferred Michelle to the bed while still strapped to the board. Becca stayed out of the room to redirect some of the other resources around the department. One of the new nurses Jake didn't know was going to handle this case. She took the report from Jake, a brief synopsis of what had happened and what he'd done up to that point, meds given, allergies (if any) and mental status. The nurse signed his transfer and care report, and the transport agreement for the patient as she couldn't see to sign. Dris took the stretcher to start decontamination and prepping it for the next run while Jake went to the EMS room to start the paperwork.

Jake was a bit bummed for not being harassed by Nurse Becca more. It was usually a highlight of his day.

The sun was shining, he'd gotten his nasty call out of the way early, and the rig was clean and fully stocked for a change. Aside from the odd stubbed toe and "feeling faint" call, the rest of the day went pretty smoothly.

- TWENTY-TWO -

It was back to that time of day again: 5:30 p.m. The last few minutes before the end of his first day back. The day had been a busy one for sure, but not crazy. They averaged about a call every 2 hours, which was manageable. He just wished some people would learn to take care of themselves. A twisted ankle may need to be x-rayed, but if you have a spouse there that can drive you, don't call an ambulance. Jake was getting more and more frustrated with people who saw them as glorified taxi services. It used to be the idea of the homeless or the mentally unstable, but now it seemed that regular folks were doing it more and more. Jake was just finishing up what he hoped would be the last inventory check of the day. He had a few vials of meds that needed to be swapped out before they expired.

"Seriously, I've never used Haldol in almost 15 years. Why the hell do they still stock it?" Jake asked Dris as if he had the answer.

Dris went on to espouse the extraordinary uses for it in times of need. Jake just shook his head. *Greenhorns*, he thought, even if Dris wasn't as green as most. Jake liked the greenhorns more so than the usual career folks. They asked questions he hadn't thought to ask, so it kept him thinking outside of the box in respect to the protocols.

Jake had counted four vials of medication that had another month to go before they expired. Generally, they were swapped out at a hospital who was more likely to use them before the expiration date, and since it was usually a straight swap, and both inventories stayed the same, it was a pretty easy transaction. Only the dates changed.

The station tones went off, and Jake just hung his head with a heavy slump and slowly put the vials back into the drug box without looking.

"Medic 742 – all available units, Rescue Squad 742 – all available units, Medic Engine 718, Tower 718, Medic 705 – all units, Engine Medic 705, Tower 705, Medic Engine 719, Tower 719, Battalion Chief 704, HazMat 707, Engine medic 721, Tower 725, Medic Engine 725, Medic 725..." the call began.

Jake knew it was something big just by all the gear they were calling in, parts of 3 separate battalions from what he could tell.

"Medic 723, Engine Medic 723, Tower 723, Medic Engine 716, Ariel 716..." it continued.

"Jesus Christ! Get in and start it up. I'll get the doors and the street light," Jake said to Dris who was just sitting there listening to all the units being called in.

Some of the federal fire departments at NIH and Bethesda Medical center were called in as well.

"...Engine 726, respond Metro derailment, possible MCI, repeat Possible Mass Casualty Incident, Wheaton Metro station, Intersection of Reedie Drive and Georgia Avenue, 1737."

Dris fired up the ambulance with the engines opening up beside them. The firefighters could get their ass going when they needed to. Dris pulled the ambulance out into the intersection to block traffic so the engines could get out too. Together, the three vehicles raced up University Boulevard and hung the hard right onto Georgia Avenue. They could see the black column of smoke rising over the houses.

"*That* is from a *train* derailment?" Dris said as calmly as he could.

"Not good," Jake replied, reaching for the mic.

He waited for a free second on the radio to acknowledge-en route which was aggravating; it's not like they'd respond anyway.

"Fuck me," Dris responded just as Jake keyed the mic.

Jake flinched, but it was too late. He wasn't sure if it actually went out over the radio, but he chuckled at the possibility.

Comms was coming fast and heavy with the information.

"All units, Tactical channels 1 and 2 are active, Operations channel 1 is active. Medic 742 has Incident Command. All units switch to Tac-1 after acknowledging. All units switch to Tac-1 after acknowledging."

Comms continued with station back-fill alerts, some from within the County. More than a few from neighboring DC, Prince George's County, Fairfax County and even a bariatric unit from Frederick County. It was at moments like this when it didn't matter if you were a volunteer or a municipal employee. There were people that needed help and that was all the mattered. Any and all personal feelings or prejudices were put on hold. The only thing that mattered was the person next to you and getting to the people in front of you.

"A train derailment and a tunnel fire. Well, let's hope all those drills we've done in the last few years have paid off," Jake said.

"I've only been in one drill with Metro and I just sat in the ambulance," Dris replied hesitantly.

"Okay, no sweat. You've been in fires and you've been in car wrecks. Have you been in a bus wreck?" Jake asked, more to steel his own nerves than anything.

Dris shook his head no.

"Well, just bring your game face. It's nothing you haven't seen before; You just haven't seen it all at once. There are two sets of SCBAs in the back with the blue turnouts, this is what they're for. We may get there and it turns out to be a brake fire or something stupid," Jake explained, trying to be optimistic.

"Park over there, across the street. It should be upwind of everything," Jake instructed.

"Battalion Chief 704 has incident command" another report from Comms as the higher ranking officers arrived on scene.

Dris had to cross 4 lanes of traffic and the concrete median to get there, but they were in a good spot to get out when needed and they weren't in the way of the fire apparatus still flooding in.

Three more ambulances followed behind them, lining up a good stretch for evacuating any patients. Some of the engines had parked along Georgia Avenue; some staged along Reedie Drive and pulled into the bus depot directly in front of the stairs leading down to the subway.

Thankfully, this was one of the more recently refurbished stations, so the water connections were built into the building's substructure. They still had no idea what they were going to face down there. The convenience store next to the entrance was covered in the foul smelling smoke. Most of the people in the building had been evacuated.

Jake and Dris grabbed their gear and headed over to the command center that the Battalion Chief had set up a block from the Metro station. There were already two teams of firefighters in the tunnel. HazMat was on the way as was the Urban Search and Rescue Team or USAR, for all the good they could do in this immediate situation. The problem they were having was egress. The building itself and the manner in which the exit to the station was set up was a pinch point for large numbers of people exiting.

One crew had set up the multi-colored tarp used for MCI events. Almost everyone coming out of the tunnel was immediately shunted to the green section for the able bodied to be evaluated. Some would be downgraded to yellow or even red, but for the time being, the ability to walk marked you as walking wounded.

There were some who were being carried out; some who passed out as soon as they hit the fresher air. These folks were designated 'yellow', as were those with preexisting conditions, smoke inhalation, burns, and a few other relatively minor injuries. No one as of yet had come out that was considered red or in need of immediate treatment, let alone the dead or obviously dying, that would be placed in the black section.

In this situation, they would most likely be left where they lay in order to tend to the ones that could be saved. Triage was a lot like playing God, deciding who could be saved with minimal work and who would be left most likely to die. Both fire and EMS crews drilled for MCI calls, but no one from the greenhorn-rookie to the grizzled and retired wished to ever have to triage.

The battalion Chief saw Jake and Dris and immediately sent them with the next team of firefighters. There was a full-stop of the Metro Red-Line. No trains were moving at all on that line. They suited up as they were walking, checking each other's mask seals and verifying that everything was secured. The trauma bags and oxygen bottles were a lot bulkier when wearing turnouts. It wasn't something they'd thought about in the drills they been in or the tabletop exercises they'd run through. The turnouts and the SCBAs all in all weighed over 30 pounds, even with the carbon fiber air tanks. Add to that the individual bags for trauma and airway kits, Dris even grabbed the pediatric bag. Jake still hated that damn Broselow bag.

He'd never worked with Dris in the shit-storm of a single call-gone-bad let alone something like this. He wished Erik was here. Erik would calm him down. Now it was his turn to calm Dris down, but to do that, Jake had to control his own rising fear levels, understand the situation and turn it into something useful.

Erik had told him a few things about how he had to keep his head together in a fire-fight while in Afghanistan. At least here there was no one shooting at them. Still, he thought there might be a similarity, willingly walking into their own variation of a fire-fight.

Jake and Dris put their nitrile gloves on, and then their extrication gloves over them and fell in line behind of couple of firefighters. They followed them down with a team of others into the smoke and darkness. That entrance stairway really was a hindrance to foot traffic, as were the escalators further in, but as the escalator was out of order, they were essentially was just sets of stairs now. They opened up further down. Everyone turned on their helmet lights and put one hand on the rail and those that weren't carrying anything put their free hand on the shoulder of the man in front of them.

Dris walked behind Jake, his free hand on Jake's shoulder. The further down, the darker and thicker the smoke, the stronger

Dris' grip got. At one point the lights were worthless. The fans in the station were either offline or being overwhelmed. If there was airflow, they couldn't see or feel it.

Fuck! Jake thought. 5:30-rush hour and it was the second or third-to-last stop on the line. The train was more than likely pretty full.

As they approached the platform, they could see flashing yellow and red lights in the air. Some of the white emergency lights had come on, and a few of the subway cars showed that they were at different angles, some just sticking up in the air, others wedged between the two platforms. One subway train was still partially in the tunnel.

Jake began to see the picture of what happened. Somehow a train was stopped in the station while another rear-ended it, destroying the last two or three cars of the one stopped and what looked like the first two of the oncoming train. That is where the most carnage would be and where the most help would be needed. It had been 20 minutes since they got the call.

The smoke was getting thicker. Firefighters were running around, some looking to shore-up the trains, some working triage where they could get into a car, and some were extricating people that were easily extricated. All of them were looking for the sources of the smoke and possible fire.

Jake grabbed Dris by the shoulder and headed over to what they thought was the impact point of the trains. The crews were still checking and securing what they could in the smoke filled station. Jake and Dris found a place to crawl into one of the more shattered train cars. Pushing their bags in first, luckily, they didn't have to take their air packs off. Surprisingly, the passenger compartment was mostly intact. It was wobbly as they stood up, shaky and not overly stable. They stood up and the side of the car they were on would tilt with their weight.

Some passengers were unconscious, some dead, and of course some in a state in between. Jake and Dris were forced to step over people, checking pulses as they walked the length of the car. People would become hysterical as they awoke. A few started screaming and running in any direction they could.

"Dris! We need to calm these people down!" Jake had to yell through his mask, and above the shrieks of the passengers. "Get them over towards the hole, but don't let them leave, there's still too much smoke out there!"

Dris started herding those few that he could towards the hole that they crawled through to get in. There were initially six people that were ambulatory. When they all walked towards the side of the train car, the whole car shifted and dropped three inches.

It was then Jake realized that the passenger car they were in was resting on top of another. The lights from their helmets illuminated the car's occupants. Most of the people were hurt, but not too bad. Some broken bones and more than a few lacerations. A lot of the people were even standing up and staring at them, for all of their hysteria.

"Dris, you got this car. I've got to get below and see if anyone's down below."

"What!?" Dris asked a bit alarmed.

"It looks like most of them are just in shock. You probably have a few broken bones, but you can do the triage. You know the drill, keep the 'greens' here and try to calm them down until we can get them out with too much movement," Jake said.

"There still a lot of smoke. There may be a few that are really fucked up. Treat the ones you can. I'm going to check out the car below us. I should be able to hear you if you need me. If not, my radio is on the Tac-2," Jake finished.

Dris checked his radio and made sure the volume was up. He took a deep breath and said, "Got it."

Jake walked over to the hole, putting a calming hand on Dris' shoulder.

"Dris, relax. You got this. We're not alone. If you get jammed up, stop, breathe and think. If they're five seconds from death, no amount of freaking out will help either of you."

Jake couldn't help but think that it would've sounded better if they didn't have masks on. Jake crawled back out of the hole they'd come in and started looking for a way into the train car on the bottom.

The fire crews deemed the scene safe for lighting which soon paved the way for the air-movers, essentially just big fans to replace the ones in the station that were malfunctioning. Some engineers were there from Metro to work on the station fans. With the extra lighting and a few other firefighters, Jake was able to find a way into the crushed subway car through what was left of one of the windows.

The impact of the crash crumpled the two cars on the end of the train that was stopped in the station, shearing the last car in half, killing everyone inside almost instantly. The second car from the end, the one Jake had crawled into, had been crushed by the weight and speed of the oncoming train. The car was twisted, but still resting on the rails about three feet below the pedestrian platform. The impact had destroyed all the windows, but because they were hardened plexiglass, they either popped from their frames or melted from the heat. There was twisted metal with sheared edges. The cheap carpeting in the subway car had been ripped and burned. Some pockets of flame were burning themselves out. The emergency lights were shattered and sending sparks through the car, lighting what little carpeting remained.

Crawling through the window required him to crawl over a body torn in half by the blunt force of the standing pole near a seat. The blood was dark and sticky. It turned out to be a woman, her mouth still agape in the surprise that filled her last few seconds of life. The blood had soaked through her clothes, still trying to hold the two pieces together. In front of him laid what looked to be a man, dead or unconscious. His pant leg had caught a flame and still he didn't move.

"Is anyone here?" Jake yelled, still squatting.

Jake could only rise to his knees; the ceiling had collapsed down. The smoke wafted through the car, which was eerily silent considering the conditions outside. Someone raised a hand about halfway in, on the floor to the right. Jake scampered over as fast as he could, throwing purses and backpacks to the side. He reached the person raising their hand, an older woman, Jake believed to be in her late 60's or so.

Her legs disappeared under the remains of the seats, the growing pool of blood around her couldn't be differentiated between hers and that of anyone else's. Jake said nothing, taking in the scene, trying to figure out how far along she was in the process of dying. Her eyes the only thing speaking to him. As he got to her, he grabbed her hand, holding it to his chest. The lights sparking behind him, his breathing into the mask the only sounds he could hear. Her other hand reached up, cupping the right side of his mask. Her eyes glistened, reflecting the sparks.

"I'm here," Jake said, "Help is on the way. Stay with me."

She smiled at him, her eyes expressing the relief she felt. She mouthed a "Thank you." to Jake, and exhaled her last breath, the smile still on her lips. Her eyes glazed over, staring off into nothing. Yet another person he wasn't able to help.

Jake sighed audibly. Still holding her hand, he reached over and grabbed what he believed to be her purse and placed it next to her, laying her hand on top of it. He knew he had to push through. He had no time to reflect, considering there could be more people that needed his help. He had to move on.

Looking through the length of the car, he saw bodies haphazardly piled on top of each other. Some people were still sitting in the seats, their heads and shoulders disappearing into the ceiling of the train, assuming they were still attached. Blood was still dripping from the hanging-straps and poles just 3 or 4 feet above the floor. The entire floor of the subway car was covered in all manner of possessions, purses, backpacks, and phones littered among the blood, intestines and severed limbs. Jake heard a cough deeper into the car. He crawled further in, trying to avoid the bodies and large pieces of debris. There was more coughing on the right, some moaning on the left.

Jake grabbed his radio and said, "Survivors! We have survivors on the bottom cars! We need extrication in the bottom car!"

He hoped there were enough people on Tac-2 to know who and where he was and that there actually were cars underneath he

"We have survivors in the bottom train cars," Jake said, breathing heavily into the mask.

"Jake! My alarm! I've only got a few minutes of air left. We have to leave!" Dris yelled over the radio, a more than a slight panic in his voice. He was hangin' tough though.

The high pitch alarm evident over the radio, signaling he only had about 15 minutes of air left. Just then, Jake's went off as well.

"Go! I'm right behind you. Take someone if you can," Jake said, unaware that Dris was working with other firefighters, some of which were paramedics as well.

Dris and the firefighters evacuated nine people, with another 17 being worked on. Jake was still alone in the bottom train car. He had identified only three or four people that were still alive, but unable to determine if they were workable. He needed to get the attention of the other rescue workers.

"We're getting a few out now. I've told them where you are, but they're having a problem getting into the car. They're bringing in the spreaders, but they have to make sure everything is secure first."

Figures, Jake thought. *Everything by the fucking book.* He understood the reasoning of course, but he still thought it a bit strange that one of "their own" was already in here, why couldn't they follow? Just then the roof of the train car jerked, the weight shifting causing the roof to collapse down another 6 or 8 inches. Jake, still on his knees, ducked down, bringing an abrupt end to his musings.

As he turned around, his knee slid in the blood. His gloved hands were covered in blood, indistinguishable from the gore itself. Shifting to catch himself, he looked under the rows of the seats. There on the right side, just before the window he came through was a baby's car seat. He saw legs dangling over the edge. A hard swallow got stuck in his throat.

"Please, God in heaven. Don't do this to me," he caught himself praying.

Jake reached over to drag the baby seat from under the seat but it was stuck. The seat had partially collapsed with a passenger above it. He laid down on his stomach, reaching for the child, his face inches from the pools of blood, his turnouts now covered in the gory soup.

The smell of smoke together with the burned blood almost made him puke. The baby was still strapped in, which was a good sign. He ran his hand down to check for a femoral pulse and found it. He exhaled audibly and quickened his pace.

The air pack alarm was still sounding, but he couldn't hear much over his own breathing and heartbeat. He reached an arm over and unbuckled the chest lock, but the seat prevented the straps from sliding loose. He reached down inside his turnout pants and grabbed his folding knife. The blade slid easily through the nylon straps, freeing the baby. He needed to get out of the car. Between the stench, the heat and flames, the carnage around him, and of course the alarm, his resolve was weakening. He felt a twinge of panic. Jake grabbed the child without much thought to immobilizing. He figured if the trauma had already occurred, there wasn't much he could do about it now, besides, babies bounced, didn't they?

Jake held the child, a girl about three months old, to his chest and could see her chest rising, but she wasn't crying. Still he kept low to the floor and belly-crawled through the bloody bowels and fiery clothing. Upon making it the window, he was met by three firefighters. Jake handed the little girl to one of them; the other two helped him slide out of the window. One was nice enough to let him know his alarm was going off.

Firefighters. Masters of the obvious, Jake thought, though he had to admit that they were the first ones in, no questions asked, and that took big brass, diamond-plated balls.

Once he was on his feet and gathered his senses, the firefighter handed the baby girl back to him. Jake took his mask off and covered the baby's head for the walk back to the surface. Most of the passengers that could be moved top-side had been, so the pinch-point at the entrance wasn't nearly as much of a problem.

There was a medic unit parked just down and across the street from the entrance. Staci Laroux was the paramedic tending the Rehab rig and jumped into action as soon as she saw Jake approach with the baby. He'd seen her around in the various hospitals, but hadn't had a chance to work with her. All Jake knew was she that she was another greenhorn. Her partner was Sam, who Jake had partnered up with before.

Handing off the child, Staci took her and laid her on the stretcher. She was breathing but unconscious, and covered in blood as Jake had held her against his turnouts. Her pupils were equal and reactive. Her pressure was 95/48 and a good, strong pulse. It was almost like she was asleep. Except for the bruising on her shoulder from the car seat strap, there was no obvious trauma. She had very little hair, her skull and spine were intact, though she her core temperature was just over 100 degrees. They weren't sure if it was from the environment or if she was sick. Her oxygen saturation wasn't the best, so Staci added some blow-by O2. Jake let Staci do her thing. She already had a few saline bags spiked and waiting.

"No time to run our yaps people, we're leaving. Now! Jake you stay with the rig; we've got to move," Staci ordered.

Staci was a greenhorn, but she knew when and how to put people in their place.

Jake was about to protest his patient effectively being stolen from him, but he saw the look in Staci's eyes and knew it was not the moment to be arguing over patients. She was after all a paramedic too, so there was really no issue aside from ego. Dris, who had taken off his turnout coat was already outside trying to help with triage and rehab, walked back to the rig where Staci and Sam were just getting going.

"Dris, toss Sam the keys to the rig. We're taking over the rehab station," Jake stated.

Dris followed Jake's lead and fished around in his turnouts for the keys and tossed them to Sam who was already behind since Staci took off running for their ambulance with the baby girl and a bag of saline.

This left Jake somewhat deflated, but overall he was happy to be out of the subway tunnel. He looked and felt like he'd just survived the 5th level of hell. As he stripped out of his turnouts, he couldn't help but smear blood all over his regular duty uniform. There was just no escaping it. His job now was to assist and rehab the firefighters as they came out, check their vitals to make sure they were still fit for duty and to tend to any emergent patients that came out in dire need, as in the baby girl he brought out. It was set up a bit too quickly. The safety officer was standing directly in front of the entrance checking names and taking Velcro badges of the firefighters as they went in. Neither Jake nor Dris ever handed theirs over.

At this point it, the hysteria of the scene had died down somewhat. The car Jake was in was by far the worst. There were still a few more patients left alive down below that were being cut out of the cars. Fresh teams were being cycled in while the original crews were taking their rest and doing a little bit of cleanup, getting some water and some rest.

Dris was very busy. Many firefighters avoided Jake due to his being covered in blood and filth. That's how Jake could tell the new guys from the old, or at least more experienced fire fighters. The older guys didn't care if he was covered in blood and saw it as a sign that he worked his ass off.

Jake could see the bank of lights from the television crews, and the podium that had been set up for the big wigs from the county to give reports. Generally, it was the communications officer, but as this was effectively national news, that position had been usurped by the brass higher up. Jake felt his phone buzz and chirp in his pocket. Whoever it was, they were going to have to wait.

A few more hours went by and the teams were beginning their cleanup, waiting for the inspectors to get there. Staci had returned with Jake's ambulance, and their rehab station was being shut down.

All passengers that could be removed, had been. 209 passengers were taken to hospitals, 37 passengers that lost their lives, 24 of which were still in trapped in the wreckage of the trains, and would probably be there for at least another day while the situation was sorted out. There were three firefighters taken to hospitals for smoke inhalation, though it was "mostly precautionary" per the communications officer, so that could mean anything.

Jake's phone had buzzed off and on for the last few hours. The one time he checked his phone, it was a text from Erik, so he assumed that the rest were his friends wanting updates. He had managed to shed the blood soaked turnouts, but his uniform was pretty much ruined. There was no amount of bleach and starch that could save his shirt; maybe his socks and boots were all that could be salvaged. Maybe.

As the scene calmed down, Dris and Jake were both relieved and told to go back in-service. There was no real need for 'decon' as their unit was only used for transport, though Jake's turnouts were out of service. Staci and Sam made sure to restock whatever they had used. Not that Jake cared. He was off the clock as soon as he got back to the station and made the official hand off to the volunteers.

Jake grabbed the mic, "County, Medic 705 clear of the scene. We're headed back to The House."

At this point most of the people on-scene were bushed and the folks in Comms knew to cut them some slack.

"Copy Medic 705, clear of the scene, returning to station 5. 2257."

Dris drove as Jake just stared out the window for the 10-minute drive back to the station. There was no talking between the two. Dris was basically in shock. He and Jake would have to have a talk. Jake was just debating on the timing. Was it better to do it right after everything? Or better to wait until everything had sunk in? In any case, Jake realized that he was now the mentor. He was the "old career guy who'd been through everything", at least to the greenhorns. Certainly after this call, the rookies were that much closer to being the "old career guys."

Jake took the last few minutes of the ride to check his phone, and call to see where the rest of the guys on the call were meeting up. He didn't want Dris alone at this point, and figured the more, the merrier. Being surrounded by people who'd gone through the same thing had a calming effect, as well as a bonding effect.

It turned out that it wasn't his friends just looking for updates. It was Erik and Kelly all sending him screenshots from the news. He was caught on camera bringing the baby girl out, both covered in blood, his face dripping with blood, sweat and dirt, His mask protecting the child from smoke inhalation. Erik had sent a photo of him sitting on the back of the ambulance looking down at his hands. He'd taken his turnout coat off, his uniform still covered in blood, his face smeared as well.

Jake chuckled at the photos because he knew what was coming next, from the perspective of the press anyway. There was a text from Terra as well. She'd heard of the train wreck all the way out in Asia. She was making sure he was safe, probably having already seen the shots of him coming out of the tunnel.

As they backed the ambulance into the bay at the firehouse, Dris was still very quiet. It was concerning. Jake remembered being shocked at his first bad call. Hopefully this wasn't Dris' first rodeo.

Speaking of firsts, he hadn't heard how the baby was doing aside from "good pressure, breathing normally." Jake made a mental note to check with Staci. It had been just over six hours since they got the call. It was almost 11 at night and he was still covered in blood. He tried to look on the bright side. *Somethings never change*, he thought, and a smirk crossed his face, that is until he thought about all the paperwork that was going to be required for this. He logged into the automated call documentation system to check how far along the process was in assigning the calls. There it was, though he didn't know where to begin.

At 1 a.m. Jake threw his hands up in defeat. The paperwork had won for the night. He decided the report could wait. He was shattered and needed some sleep.

Jake and Dris both decided to spend the night at the firehouse. It was the logical thing to do, considering they had to be back on shift and ready to do it all over again in five short hours. The Volunteers can take it until then.

EMS never stops. It doesn't even *slowdown* in the face of disaster.

In the end, the day's events were yet more memories to store away. Some to keep, and some to try to forget. At the very least, he was responsible for helping someone stay alive to have more memories, and he was there for someone's relief and last memory as they passed. Both the blessing and the curse of an EMS life.

ABOUT THE AUTHOR

N.L. Seitz spends his free time reading technical books, and RSS feeds, spends time at a local Volunteer Fire Department and harasses the doctors and nurses at the local ED when he gets the chance. With help from his wife and children, Mr. Seitz tries to keep dogs, cats, chickens and bees in some semblance of order.